MAINLY BY MOONLIGHT

Book Two of the Mage Web Series

C. LaVielle

DRAGON'S EGG PRESS
Portland, Oregon
2018

This book is for my father
Frank Millin Mellinger
1910–2001

We live our lives mainly by moonlight,
Dancing in the dazzle
And dreading what lurks in the dark shadows.
Everything is black or white,
This or that.
We see no confusing shades of gray.

From the collected works of Krios

1

olly Adair stalked up the steps to Ulysses S. Grant High School. The row of columns across the entrance made it look like a gaping mouth lined with ivory fangs. Students crowded all around her. Some were laughing and messing around, but most walked silently. She knew the exact location of each one. She sensed no threat, so she ignored them.

And they ignored her.

As she pulled open one of the six front doors, the roaring pandemonium of the biggest, edgiest high school in Portland lashed out and smashed her back onto the guy behind her.

"Hey, watch it!" he said and shoved past.

Shoulda seen that coming, Molly thought as she franticly adjusted her shields. She leaned against the wall between the doors as students streamed past. The physical and psychic noise was deafening. It surged into her brain on a dark wave of angst and hormones. Pierced and tattooed teens howled and high-fived friends they hadn't seen all summer. Students of all colors, scents, shapes, and sizes bumped and boogied their way down the hall, yelling at each other in barely intelligible English.

This wasn't anything like Concord Academy.

After she'd tuned out most of the noise her brain was still twitching, but she could at least think again. She pulled out the map and class schedule the school had sent. Her locker and first-period English class were to the right. She nudged her way through jammed-up, jostling teens and headed down a linoleum-tiled hallway lined with gray lockers and black-and-white pictures of long-gone sports teams.

Starting her junior year in a new school totally sucked. She had begged her grandmother to homeschool her. The kids at Grant would never understand her—she wouldn't fit in at all.

Gram had pointed out that we hardly understand anything about anybody anyway—even those who are closest to us; and that yes, of course the kids at Grant would never understand her. They weren't mages. But that was the whole point. Molly needed to learn to blend into a world filled with non-mages, and high school was an excellent place to start. Perhaps if Molly looked for things she had in common with her classmates instead of concentrating on the differences, she might be surprised at how alike they were. And besides, she was new to Portland, and school was an excellent place to make friends and "integrate into the community."

End of topic.

Much as she loved Gram, arguing with her was worse than useless.

As she opened her combination lock, a tall, scruffy guy who looked like he would rather kill you than talk to you, jerked open the locker next to hers. Anger flickered all around him. Molly prepared for an attack, reached a bit further into his aura, and relaxed. The dude was paralyzed with fear, and he'd been that way a long time. It was making him angry and frustrated, but not at her. Molly knew all about fear. Just a few months ago it had been her constant companion. She stifled an impulse to grab the guy by the shoulders, give him a shake, and tell him that the only way to get rid of fear was to look it in the face and deal with it.

Maybe Gram was right.

Maybe she did have more in common with the students here than she'd thought.

She clicked the lock closed on her locker.

A girl who looked like she'd just stepped out of the fashion pages of *Teen Vogue* walked by with a bunch of her friends. Her shining blond hair bounced around her head in a mass of perfectly trimmed curls. Her red mini-skirt and tiny black boots set off her swaying hips, and her trilling laughter cascaded through the halls. Any girl would have loved to be in her fashionable shoes. But waves of shame and guilt pulsed out from this paragon. It wasn't clear exactly what the problem was, but Molly felt strong images of a father figure. Maybe she wouldn't want to be this girl after all.

Heading for English class, she passed a group of Goths lurking in a doorway, oozing gloom and doom—except for the one in the middle. This was the Gothiest Goth of them all. Dracula would have been smitten. Unfortunately, she radiated happiness and well-being—and fear that she would blow her cover.

Molly snickered.

A skinny, nerdy looking kid was pushing his way down the wrong side of the hall, struggling against the oncoming bodies like a salmon swimming upstream. Something about him caught Molly's eye. As he came nearer, the big, black dude in front of her reached out and shoved him. It wasn't an angry shove; the move was made with casual enjoyment. The skinny kid slammed into the lockers.

Molly's temper flared. She hated bullies with a deep, abiding passion. The jerk in front of her was small time compared to some she'd dealt with, but definitely a bully. Anger sparked her trained reflexes into action. And then she remembered Asmodius's exasperated plea: "Why can't you think before you act? Use your power wisely." Okay fine, she wouldn't kick the guy's feet out from under him, but she couldn't just let this go.

"Hey, why'd you do that?" she said, touching the bully on the back of his shoulder. "You should help him pick up his stuff."

He swung around and glared at her. "The nerd needed a lesson, and it looks like you need one too." He reached out to grab her T-shirt, but she twisted out of the way, shoved him hard and kicked his feet out from under him.

This wasn't going well.

How do you reason with an obnoxious idiot?

Molly's skin crawled as the deafening roar of the hall dropped a few decibels. Everyone had stopped to stare, forming a clot that jammed the wide hallway. She scanned the crowd for any threat and found none, just curiosity, amusement, and a bit of apprehension. She backed away and dropped into fighter's stance. Now what was she gonna do? She didn't want to fight the jerk, but she didn't want him pounding on her either. The bully surged to his feet with amazing quickness for such a big guy and reached for her again.

A tall, black Amazon glided between them.

"Just who you think you're messin' with, Bro'? Don'cha know she was gonna kick your sorry crotch an' drop you?"

Yup, that was just what she'd had in mind. Thank the gods it hadn't come to that.

"Aw, Shandra, I was just foolin' around."

"Well, do your foolin' on the mat next time—with someone your own size!"

As he went stomping off through the crowd, the Amazon turned to Molly and said, "You got fine moves, girl. You know how to fight and you got attitude. We need you on the wrestling team. And to keep yourself in shape till next quarter, you'd better join the soccer team."

Molly stared up at the young woman in front of her in amazement. Her skin was a rich mahogany. Long dreads topped a tall, muscular body. Mischievous, brown eyes glinted dangerously, and a small gold ring gleamed in her right nostril. She was totally awesome.

"Where do I sign up?" was all Molly could say.

"Meet me at the soccer field after school." She slapped Molly's shoulder and headed down the hall.

The crowd had broken up and everyone was rushing to first period, except for the skinny kid.

"Thanks," he said. "Seeing Zach Jefferson fall on his ass was truly fabulous." He grinned down at her. His eyes were almost black, and they sparkled with intelligence. Electric blue magic crackled and snapped around him. Molly gasped in surprise and took a step back.

"Nice to meet you, Molly Adair, I'm Adam Aubrey, and I'm pretty sure we have first-period English together."

He wasn't skinny.

Lanky, maybe, but definitely not skinny.

"You're a mage!"

"Shhh. Quit yelling and quit staring at me like that."

"How do you know my name?" Molly's whisper was almost a hiss. "And how do you know I have English first period?"

"We know your name and we know your schedule, and we know who you are because I'm the best damn hacker in Portland." He grinned, making quick keyboarding motions with long, slender fingers.

"We? There are more of us?"

But Adam was on his way to class.

Molly hurried after him. "Well, are there?"

"Of course there are. You should have us all identified by the end of the day. Grant's the magnet school for magic. Kids from all over the West Coast come here to train. But the other students don't know about us, and all Hades would break loose if they did, so watch what you say."

2

Tuesday, September 6 ◆ 8:10 AM

nglish was a total blank. Her brain flipped spastically between shock and excitement. She kept trying to imagine what a magnet school for mages would be like and came up with nothing but questions.

On her way to physics she passed a big guy with a smile so brilliant it could sell anything. A blond was draped over one arm and a dusky brunette over the other. His espresso-dark skin glowed, and crashing waves of boisterous energy nearly hid the mage magic in his aura. The dude had "jock" and "senior" written all over him.

A shy mouse of a girl who radiated forest-green magic glanced at her, smiled a quick, sweet smile, then blushed and ducked into her classroom.

Her physics lab partner was a geeky mage named Gareth Strath. But the only comment he made about magic was a whispered, "Aw, c'mon, Molly. You're throwing the instruments off. You've got to do a better job of shielding or we're gonna flunk."

On her way to U.S. History, she spotted a compact, gray man coming toward her. His hair was gray, his suit was gray, even his skin had a gray tinge. He moved easily through the crowded halls, because students scrambled to get out of his way. His fierce, gray eyes searched everywhere for offenders in need of correction. She imagined that very few escaped him—he was a mage.

He scowled at her as he approached. "Miss Adair, come to my office, immediately." He stalked off and Molly followed.

Now what?

The man slammed into the school offices and through a door on the right, which said, in big, silver letters, "Thaddeus Rathkin, Principal."

Oh shit.

All the secretaries stared at Molly as she trailed along in the angry man's wake. Was that pity she saw in their eyes?

Bracing herself, she entered Mr. Rathkin's lair.

He was already seated behind a huge oak desk. The room was dark. Even though there was a floor to ceiling window, it was shrouded in heavy drapes. The only light in the room came from a desk lamp with a green glass shade. Other than the blotter, it was the only thing on the desk. Nothing relieved the blankness of the walls except for a few framed diplomas and a bookcase. But the room writhed with dark, heavy vibes.

"Close the door," he said.

Molly turned and pushed the door closed. Her hands were cold and still as steel.

She looked around for a chair. There wasn't one.

Just as well. She had a feeling it would be better to deal with this standing up.

Mr. Rathkin leaned back in his leather chair and glared at her over steepled fingers.

"Miss Adair," he said quietly, "Grant has been a magnet school for mages since it was founded in 1924, and yet very few Portlanders are aware of the program. Magic isn't an issue here. Do you know why that is?"

Molly was speechless. The man bristled with power and rage.

"Answer me!" he shouted.

"No, sir." What was he so pissed about?

"Because," he said in a low, deadly voice, "mages do not pick fights with non-mages ten minutes after they walk in the building! We are here to serve our fellow human beings, not fight with them. You are trouble, Miss Adair, and I don't like trouble. It makes Grant visible in a negative way and endangers the magic program. I will overlook this first incident. No harm was done, thanks to Miss Sheehan. But if I ever hear that you've so much as looked crooked at another student, mage or non-mage, I will have you expelled. Is that perfectly clear?"

"Yes, sir." Her answer was prompt. She didn't want to hear that deafening roar again.

—

Even on the first day of school the cafeteria reeked with an unpleasant medley of stale tomato sauce, onions, overcooked vegetables, and grease. And Molly knew it would probably smell the same way tomorrow and tomorrow and tomorrow, no matter what was being served. She had spotted thirteen students who were mages, and one more was standing at the opposite door and waving at her. Her aura glowed a calm blue-green.

"Oh good, she's here. Let's go." Molly jumped in surprise as Adam appeared beside her, touched her elbow, and guided her toward his friend. The gesture was casual, but intimate enough to make Molly feel like she had known Adam Aubrey all her life. "Nobody eats in the cafeteria," he said. "It's the first day, so we've decided to celebrate and go to The General's for pizza."

"I'm Diana Andrusko," the girl said. A warm, well-tanned hand gripped hers with surprising strength. Sapphire eyes sparkled into hers. The face they inhabited was more striking than beautiful—the nose was too large and the eyes were set a bit too far apart—but it was framed by a glorious mane of black hair prematurely streaked with gray. "Adam says you touched up Zach Jefferson," she said. "That does my heart good, but it was not a wise thing to do."

"Yeah, it got me a trip to the principal's office."

Two pairs of eyes and two sets of lips went round with horror.

"Amazing," said Diana. "Most students are in total shock when they come out of there, and they jump at sudden noises for days. You look perfectly fine."

"Rathkin is a scary dude," Molly said, as they headed out of the cafeteria. She didn't mention that she'd faced opponents far more terrifying than an angry principal.

"I can't believe he found out about it," Diana said.

"He's got eyes all over the school. He probably even knows when we take a dump!" Adam stomped up the steps. "What did Old Iron Ass have to say?"

"He said I was trouble, and he'd expel me if I, and I quote, 'so much as look crooked at another student,'" Molly said, smiling at the principal's nickname.

"He'll do it," Diana said, touching her hand. "Be careful."

"Yeah, sure," Molly pushed open the door. The sun had burned away the morning clouds and the sky was a heart-stopping blue. A cool breeze ruffled the leaves of the trees dotting the school's park-like grounds. She took a breath of fresh air as she strolled down the sidewalk between her two new friends and grinned. Grant wasn't anything like she'd expected. It was tough and loud and monstrous.

But there were mages here and the halls shimmered with magic.

⸺

A horde of students followed them down the street and into The General's. Molly and Diana each ordered two slices of the pepperoni and sausage pizza, and Adam ordered three slices of the vegetarian. As they sat down at one of the sidewalk picnic tables, two guys at the next table looked curiously at Molly, stared pointedly past Adam and Diana, and gathered up their pizza. They were mages.

"What was that all about?" Molly asked, watching them move down a table and squeeze in beside a chattering group of girls.

"Um, Diana and I aren't the most popular mages at Grant." Adam looked at her with an odd combination of anger and embarrassment. His voice was so quiet that Molly could barely hear it over the roar of traffic on Broadway. "We both just moved here last year. Diana's from Ukraine and I'm from Brooklyn."

Molly could sympathize. Switching high schools was a bitch. And now that she knew where they were from, Molly realized that they both had a slight hint of an accent, but there was really nothing else to set them apart from all the other students. What was the problem?

"My family moved here in hopes of making a fresh start." Diana said watching her closely. Her gaze sent shivers up Molly's spine. "There is a history of lycanthropy in my family."

"What?"

"Her maternal grandparents are werewolves," Adam said.

Molly stared at her friend and realized she was looking into the focused, watchful eyes of a predator. Maybe Diana's grandparents weren't the only werewolves in the family.

"Way cool," she finally said, trying to picture Gram as a werewolf. It didn't work.

"None of the other mages seem to think so," Diana said with a relieved sigh, and she was suddenly a girl with sparkling blue eyes again.

"But how did they find out? I mean, isn't that confidential information?"

"From Theo—that's short for Theophilus Aloysius Peregrine III. He's the blond guy who just dissed us. He's almost as good a hacker as I am. His faithful sidekick is Jeb Dorfman. Not real bright, but mean as a snake," Adam said. "We both found out about Diana's grandparents, but Theo spread it all over school. At least he had the sense to just tell the mages. And you can bet that Theo has also made sure every mage at Grant knows that you're from Concord, Massachusetts; your parents died last May; and you came here last summer to live with your grandmother, who, incidentally is one of the most dreaded instructors in the Web. I'm also sure that he dug a little bit further and discovered that you spent your summer in Damia training with Asmodius and Tamerlane."

She looked up and found herself staring into Theo's pale amber eyes. He gave her a sly smile and turned back to his friend, almost as if he'd heard everything Adam had said. Molly decided that Theophilus Aloysius Peregrine III was someone to avoid. Information was power and anyone who used it to hurt others was nothing but a bully in intellectual disguise. She turned to Diana. "That totally sucks. But why are they making such a big deal about it? I mean, it's just history."

"Ah, you haven't taken the...oof," Diana said as Adam elbowed her in the ribs.

"Lycanthropy runs in families and always skips a generation," he said.

"So, if it skips generations that means you're a werewolf." She'd been right. Molly gazed at the quiet young woman across the table with new respect and a touch of fear. But what had Diana been about to say? There was so much going on here that she didn't understand.

"The trait doesn't get inherited very often and doesn't show up until adulthood, but yes, I probably am. My temper is awful at full moon and I get, um, hungry." Diana's kind, blue eyes flared for the briefest moment with savage darkness.

The tiny hairs on the back of Molly's neck stiffened.

A werewolf would be a powerful and dangerous friend to have, which was just fine. Molly thrived on danger. She had a million questions to ask her, but they weren't the sort you'd ask someone you'd just met a few minutes ago. Her new friends were watching her closely, waiting for her reaction.

"Are you gonna eat that?" Molly asked, pointing at Diana's full plate.

"Keep your paws off my pizza." Diana grinned and reached for her lunch. Adam started in on his last slice looking distinctly relieved.

"So what's wrong with you?" Molly asked him as she finished off her pizza and started on her drink. "Are you a werewolf too?"

"Nope, guilt by association I guess. When I found out what Theo'd done to Diana, I called him on it in front of a bunch of other mages. He didn't like that."

"You've also made a few enemies." Diana said in between bites. "Rathkin is bad enough, but Zach Jefferson is mean as a rabid pit bull and sharp as that switchblade he smuggles into school. He is one of Micah Ortiz's thugs."

"Who's Micah Ortiz?" Molly asked, reaching for Diana's second slice. Diana slapped her hand away.

"He's a gang leader that's managed to stay in school." Adam replied through clenched teeth. "He's a senior and he makes Zach Jefferson look like a harmless idiot. And he's a mage." Then he grinned wickedly. "Welcome to Grant, Molly!"

"Sounds like it won't be boring," she replied and finished her drink. "So, there aren't any magic classes offered at Grant—where are they?"

Adam and Diana blinked in unison, and their faces went blank.

"You'll find out soon." Adam said, looking around nervously, although it would have been impossible to overhear their conversation. They had a table to themselves and no one was paying the slightest bit of attention to them.

"So tell us about your summer in Damia," Diana said, hastily changing the subject. "It must have been fantastic. Working magic is so easy there."

"I wouldn't exactly call it fantastic," Molly replied. "I'd only been at Gram's a few days before I got sent to Damia. I didn't know anything about magic and totally freaked." She gave them a quick rundown of the summer she'd spent traveling through Damia with Asmodius, a mage who was a black cat. How she had learned swordcraft from the warrior mage, Tamerlane, and how Brigga, the goddess of smith-craft had forged her a sentient sword named Flick.

"I can feel the bond you have with your sword," Diana said. "It must be hard to leave it at home."

Molly jumped in surprise and Diana smiled innocently. There was no such thing as privacy when you were surrounded by mages. But no way was she going to tell them that Flick was just an arm's length away. She couldn't go strolling around Portland with a sword through her belt, so her grandmother had placed Flick in one of the gazillion other universes in the multiverse—a parallel universe that was literally an arm's length away, a pocket between the worlds. Then she taught Molly how to reach through the dimensions and get it. So Flick was always nearby, just in case. Which was a good thing; because, if she was honest with herself, she had to admit that she felt sort of lonesome and useless without it.

"Um, yeah, it's hard." She was such a lousy liar.

Diana looked at her oddly, but before she could ask any more questions, Adam cut in.

"Tamerlane is awesome. And his house is so full of spells and spirits you can almost see them slithering around the furniture." Adam said, making slithery movements with his fingers. "I've seen Asmodius there," he continued. "He looks totally evil. What's he like?"

Molly smiled at the thought of her brilliant, ruthless teacher.

"He's not quite as bad as he looks."

"So, if you didn't know anything about magic and you'd just got here, why did you go to Damia?" Diana asked.

Molly shifted uncomfortably on the bench. She really didn't want to talk about her parents' horrible death and how depressed and scared she'd been. She and her grandmother had fought like two dragons, and life had been miserable until Gram had sent her on a quest through Damia.

"Oops, just look at the time," Adam said, coming to her rescue. Diana took the hint and stood up.

"We'd better get back or we'll be late," she said. "Molly, you've got study hall next period. Get a pass to the library; it's quieter and you'll get more done."

Theo and Jeb walked past their table and the sun went behind a cloud.

A cool breeze sent goose bumps swarming up Molly's arms.

3

Tuesday, September 6 • Noon

olly pushed open the library door. Soft light and the dry, papery smell of books filled the spacious room. Her eyes were immediately drawn to the totally amazing mural above the back bookcases. It was crowded with people—famous people, complete with some of the words that had made them famous. And they weren't just dead white guys. There was Martin Luther King with part of his "I have a dream..." speech, and Black Elk, and Florence Nightingale. You could get lost in it.

And the room was alive with magic.

The woman behind the counter was a mage, but her glowing lavender aura didn't account for even a small chunk of the vibes in the room. As Molly handed over her pass, the librarian peered owlishly at her through thick, round glasses and said, "Welcome, I'm Ms. Neal. Were you looking for anything special?"

"Where is all this magic coming from?" Molly whispered.

Ms. Neal tucked her shoulder-length brown hair behind her ears and leaned forward. Her mischievous grin emphasized her high cheekbones and narrowed her eyes to gleeful slits.

"All libraries are full of magic, dear. It's the books, you know. However, you are correct, this library holds more magic than most. When you find where it's coming from, your question will be answered. Unfortunately, as with most answers, it will only serve to bring up more questions. But then, life is like that, isn't it?" Her eyes, magnified by the thick lenses, glinted with amusement.

"Um, yes, ma'am."

Turning away from Ms. Neal's desk and facing the mural, she could feel tingles on her left side but not on her right. There were a few other mages in the library and they were all watching her. Molly looked each of them in the eye and started walking to her left. With every step she took, the tingle grew stronger. It wrapped itself around her, and she had the unsettling feeling of being carefully dissected, studied, and reassembled.

She arrived in the economics section facing a narrow bookcase. It held one book, which nestled on a shelf just above eye level. It was black and scaly looking and way too tall to stand upright on the shelf, so it lay flat with its blank spine facing out. It stirred ever so slightly and made faint whuffling, snorting sounds. Molly's heart raced in excitement.

It was the Librarian from Tamerlane's library in Damia—or at least its twin. A very different sort of librarian from Ms. Neal.

She remembered her weapons instructor's tiny house tucked away in the Wildwood above the River Selene. Its living room had two comfortable, overstuffed chairs separated by a small table that was always piled with stacks of restlessly shifting books and papers and pipes. The Librarian snoozed in the middle of a wall of packed bookcases that loomed behind the chairs.

So what was the Librarian doing here?

If you will but still your mind and allow it to approximate a limpid and receptive pool, I shall proceed to enlighten you.

The voice was small, but it vibrated every cell in her body. The library slipped slightly out of focus and lines of power that she'd been only vaguely aware of now glowed all around her, begging to be manipulated and used. Molly was too surprised to do anything but obey the Librarian and open her mind.

"Ah, well done."

The voice was much louder now and throbbed with power.

"Please be so kind as to quit standing in front of me and gawking. Take a book from one of the neighboring shelves and pretend to read it; we shall be much less conspicuous."

Molly grabbed a nearby book and opened it.

"Excellent choice. Do remember to turn the occasional page. Now, hear and attend, and I shall elucidate:

"Cast your mind back—back before your parents died. Back before your first memory of your mother looking down at you in your crib. Back before the founding of this country. Back before even the first knight in shining armor walked the earth. Go back to the third century before the time of the Christians, just after Alexander the Great went out for a hike with the boys, conquered the world, and managed to die childless at the age of thirty-two. Alexandria, his city, the jewel of the Mediterranean, was set on the coast, where the Nile Delta meets the sea and sweet breezes cool the land; it was destined to become a great center of commerce, wealth, culture, and scholarship."

The library disappeared and Molly found herself looking down on a dazzling white city curling around a brilliant blue bay. Ornate sedan chairs carried by hefty men moved sedately along broad, straight streets lined with regal palm trees and hanging baskets filled with flowers. Fresh Mediterranean breezes wafted through the city, stirring the palm fronds and spreading the perfume of flowers everywhere. Bright sunlight baked her body.

She spun around and looked north, toward the Mediterranean, and a huge, three-tiered tower of honey-colored stone blocks glowed in the sun. It seemed to float above an island that was connected to the mainland by an arc of land that formed the west side of the harbor. A statue of a man holding aloft a three-pronged spear balanced at its peak, beckoning ships in.

"Ptolemy and his son, Ptolemy II, Philadelphios, built the great Pharos of Alexandria. It was, indeed, one of the seven wonders of the ancient world.

"But even the great Pharos was as nothing compared to the Royal Library at Alexandria. Talented mages and scholars came there from all over the known world to study, do research, and learn from each other."

Molly's view turned toward the northeast portion of the city and zoomed in on what looked like a university campus. Situated near the palace grounds, it consisted of several white marble buildings. Shaded walkways meandered through gardens filled with fragrant flowers, splashing fountains and songbirds. Three magnificent buildings dominated the campus. She walked through the huge, wooden door of the center building and into an immense space flooded with light from dozens of skylights. The smell of exotic woods, dust, and ancient paper clung to everything, even the robes of the scholars seated at the study spaces dotted around the floor. Thousands of wooden pigeonholes stuffed with papyrus scrolls lined the interior walls and partitions. Two long corridors connected this building with the two others and contained the stacks—row upon row of partitions filled with even more scrolls. Carved into one of the marble walls of the central building was an inscription that read, "The Place of the Cure of the Soul."

The Librarian continued:

"Hundreds of mages and their families called this paradise home. And they brought books—thousands of books containing all the magical knowledge of the world. Others traveled the seas and caravan routes and brought more books and more knowledge. Great advances were made in our understanding of the ways of the multiverse.

"And I, I was the one who made it possible. Fluent in all the languages of the worlds, able to keep a huge library's wealth of information in my head, skilled at transporting objects and people in time and space, I coiled invisibly through the library in a parallel universe and kept it organized and all its information accessible. A mage only needed to ask, and the scrolls she wanted would appear on her desk. If she needed information on a subject, I found the sources for her and delivered them. I could travel instantly to other libraries in the world and bring back books from those as well.

"But I was not as you see me now, oh, my stars and planets no—I was a fierce and powerful dragon, and I guarded my scrolls jealously. The libraries of the world were my treasure trove, and the Royal Alexandrian Library was my nest. It was a very exclusive facility. Any unauthorized person who tried to "borrow" scrolls incurred my wrath. And any mage or scholar who lost or damaged a scroll...only did it once."

This was all quite fascinating, but Molly knew enough about dragons to know that there was something the Librarian wasn't telling her.

So, whose dragon are you?

A sulky silence followed.

I mean, you're not a wild dragon, so you must belong to someone.

"Ahem. Well, if you must know...the first editor and head librarian of the Royal Alexandrian Library was a man named Zenodotus. He was a wise and powerful mage and conceived the idea of using his dragon to assist him with the library. And so he taught me all that he knew about the library and how it was organized and showed me my duties. It was a most appropriate use of my talents and powers, and I soon made myself indispensable."

But what about when he died? Why are you still here? I thought we were sort of stuck to our dragons, like, they're a part of us.

Molly turned a page.

"And you understand correctly, little one. But, as I said, he was a wise mage, and foresaw that very problem. After years of research and consultation with hundreds of mages, he discovered a way to reorganize himself. And so, when he died, I became a separate entity and his spirit found a wild dragon, tamed it, and took it for its own. I continued on as the invisible Librarian at Alexandria, and Zenodotus was able to continue the rest of his journey through the multiverse. Everyone was happy."

Except, maybe, the wild dragon.

The incense-like smell of sea air, flowers, and exotic woods surrounded Molly and she was back in the Royal Library. One by one, the patrons looked up from their studies, stretched or rubbed their eyes, and stacked their scrolls to one side of their study area. The regular scholars strolled out of the library, but the mages remained. More mages arrived, dressed in long robes and turbans or short, sleeveless tunics. Some wore their tunics over loose trousers pulled tight at the ankles. The clothes were of every fabric and color imaginable. Some were men and some were women. Some had dark skin and some were pale. But none of them looked like they were having a good day. In fact, they looked dangerous. They clustered in tight groups and glared suspiciously at each other. Soon the room was packed. It thrummed with power and pulsed with unease.

"Now, as I was saying," the voice in her head continued, "the Ptolemies, the ruling dynasty of Egypt at the time, had supported the Royal Library, the mages, the scholars, and their research for over two centuries. Then Julius Caesar and over 2,000 legionaries arrived in Egypt, chasing after Pompey, his rival for the consulship of Rome. He immediately became entangled in the dispute between Cleopatra VII and Ptolemy VIII over who should rule

Egypt. The Ptolemy dynasty's days were numbered, and Rome would soon be our new patron, no matter which Ptolemy won."

Molly felt a surge of power and both she and the Alexandrian mages looked up.

A dragon's head materialized, filling the airy space below the skylights. It was covered with huge, black scales that gleamed like glass and slid over each other with shushing sounds. It opened its mouth, revealing fangs the size of javelins and a faint stench of sulfur. Its slitted, reptilian eyes regarded them all with a look that made Molly feel like a cross between a naughty child, a worm under a dissecting scope, and a tasty morsel. She shuddered and forced herself to "look" at the monster more closely. She couldn't actually see the body with her eyes, but a part of her mind sensed it and informed her of its presence. It extended into the neighboring dimensions and wrapped itself around the library and university complex. It was much larger and stronger than Riada, her own dragon.

"And what have you found?" the dragon asked in a voice that reverberated through the building.

Molly looked back at the mages and was surprised to see neither fear nor awe in their faces. They regarded the Librarian with irritable suspicion.

"I sacrificed a white goat and examined the entrails," said a fat, oily looking mage in a scarlet robe and pink-plumed turban, "and saw victory for the Roman Empire."

"My colleagues and I have consulted the stars," said a tall, emaciated man in a simple robe that had once been white but was now smudged with ink and a variety of other less savory things. "Victory for Rome."

"I jumped one year ahead," said a petite woman, who looked like a younger version of Gram. "Cleopatra wore the double crown of Egypt, but Rome ruled."

"Now will you believe that something must be done?" the dragon asked. "The Romans will not be generous, hands-off patrons like the Ptolemies. If you hadn't noticed, they have a huge empire to support and enlarge. They are not going to spend good denari supporting hundreds of mages and their families unless we use our magic to help them win territory and make money."

"And there was another problem that I, of course, didn't mention," the Librarian said to Molly. "Mages can be stubborn, arrogant, and very testy. In short, they do not excel in communal living. Factions had taken root and grown strong in the library. Tiny, worthless empires were constantly being built, vehemently defended, and demolished. It was obvious to me that the time had come to move the library. But where could we find another stable, undemanding, wealthy patron? I searched the world over and found only a few places. The Chinese Empire appeared to be most the promising, but its culture was so foreign, and it was so far away that I doubted that the mages would be happy there. And, of course, being somewhere else wouldn't give the mages more congenial temperaments.

"Besides, Chinese dragons are much too jolly and complacent. I would have started biting their heads off—a definite diplomatic taboo."

Molly snickered as she turned her attention to the scene playing out before her. The mages were grumbling among themselves. Then arguments broke out and shouts echoed through the library.

"So what do you think we should do?" a young mage shouted as he glared up at the dragon.

"Ahem," said the Librarian and waited patiently until everyone had stopped arguing. "We must move the library, of course," it replied.

"Impossible!"

"Alexandria is our home!"

"There's nowhere else that is suitable!"

"We won't move it all to one place," the dragon replied. "You will disperse throughout the Roman Empire and set up your own homes. I will divide the library and house a portion of it with each of you."

"Turn a page."

What? Grant High School library appeared around her.

"You haven't turned a page in quite some time."

Molly turned a page.

"Do remember to turn a few more during the course of your instruction, I don't want to have to stop and remind you again.

"Now, to continue. As with any new and brilliant idea, mine was met with violent opposition and thunderous objections. The real problem the mages had with it was that they would actually have to work for a living. However, none of them voiced that particular complaint for obvious reasons. But I thought working would be good for them. And if they had to support themselves as physicians, apothecaries, engineers, astrologers, priests, teachers, et cetera, they would be much more accessible than they were now. And the world was desperate for their skills.

"It would also separate them and cut down on the constant infighting.

"But, most importantly, it would keep the library even safer than it had been in Alexandria, because, split into small portions and scattered throughout the empire, no one would even be aware that it existed."

Back in the Alexandria library, the mages glared speechlessly up at the Librarian as if it had just sentenced them to death. Molly watched their faces as they began to consider the plan and the arguments for and against it. Then, they took one great communal breath and began trying their arguments out on each other. The walls echoed with their shouting and cursing.

"How will we educate our children if we're scattered all over the world?" a woman dressed in flowing green robes screamed up at the Librarian.

"Ahem," said the Librarian, and waited for silence. "I will help you build an academy at the center of the circle of time, the place that is not a place and the time that is not a time. It will be independent of all pasts, presents, and futures, a bubble in time and space. The class schedules you create will also be independent of time and space. You may build entryways into it from anywhere on earth, and your children will enter and leave the Academy through them. The instructors will jump ahead or use the entryways to teach their classes."

As they were considering this possibility, an elegant man in a long, black robe said, "We must have all the resources available for study if we are to make any progress in our research."

The Librarian vanished.

Not just the part of it they could see, but all of it. The mages gasped, and Molly saw true fear in each of their eyes. However, the fear was replaced by curiosity as a book with a scaly, black cover, just like the one in the Grant Library, appeared beside each of them.

"And each book spoke to each mage, as I am now speaking to you," the Librarian said to her, "for indeed, I was each book and each book was I."

All the mages jumped as their books said, "Open me and behold all the contents of the library of Alexandria." They had never seen a book before, since books hadn't been invented quite yet, but they figured it out quickly. There was a furious rustling of pages as each mage searched out scrolls he or she knew should be there. And, of course, they found them all.

"Now find something that you wish to read and tap the title twice," the Librarian said.

Each mage paged through the book, found a favorite scroll and tapped. The requested work appeared on the table next to him or her.

"'I will be always with you in your libraries to bring you scrolls—and books too, for they are the scrolls of the future. As your numbers and the numbers of scrolls and books increase over the years, I will replicate myself to manage the new libraries."

There was silence as they thought this over and came up with their next objection.

"But we would be stealing! We have no right to those scrolls!" said a handsome man with intense, blue eyes.

All the librarians snorted in unison.

"Since when did you ever lose sleep over "borrowing" a scroll you needed, Pindar? But actually, you wouldn't be stealing them. The only scrolls you will take with you are the ones you and your fellow mages have donated. In the twoplus centuries that you and your ancestors have lived here, you have contributed almost three hundred thousand scrolls. But you will also have access to all the ones that remain in this library and several others. Those scrolls are marked in blue on my pages."

"They may, in fact, be ours," said Pindar, "but Caesar and the Ptolemies won't see it that way. How are we going to explain all those missing scrolls? Caesar will have us hunted to the ends of the earth."

"Caesar will never suspect you of taking the scrolls, because you will be wailing and gnashing your teeth right here in the Library when they disappear," replied the Librarian. "Now hear and attend and listen—this is what we shall do."

Molly watched as the days went by and the mages decided where they were going to live and packed up their belongings. One at a time the Librarian jumped them to their new homes. They went as far away as the British Isles and as close as down the street. Each new household had a room full of empty pigeonholes and the Librarian in book form snoozed contentedly in each one.

Soon all the mages had secretly established their households and returned to Alexandria.

And they waited.

Molly turned a page in her book.

"Caesar came through for us admirably," the Librarian said.

The peaceful rooms of the library disappeared and she was cowering behind a potted palm in a corner of a courtyard. It was dark, and the clang of weapons and shouts and screams echoed off the walls. A small bunch of Roman legionaries in ragged, red-plumed helmets hacked desperately at a host of Egyptians in white kilts brandishing spears and narrow shields. One was backing toward her hiding place, parrying the spear strokes of a tall Egyptian, and pounding the man's shield with his short sword. They fought with such savage skill and intensity that Molly was breathless with fear and awe. The Roman slipped in a puddle of blood and dropped his shield for one fatal moment. The Egyptian's eyes widened with triumph, and he plunged his spear into his enemy's chest. Molly cringed as the point of the spear sprouted out of the soldier's back and blood spattered on the wall behind her. The Egyptian soldier yanked out his spear and looked around for his next victim as the Roman dropped back behind the palm tree. His head and shoulders landed on her lap. He was hot and heavy and covered with sweat that stank of fear and desperation. The dying man looked up into the stars as blood gushed from his wound. His glazed eyes snapped into focus and he smiled at an invisible something. His breath gurgled in his throat, and his legs kicked a desperate rhythm on the stones. And he was dead. Molly shuddered, backed away from the body, and peered out from behind the pot and past the fierce battle in the courtyard.

The city was an inferno. All the ships in the harbor and most of the nearby warehouses, granaries, and shops were in flames. Firelight glowed red gold on the black water and cast gruesome shadows against the bloody walls of the courtyard. Acrid smoke choked the city.

She was back in the Alexandria Library. Most of it was reduced to a smoldering heap of charred marble. Only the central building had been saved.

The Librarian continued its story.

"As the city assessed the damage, the mages did marvelous wailings and gnashings of teeth and recounted the story of the fire and how they had managed, at the risk of their own lives, to save the scrolls that remained. Of course, none of the scrolls were really burned. I had transported them across the empire to the mages' new libraries, put the ones that were left in the central library, and set fire to the empty stacks. Caesar, of course, denied that the fire went as far as the library, but no one believed him. It was hard to argue with the evidence."

"Cool," Molly said. But her voice shook.

"And that is the story of how I created the Mage Web. This particular library is a part of that network and is used by the young mages at this institution of learning to continue their education. If you wish to join them, be seated at that study carrel."

With a start, Molly found herself back in the Grant High School library. Visions of sundrenched cities with fabulous libraries full of scrolls and Roman legionaries fighting to the death in the flames around Alexandria harbor collapsed in her mind like a house of cards. She blinked a few times, shrugged the stiffness out of her shoulders, and replaced the book on the shelf. Lines of power still glowed all around her. The Librarian had not only accepted her into the Web, it had also amped up her magical abilities.

Her mind was an exhausted blank as she turned and settled into the nearest study carrel. Its sides and front were higher than the other study carrels—the one place in the library where she was invisible to everyone except Ms. Neal. Chief Joseph gazed out of the mural directly in front of her. To his right was a portrait of Charles Lindbergh. An eagle soared over Lindbergh's left shoulder. Molly felt herself flying up to meet them.

And then she just kept going.

4

Tesseract Academy • No Time. Any Time.

olly's feet touched down on a seriously polished checkerboard-tile floor. Her backpack appeared like an afterthought beside her. An impression of walls and a ceiling surrounded her, but when she actually looked at them there was only mind-muddling emptiness. What was on the other side of those walls that weren't walls? She was about to find out when a gentle but insistent voice said, "I wouldn't go there if I were you."

She spun around and found herself standing in front of a narrow clerk's desk that looked like it had come straight out of a stage set for *A Christmas Carol.*

It hadn't been there a few seconds ago.

And neither had the man perched behind it.

He was peering down at her through half-moon glasses that balanced precariously on his monstrous beak of a nose. The top of his head was perfectly bald, and his remaining hair was swept back in white, feathery wings. He wore a dark brown three-piece suit with broad lapels, set off by a large, yellow bowtie. She couldn't see them, but Molly was sure that if she could, his shoes would be dark brown with big brass buckles and polished to within an inch of their lives. In his hand was the huge plume of a quill pen. In fact everything about this man was large, except his actual size. He was tiny and thin—almost to the point of emaciation.

"Ah, Miss Adair," he said in a dry, precise voice. "Welcome to Tesseract Academy. I am Mr. Finch, the secretary. Now, about your course of study—students usually begin here their freshman year in high school and graduate in their senior year. Unfortunately, you are beginning in your junior year, a full two years behind your peers. Even with special tutoring and all the work you have already done, you will need to spend three quarters at the Academy this year and three next year instead of the normal two per year. You are right on track, if not a bit ahead, in your regular high school curriculum."

"Whoa, whoa, wait a minute. Go over that again." Things were not getting clearer and her eyes started to cross.

"Oh, dear, I had hoped The Librarian would educate you about the Academy, but I imagine it just talked about itself as usual. Dealing with dragons can be quite tiresome. I'll have to start at the beginning," he said, sitting up a bit straighter, capturing his glasses as they slid off the end of his nose, and resettling them exactly halfway up the long slope.

"Did it mention that the Mage Web established Tesseract Academy when they left Alexandria in order to train the following generations of mages to continue the great work of self-discovery, exploring the fabric of the universe, and serving humanity? The secretary peered down at her hopefully.

"Um, yeah, it did. Mostly."

"And did it inform you that you have been accepted as a student here?"

"Yes." Molly wasn't real clear about the universe fabric and serving humanity, but she was sure the Librarian had invited her to learn magic with her friends.

"Ah, good. Did it bother to mention that the students are, for the most part, children of mages—at least those offspring who show interest and aptitude?"

"Yeah. But where do the others come from?"

"Mages are constantly spotting magically talented youngsters. When they do, they suggest that they visit the nearest library in the network. If the candidate can sense the presence of the Librarian, it assesses whether or not the youngster would make a good mage. If it thinks he or she would, it offers the candidate a magical education, much as it probably did with you. If the candidate accepts, arrangements are made and he or she is transported here. But if the Librarian judges a candidate to be unfit, it immediately casts a spell of erasure, which causes them to forget the magical presence in the library and the person who suggested the visit."

So that's how they kept it secret.

The Librarian could erase people's minds.

Lucky for the mages. They used to burn women that they just *suspected* of being witches; imagine what they would do to a group of powerful magicians. And if, by some miracle, they did know that mages existed and didn't kill them, they would want to use mage magic for their own ends. The mages that Molly knew didn't play well with others—much less take orders from them.

Things would get ugly real quick.

No wonder Gram had been so vague about continuing her magical education and her new friends had quickly changed the subject when she asked them about it—she hadn't been okayed by the Librarian yet. Things were beginning to make sense. Sort of.

"The curriculum of Tesseract Academy has changed very little over the centuries," Mr. Finch continued. "The western esoteric civilizations class has, of course, expanded with time. Introductory calculus has been required as a regular math credit since Gottfried Leibniz and Isaac Newton, one of our mages, developed it. And then there're relativity and quantum mechanics, but these disciplines merely served to further define and quantify what the mages already knew. But I digress." Sticking his quill pen carefully back in its stand next to the bottle of ink in the ink well, he shuffled through a stack of papers set squarely on the upper right hand corner of his desk. With a flourish, he produced a sheet of paper and handed it down to her. "Here is a copy of the curriculum. I will give you a few minutes to look it over," he said, and went back to his paperwork.

Molly felt a nudge against the back of her legs and turned to see that a ladder-back chair with a raffia weave seat had materialized behind her. She eased down carefully, in case it decided to dematerialize, and studied the paper. But the words waltzed giddily across the page and her thoughts raced in circles.

This was so cool. She wondered what the rest of the Academy would be like. Would it be like floating in outer space? Would it look like the original Library at Alexandria? Would it look like Oxford or Cambridge? She couldn't wait to see it. And Isaac freaking Newton was one of the mages! These were folks who made history and then rewrote it, and as far as she could tell *no one else knew they existed*—or maybe they were one of those secrets the exiting U.S. president told the incoming one.

She turned her attention back to the curriculum. She read it over and then she read it again. The only sound was the scratching of Mr. Finch's pen and the occasional rustle of paper.

She read it a third time and swore softly. The secretary scowled down at her.

She couldn't believe they expected her to do all this.

To graduate from Tesseract Academy, she would have to complete the college prep program she'd already begun back in Concord plus all the course work for the Academy. And there was a ton of it. And this didn't even include the make-up work she would have to do because she was two years behind in her magic courses.

"This is ridiculous! It'll take me at least three years."

"Actually, you're going to have to do it in two," the secretary replied.

"Why!?" Molly leaped up from the chair and glared at the man behind the desk. The curriculum sheet crumpled in her fist.

"Your grandmother insisted, you'll have to talk to her," he said peeking timidly out from behind his quill pen. "It's doable, really it is."

"I don't see how."

"I was starting to explain that to you when you arrived," he said, repositioning his glasses.

"So tell me now."

"Instead of two three-months a year, you will have to do three, and..."

"What's a three-month?"

"Twice a year, the young mages spend three months at Tesseract Academy doing course work. The first three-month is done either fall, winter, or spring term, and when it is completed, students return to their regular schools just a few minutes after they left three months before. That way they don't lose any time at their regular schools."

"What about the other one?"

"I was just getting to that. The second three-month is done in summer. Students leave in June and return the end of August. This minimizes the amount that they age. As it is, after timing it back from four three-months and all the overtime from your daily Academy classes, you will be more than a year older than the age on your birth certificate when you graduate."

She looked down at the curriculum sheet and forced her brain to quit twitching and start functioning. Some quick math informed her that even if she did spend four quarters out of time, it still looked impossible. It would have been almost impossible even if she'd started her freshman year like everyone else. Molly glared at Mr. Finch and firmly suppressed an urge to grab the smug little man and shake him till his glasses flew off. She reminded herself that the secretary hadn't designed this stupid curriculum sheet, the mages had. And it was her grandmother who had decided that she could do the impossible and graduate in two years. Arguing with Mr. Finch would be mean and unproductive.

On the plus side, most of the classes looked pretty interesting. But she had some reservations about the Magical Ethics, Etiquette, and Philosophy class and Introduction to Quantum Physics, and she had no idea what Psychoactive Ethnobotany was.

It looked like she had to choose a course of study. There were three possibilities.

"So tell me about these three lodges. I can't decide which one I want to be in until I know more."

"Quite so, Miss Adair, quite so," he said, flourishing his pen at her. "I am more than happy to explain. The lodges were formed to accommodate the diverse interests of the mages. The Ouroboros Lodge was created to suit those students who wish to become scholars, scientists, engineers, economists, and the like. The courses are designed to strengthen the student's ability to frame questions, solve problems, and work advanced magic.

"Unicorn Lodge is for students who wish to become doctors, herbalists, naturopaths, nurses, health care professionals, environmentalists, and gardeners—anything to do with living things and their health and well-being.

"The Dragon Lodge is for students who wish to become artists, performers, lawyers, diviners, social workers, politicians, priests, preachers, marketers, sales representatives, etc. These students are trained to use their energy to not only understand but also influence people's hearts and minds. When they graduate from the Academy they use their talents to become the eyes, ears, and voice of the Web."

She wondered which lodge Adam was in. Diana would probably be in Unicorn Lodge since she'd said she wanted to be a naturopath. Molly doubted that Adam would be in the Unicorn Lodge, so they couldn't all be together. And which lodge was Theo in?

"Do I have to decide now?" She really wanted to find out who was in what lodge first.

"You will make your course choices tomorrow when you meet with the adept who will be your adviser. However, the Academy makes the final decision about which lodge you join."

"You mean I can't even pick my own lodge?" Molly's shaky temper was about to blow. She began pacing.

"Of course you may, and the Academy approves most students' choices. However, once in a great while, it doesn't."

"So you or the Librarian or some mage I've never met gets to tell me what I can study?"

"No, Tesseract Academy does. If it doesn't like your choice, it chooses a lodge for you. Over the centuries it has become a sentient being."

Molly stopped in mid pace and stared at Mr. Finch.

This was insane.

"I can't believe the mages let a school dictate what classes their kids can take."

"They don't have much choice. It only allows students into the classes it approves," the secretary said, sticking his quill pen back in its stand.

"So why can't we just go to the classes we want?"

"You misunderstood. The school literally hides every class from the student except the ones he's supposed to be taking."

"That's impossible."

"Not at Tesseract Academy."

This was getting spooky. Maybe she didn't want to join the Academy after all.

"And it's not fair," said Molly, stamping her foot.

"Maybe not, but the system works well. Most students still get to study whatever they want, and the ones that don't soon realize that the Academy's choice was better after all," the secretary replied, smiling complacently.

Molly was furious. They'd just dumped a ton of work into her already full schedule and her grandmother was making her do it all in two years. And to top it all off, she might not even get to study what she wanted—some stupid school that didn't know squat about her was gonna decide what she'd be when she grew up.

"So who's my adviser and when do I get to see him? And what's an adept?"

"Tomorrow, the Librarian in your school's library will take you there. All advisers and instructors in the Web are adepts, mages who have reached the upper levels of magical competency."

"So who's my adviser?"

"They don't tell me things like that."

"Of course they don't," Molly said through clenched teeth.

"Now don't get snappy with me, young lady," the secretary said, snatching up his plumed pen and shaking it at her. "This will take you back to..." he consulted a sheet of paper "Grant High School library." He waved his pen toward a wood panel door with a brass knob that had appeared to her right.

"Now, if you will excuse me, in just a few minutes I have another incoming student and I must get his paperwork in order." He stuck his pen back in its stand and began going through a new stack of papers that had just appeared on the upper left corner of his desk.

There was, of course, nothing left for her to do but walk through the door.

5

Tuesday, September 6 • Early Afternoon

olly's brain was reeling in anger and confusion as she hurried out of the library and headed for her sixth-period class. When she sensed trouble coming up fast behind her and to the left, she didn't think about being in a roaring hallway crowded with students, and she didn't think about the principal's warning. Her instincts took over and she lunged away from it and reached for Flick.

A quick hand appeared, grabbed her right wrist, and snatched it back before she'd even touched her sword. "Bad move, Miss Molly. We wouldn't want your tight little ass thrown out of here for sword fighting, now would we?"

The trouble on her left arrived and clamped its arm around her waist, pinning her left arm to her side. Molly looked up into

Zach Jefferson's mean, toothy smile. So who had grabbed her hand? And who was draping a leather clad arm casually around her shoulders? She hadn't sensed anyone on her right. She turned and found herself staring at her own face glaring into a pair of mirror lens aviator glasses. The black leather jacket creaked ominously as the guy tightened his grip on her shoulders. His thin lips curled into a cruel smile. Purple-black mage energy flared angrily around him. He wasn't a whole lot taller than she was, but he radiated power. They were frog-marching her down the hall, but no one showed any concern. It probably looked like she was strolling along with two guys draped over her—not an uncommon sight.

"Allow me to introduce myself." The mage's voice was a soft purr dancing over cold steel. "My name is Micah Ortiz, and I believe you've already met Zach. He says you've been interfering with his business. You're new here, so I'll give you a quick catch-up lesson. I will only explain this once, so pay attention." He squeezed her just a bit more tightly and so did Zach. Molly found that she couldn't breathe.

They headed upstairs.

"If you ever mess with me or any of my men again, I'll get you. And you'll wish you were dead."

Molly's lungs screamed for air and her pulse pounded in her head as they marched her along the second floor hallway.

They came to a stop in front of the door to her sixth-period class. Her captors smiled down at her like two amiable alligators, patted her on the shoulders and turned to walk away. Air flooded into her lungs.

"Wait a minute. How did you know Rathkin threatened to expel me?" she gasped.

Micah snapped around and leaned in close as a lover, and Molly found herself staring into those disconcerting lenses once more. He smelled faintly of leather and peppermint.

"That's my business, not yours. And it's best to stay out of my business."

He turned and vanished into the press of students.

Molly glared after him, shaking with rage. She was furious with herself for letting those two losers sneak up and grab her, but mostly she was furious with Micah. How dare he threaten her and order her around? Who did he think he was? She clenched her fists and stalked into Pre-Calculus.

Adam and Diana were already there. They grinned and waved and gave her the thumbs up sign as she walked toward them. For a moment Molly couldn't figure out what they were so hyped about. Then she remembered that it had only been one period ago that Diana had suggested she study in the library.

Still shaken from her encounters with Micah, Mr. Finch, and the Librarian, Molly smiled vaguely at them, but then her gaze sharpened. "How did you know the Librarian accepted me?"

"We knew last week, as soon as Krios recorded your first Greek Mythology grade," Adam replied, wriggling his hacking fingers at her. "I figured you'd be taking it this quarter, so I checked and there you were."

"What?"

"Teachers often jump ahead to teach their Academy classes. Since all times are the same at Tesseract Academy, they choose a time that's convenient for them, so sometimes the grades get recorded before you actually go to your first class."

She glared at Adam.

"Don't you ever look at my grades again, Adam Aubrey. That's just wrong."

"I just wanted to see if you made it in, I didn't even look at the grade, I never do," Adam replied. He looked totally virtuous and totally surprised that she would be having a problem with this.

Molly stared at him in amazement.

He'd missed the point.

It was like his hacker brain had forgotten what privacy was all about.

"Theo opens everyone's grades, but I don't," Adam continued. "And he sells the information, which is a ripoff because even if the grade sheet says you got an A on a test, if you goof off and blow it, that A turns to and F. I know. I did the experiment. Don't ask me how it works, but you always wind up getting the grade you earned."

"Yeah, but still," Molly began, but the bell interrupted her.

As everyone headed for their seats, Molly wondered if there really was such a thing as an ethical hacker. And she hadn't had a chance to ask Adam and Diana which lodges they were in. Then class began and she struggled to pay attention—this was going to be her hardest class. But her rebellious thoughts kept wandering back to Micah Ortiz and the smell of leather and peppermint. And the buzz of power that surrounded him.

Molly was really excited about seventh-period forensics. It was supposed to explain what all the crime-scene techs on TV were doing. And she was even more excited when she spotted the amazing, black Amazon who had kept her from totally messing up in the hall this morning.

"Hey. How's it going? My name's Molly," she said as she sat down next to her in the front row.

"Hey yourself. I'm Shandra." Mocha brown eyes twinkled as she grabbed Molly's outstretched hand in a firm thumb-opposite-thumb grip. "I hope this class is as good as they say it is. What do you think of Mr. Liu?"

Molly turned to look at their instructor and let out a squeak of surprise. He wasn't much taller than she was, and he built like a stick. But his hooded eyes glittered with a somber intensity and he radiated the same purple-black mage energy as Micah Ortiz. And he was looking straight at her. With a shiver, she turned back to Shandra, who was watching her closely.

"He looks dangerous, like he ought to be worried about forensics, instead of teaching it."

"Yeah. But it takes a thief to catch a thief," Shandra replied. "This class'll be good."

The bell rang.

"Good afternoon, ladies and gentlemen." Mr. Liu's voice was dry and precise, and it rustled like dead leaves in the wind. Students scurried to their seats and silence descended. Dropping copies of the class outline and syllabus on the front row desks for the students to pass back, he continued. "Forensic science is the application of science to criminal and civil laws. Forensic scientists collect, preserve, and analyze evidence during the course of an investigation."

"It doesn't sound real promising," Molly whispered.

Shandra snorted.

Mr. Liu shot them a look that commanded their immediate and undivided attention.

Literally.

Mages were a pain in the butt as teachers.

They were going to be using both the computer and chemistry labs for the class, and they were going to the computer lab today. The tech would assign each of them a computer and go over the rules and procedures.

The computer lab was a dim, quiet refuge. Ms. Matsuda, the tech who ran it, sat like an exotic spider at the center of her web of computers. A faint, eerie energy rippled around her, but it wasn't mage energy.

"She's new this year," Shandra whispered, "And there's something weird about her. But the guys think she's the best thing since sushi. Just look at those idiots."

Molly snickered as she watched the guys eye the lovely tech like so many lecherous old men. When they'd gotten their computer assignments one of the more enterprising ones said, "Hey, Ms. Matsuda, my computer's locked up." The tech tried to fix it from her station, but had no success. She moved toward him with the grace of a geisha, but when she noticed Molly a look of surprise flashed in her perfect, almond-shaped eyes. She tossed her head, sending a wing of gleaming black hair fanning back over her shoulder. She arrived at her admirer's station, reached down, and pressed one key. The screen sprang to life. She peered suspiciously down at him and headed back to her machines, leaving behind a hint of jasmine and sandalwood, one puzzled mage, and one smitten male.

Heads turned as Molly and Shandra walked across the parking lot toward the soccer field.

They were an odd couple.

Shandra was nearly six feet tall, gorgeous, and black. Molly was exactly five foot four inches. She knew this for sure because she kept measuring herself to see if she'd grown. A wild mass of auburn curls framed her face and way too many freckles peppered her nose and cheekbones.

But the two girls walked together like a single unit of force, basking in the late summer sunshine.

"So tell me everything you know about Micah Ortiz," Molly said.

Shandra stopped dead and stared down at her.

"He's the evil whiz kid," she said. "Why do you want to know about him?"

"What's a whiz kid?"

"You tell me. There are fourteen of you at Grant—fifteen now that you're here. Y'all are freaky. And Mr. Liu and some of the other teachers feel freaky too. So what exactly are you?"

Molly gaped at her new friend. Shandra was surrounded by strong, vital red light. And, yes, there was a hint of magic there. No wonder she could spot mages. The Librarian must have hidden from her because it decided that she wouldn't be suitable. Why?

"Close your mouth. You look like a fish." Shandra said.

"Does everybody know about us?" Molly asked.

"A few other kids can feel it, but when we try to talk about it to anyone else, they look at us like we're crazy. So, what exactly are you?"

Molly stared helplessly at her new friend.

"You're not gonna answer me, are you?"

"I'm sorry," Molly said, "I can't."

Shandra sighed and turned away.

"We are sort of freaky, I guess, but we're mostly just people. Some of us aren't so nice but most of us are—just like everyone else. Can we still hang out together?" Molly really didn't want to lose Shandra as a friend.

Shandra grinned. "Of course we can."

They linked arms, and walked onto the soccer field.

6

Tuesday, September 6 ♦ Late Afternoon

olly slammed the solid oak front door behind her, dropped her backpack, and ran upstairs to her grandmother's study. The door was open, so she stomped in and glared down at the tiny woman.

"You might have mentioned something—just a hint about what was going to happen at school would have been nice."

Gram was working at her desk in front of an array of computer screens displaying columns of figures. Soft, wispy curls of gray hair sprang out from her head, giving her a slightly Einsteinian look. The adept's welcoming smile froze. "You must know by now that I couldn't have said anything..."

"And just who do you think I am, Wonder Woman?" Molly continued. "Graduating in two years will be impossible."

"Yes, I do think you're Wonder Woman," her grandmother said. "And you can graduate in two years."

"I can't!"

She clenched her already clenched fists even harder as she noticed Gram's copy of the Librarian lounging in plain sight on the oak study table. She'd been in this room a hundred times this summer and never noticed it. Sneaky bastard.

"You're just upset. Wait until you talk to your adviser..."

"Of course I'm upset," Molly screamed. "I feel like I'm a character in a computer game, and you're at the keyboard deciding where I'm gonna go and which monster I'm gonna fight next. You've probably already picked out all my classes and decided which lodge I should join. Why should I even bother to see my adviser?"

STOP!

The two angry women froze, as an even angrier Asmodius appeared between them. He faced Molly and hissed, whiskers pulled back in a snarl of rage revealing white fangs. His black fur stood on end, his back arched, and his tail stood tall and rigid. Molly stepped back. Asmodius could be vicious and she wasn't taking any chances.

Stop, before you say something that can't be unsaid. He sat down, curled his tail around his front paws, and stared a Molly with baleful amber eyes. *You have many faults, but I was not aware that laziness and lack of confidence were among them.*

Without taking his eyes off Molly he continued. *And Estelle, be careful, or you will lose Molly too.*

Gram sank into her desk chair like she'd suddenly been deflated. She rubbed her face with both hands, sighed, and looked up at her granddaughter. "I'm sorry. I must seem like I'm sneaking around behind your back and planning your life without consulting you, but..."

"Wait, who did you lose?'

"Your father."

"But it wasn't your fault that he and Mom died in that plane crash," Molly said, watching her grandmother uneasily.

Go ahead, Estelle, tell her the story. She should know this. His voice was a mere whisper in this world.

Molly felt the blue plush chair that usually sat next to her bed appear behind her and nudge her gently. The Chair always seemed to know when she needed it. Sinking down onto her friend's ample seat, she patted its arm, sat cross-legged, and waited. She wasn't sure she wanted to hear this story. Listening to her grandmother talk about her parents was so bittersweet. She treasured every scrap of information about them she could get, but at the same time, it made her sad to the bone.

The two adepts glared at each other, but even Gram couldn't stare down Asmodius. She looked back at Molly, sat up a little straighter and said, "Have you ever wondered why you and your parents lived in Massachusetts and I live in Oregon?"

"I never gave it much thought back then, but I sure understand it now. I don't think you and Dad would have agreed about much of anything."

"You're right. We didn't. Our views of the multiverse were very different. Even though he had magical talent, all he ever wanted to do was become a medical researcher. He found the Librarian immediately, but when it told him about the Web and Tesseract Academy, he said he wasn't interested, that he'd much rather deal with facts than fantasy." Gram's face was a tragic mix of grief, confusion, and anger.

"We argued constantly. He couldn't understand why I wouldn't just leave him alone and let him live his life, and I couldn't understand why he wasn't interested in magic and the Web. He could be a mage and still do research. I never forgave him for his decision, and he never forgave me for trying to control his life." She looked down at her clenched fists, opened them, rubbed her palms together, and looked up at Molly. Her ice blue eyes shimmered with unshed tears.

"He received a scholarship to Boston University and I never saw him again. I got the occasional letter and then email, but that was all. When you were born, I pinned all my hopes of continuing the centuries-old line of Adair mages on you. But he never invited me out to meet you, so we never got to know each other."

"It's probably just as well," Molly said. She leaned back into the Chair as her brain began making connections, and suddenly her life made a bit more sense, and also a bit less sense. She began to understand that, at least in her family, there was no real good or bad; things just were what they were because the people in it were what they were. Gram was a control freak and she'd been cursed with not only a fiercely independent son, but also a fiercely independent granddaughter. "I don't get along with you any better than Dad did," she continued. "I mean, look at us now."

Her grandmother nodded sadly and said, "But my story isn't finished. Because I'm a stock broker, I jump into the future constantly, and I've gotten better than most other mages at reading whether or not it's actually this future or just a possible future. In one of those jumps I saw the plane crash that would have killed not only your father and mother, but you as well. In a panic, I called David and begged him not to go."

"What?!" Molly jumped out of the Chair. Anger at multiverse in general and her father in particular flashed through her. "You mean Dad knew and he still went?"

"Hush," said Gram, waving her back down, "and let me finish. Because your father refused the Librarian's offer, he knew nothing about magic and what an adept is capable of. He must have thought I'd had a bad dream or something, because he said that wasn't enough reason to cancel his trip. It was a very important conference, and there was no other flight that would get him there in time. And then there was that mulish refusal to listen to me. So he went and your mother went with him, but I talked him into leaving you at home. You know the rest."

Gram looked down at her hands laying palms up on her lap, and then gazed apprehensively at Molly. She looked like she was bracing for an attack.

Molly went numb with anger that she was only just now hearing this. But the anger softened as the story changed her view of reality yet again. She knew that she was supposed to have been on the plane that had crashed and killed her parents six months ago. She had just managed to let go of the terrible guilt that she had survived and they hadn't. But she hadn't known that it was

Gram who had saved her life. And she hadn't known that Gram had tried to save her parents' lives and failed because she'd totally messed up her relationship with her son. One look at her grandmother's tragic face was all it took to convince Molly that she was still struggling with this failure. She mentally kicked herself for being so emotionally clueless. Last summer she had been so busy feeling sorry for herself, that she hadn't given a thought to the obvious fact that her grandmother had also been deep in her own grief. All Molly could do was stare dumbly at her only living relative.

"I like to be in control of things," Gram continued, smiling thinly. "And you are so very important to me, and I am so very proud of you that I get a bit too involved. I promise I'll back off. But please believe me when I tell you that you must graduate in two years."

"Why?" Molly asked absentmindedly. She was still trying to absorb all this new information.

"Because after that, in most futures, someone or something starts killing off mages, and the Web and most of us cease to exist. We're pushing as many students through as we can, because we will need their help."

Molly's mind warped and shuddered and went blank. She had only just learned about the Mage Web a few hours ago, but the thought of its demise terrified her. Not because she would miss the Web, but because she was afraid for Gram and Asmodius and all the mages at Grant. And a world controlled by something powerful enough and cruel enough to kill off thousands of mages would be a nightmare. She sat paralyzed in the Chair as her brain crept back online, and she began sorting through all these revelations. She set aside most of them to think about later. In fact, she suspected she'd be thinking about them the rest of her life. But now she understood that graduating in two years had nothing to do with her and Gram and everything to do with helping the Web and all the mages in it to survive.

Okay, fine.

It looked like she'd be graduating in two years.

7

Wednesday, September 7 • Morning

he looming shadow of the Web's uncertain fate haunted Molly as she hurried up the steps to Grant High School.

"What's up, Adair. You look like you're ready to bite someone's head off."

She jumped as Adam suddenly appeared beside her. "I'm not. I'm just worried."

"If that's how you look when you're worried, I'd hate to see you when you're pissed. What's the problem?"

"Good morning!" Diana appeared on her other side. Molly jumped again. She needed to figure out how to sense mages. She hadn't felt either one of her friends approach. What if they hadn't been friends?

"Good morning yourself," she said.

"So what are you worried about?" Adam was persistent.

"Do you guys know anything about mages getting killed off and the Web disappearing?"

"What?" Diana looked horrified.

"No way!" Adam said. "What idiot told you that?"

"My grandmother."

"Oh shit."

Many questions later, Adam and Diana knew everything she did.

"I shouldn't have told you guys this. Gram asked me not to say anything. But I had to. It's awful and it'll always be on my mind and I need to be able to talk to you about it. I mean, if we're friends we should be able to talk about the big stuff we're dealing with, shouldn't we?

"Thank you for sharing," Diana said.

"Yeah, thanks," said Adam.

Neither one looked even close to grateful, but Diana gave Molly a quick hug before she left for biology II, and Adam linked arms with her as they headed for English class.

—

But her heart still raced with excitement as she hurried into the library. She couldn't wait to see who her adviser was. She had learned that Adam was in Dragon Lodge and, as she had suspected, Diana was in Unicorn Lodge. Theo was in Ouroboros Lodge. She would ask to be in Dragon Lodge.

She smiled at Ms. Neal as she plunked down in the study carrel.

Take me to my adviser please, she said to the Librarian.

Damia • Noon

She stood in the middle of Tamerlane's living room. A wall of leather-bound tomes loomed in front of her. Their green, brown, burgundy, and black spines embossed with gold and silver lettering gleamed in the warm light from the fire that crackled and snapped in the huge river-stone fireplace to her left. The fire cast shadows that shifted and lurched when they should have been standing still and stood still when they should have been shifting and lurching. Tamerlane's copy of the Librarian whuffled and snorted dreamily on its shelf. And best of all, Tamerlane was there, sprawled in his easy chair, white hair and beard and gold signet ring gleaming in the firelight. His craggy features morphed eerily with the shifting shadows, and his gray eyes glittered wickedly up at her.

Molly grinned.

There was a quick flurry of shadowy robes and he was suddenly standing in front of her. Molly hadn't even seen him get up.

"Welcome back."

His courtly bow ended with an "Oof," as Molly threw herself into his arms and hugged him fiercely.

"I'm so glad to see you. I missed you. I'm so glad you're my adviser."

"Harrumph, ah, yes, I missed you as well," he said, patting her on the shoulder and gently extricating himself from her embrace.

"Now, we've much to do. I want to get in a practice session and we need to plan your schedule."

Tamerlane gestured toward the spare room she'd slept in last summer.

"Estelle brought over several changes of clothes a few days ago. There should be something there you can wear for weapons practice."

With a whoop of joy, Molly headed into her room to change.

"I'll be out in a sec."

She slipped into a pair of running shorts and a T-shirt and frowned as she realized that Gram had probably checked to see if she'd made it into Greek Mythology before she brought the clothes to Tamerlane. Even though the room was warm, she shivered. The idea of anyone, even friends and family, jumping around in time and snooping into her life creeped her out.

Moments later she hurried out into the practice yard, shoving her sword and scabbard through her belt. Its silk hilt wrappings and gleaming scabbard exactly matched her auburn hair. This would be the first time she'd faced Tamerlane over naked blades. Her heart raced with excitement and fear. Would she be able to keep up? What if she couldn't?

Tamerlane was waiting for her. Even as she stepped toward him she began the familiar ritual of grounding and centering and focusing her mind upon the coming bout, but her mentor wasn't quite ready to begin.

"You must show me this fabulous sword that Asmodius has been raving about," he said.

Molly grinned, eager to show off her most precious possession. Tamerlane stepped back and kept his hand near his own sword as Molly drew her sword from its scabbard, but relaxed as she held the fabulous blade's hilt across her open right palm and rested its gleaming tip on her left sleeve. The patterns on the steel shimmered like sun on water and pulsed like fire. The black cat charm wrapped into the hilt regarded Tamerlane with sharp topaz eyes.

"Whoever did this certainly managed to capture the essence of Asmodius!" he said. And then he just stared. Tamerlane was so still for so long that Molly began to worry that something was wrong, but he finally said, "Amazing. Almost a living, sentient creature.

"And so beautiful.

"And so deadly.

"But was it worth your soul?" he asked, and his fierce eyes locked onto hers.

Surprise surged through Molly and caught at her breath. So Asmodius had told his friend that in return for the sword she had agreed to be Brigga's agent and under her total control. But judging from Tamerlane's look of deep concern, Asmodius had neglected to mention that he had tricked the goddess into mingling a drop of her own blood with Molly's on the steel that would become Flick. As the blade was forged, their spirits had entwined and their relationship had deepened. Because of this, Molly was not the pawn Brigga had bargained for, but a beloved sister, to be treated with care and used wisely. The goddess had been furious. She'd cursed the meddling mage and vowed revenge. Asmodius was a private creature and might not want everyone to know that there was an angry goddess after him. So, much as she wanted to tell Tamerlane that he didn't need to worry, she felt that she had to honor Asmodius' silence. All she could do was look into those compelling eyes and say, "Yes."

Greetings and well met, Tamerlane. Flick's silvery thought flashed brightly between them. Much stronger now that they were in Damia. *When can we fight? Molly says you're the best!*

Tamerlane gazed into Flick's topaz eyes and said, "How about right now?"

Excellent, Molly and I both need the exercise, and I'll finally get to fight Death Dancer.

"Who's that?" Molly asked, grateful for the magic in Damia that made it so easy to talk to her sword.

It's Tamerlane's sword. Brigga made it too. That makes it almost my brother. I've just been able to feel its presence and learn its name, since it's not very chatty.

"Well, I hope you two have a nice conversation, just don't distract me," she replied.

The moment Molly grasped Flick's hilt, Tamerlane whipped Death Dancer out of its black lacquered scabbard and sent it flashing toward her. But Flick's magic coupled with her skill were a match for the adept, and she easily countered the stroke that would have cut her torso in half. The air shattered with the bright ring of steel on steel, laced with the nearly silent overtones of the two magic blades singing fiercely to each other. Tamerlane continued to slash at Molly, who parried each of his strokes. He continued to press her back until she ducked a slash that came a bit too high. Molly lunged under her mentor's arm as it whipped past her, but her point found only empty air where Tamerlane's heart had been a moment before. His back-swing was headed for her open neck. Molly dropped and rolled and came up with a bit more breathing room.

"Well done," said Tamerlane.

For the next twenty minutes they slashed and stabbed at each other mercilessly and had a wonderful time.

Finally, exhausted and soaked with sweat, Molly called "Enough!" and the fighting slowed to a stop. But each watched the other warily as the two swords slid into their respective scabbards and snicked home at precisely the same time—and Molly didn't turn her back on her teacher until they had left the practice yard, a lesson she had learned last summer the hard way.

"Excellent, excellent!" Tamerlane enthused and headed for the kitchen. He wasn't even out of breath. "I'll make us tea while you go down to the river and refresh yourself."

—

"So, what's Tesseract Academy like? When will I get to see it? Do you teach there?" Molly asked as she inhaled her third slab of chewy brown bread and butter and washed it all down with a second mug of milky, sugary tea.

"The Academy is amazing," Tamerlane replied from across the kitchen table, "but it's difficult to describe because it's constantly changing. As Mr. Finch probably informed you, you'll be doing a three-month there for two quarters of your junior and senior years instead of just one quarter like everyone else, so you will be seeing a lot of it. And, yes, I teach Basic and Advanced Spell Casting and Sacred Geometry. Now, have you thought about which lodge you want to join and which classes you want to take?" Tamerlane asked, putting an end to any more questions. The mage moved over to his easy chair and began rummaging around in the papers and books on the table beside it.

"Dragon Lodge," she said, snatching up her copy of the curriculum. "But it's too bad they don't have a lodge for warrior mages."

"The Web doesn't have very many warrior mages right now. It's apparently fallen out of fashion. In fact, counting you, there are only eight of us." He finally located his pipe and began stuffing it with tobacco. "We all just picked a lodge and substituted our weapons training for one of its courses each year."

Molly stared at the list of Dragon Lodge courses and wished she'd thought to ask Adam which ones were worth taking and which ones weren't.

"Can I decide later?"

"Of course." Tamerlane fired up the pipe and began puffing out clouds of citrusy-cedary smoke. Molly got up and opened the front door. The house already smelled like a smoky cross between Gram's lemon furniture polish and a hamster cage full of cedar shavings.

"Now, getting back to your class schedule," he said, picking up a copy of the curriculum. "Asmodius and I have taught you everything you need to know to opt out of the Basic Skills class and the Shielding, Invoking, and Banishing classes in the core curriculum." He paused and crossed out several items in the required section, made a mark next to several others, and looked up at her.

You need to choose two classes from the Ouroboros Lodge and two from the Unicorn Lodge."

Molly plopped into the other easy chair and studied the Ouroboros Lodge classes. "I've had lots of experience in Magical Weapon and Tool construction already. Will that help me complete that class quicker?"

"It should. It depends on Thorvald, the mage who teaches the class. But the subject matter will be quite useful in your line of work. Which other one do you want?"

"How about Advanced Spell Casting?"

"Excellent choice," he said, making a note. "I teach that course. You'll take it the end of your senior year. Which two Unicorn Lodge classes do you want?"

Molly looked at her list of classes. She knew from painful experience that to survive as a warrior mage she would need to know as much about healing as possible.

"Spiritual and Physical Anatomy and Physiology, and Auric Healing," she replied.

Tamerlane raised his eyebrows in surprise, "Those are the two most difficult courses in the Unicorn Lodge curriculum, and the anatomy and physiology class takes three quarters."

"Yeah, but I'll need them."

He made a note of her choices and began arranging her schedule.

"So, during your fall three-month, you'll be staying here and taking Western Esoteric Civ; Basics of Magic; Magical Ethics, Etiquette, and Philosophy; and Circle Casting from me. The Librarian will jump you to the Academy for the Who's Who in the Magical Realms class and the two healing classes."

Molly could hardly believe her luck. She'd get to spend three whole months in Damia with Tamerlane. Unfortunately, they were going to be a very busy three months.

"We've used up enough of your time," Tamerlane stood and stretched. His pipe had gone out. "You need to return. Remember, Monday, Wednesday, and Friday you have weapons practice here with me and Tuesday and Thursday you have Greek Mythology class at the Academy."

"How do I get there?"

"The study carrel is the Grant wormhole to the Academy."

"Wormhole? Yuk, what's that?"

"It's essentially a stable tesseract, a spot where the space/time continuum between two places has been pleated, putting those two places right next to each other, even though they are light-years apart. Every school where mages are trained has its own tesseract to the Academy—hence its name. The Librarian constructed them so it wouldn't have to be constantly transporting students to and from classes. Just sit and envision the room number of the class you're headed for. Greek Mythology is room 230."

"So when will I find out if the Academy will let me take the classes I want?"

"If you make it to room 230, you're in."

8

Thursday, September 8 • Noon

 olly sat in the study carrel shivering with excitement. Finally. She was going to Tesseract Academy. She closed her eyes, and pictured the number 230.

Tesseract Academy • Daytime

The library disappeared into total blackness. Moments later her feet hit a hard surface with a thunk and she froze in terror. She was standing in the middle of a glittering night sky. Even though she could feel the surface under her feet, she couldn't see it. Her palms began to sweat, and her heart skittered in her chest. She stood glued to the solid but invisible something under her feet. A cloud of stars surrounded her like vast hula-hoop. Sparse scatters of more stars of all shapes, sizes, and colors dotted the rest of the endless space. An almost silent, ethereal arpeggio echoed through the void.

A door numbered 230 loomed directly in front of her, but she didn't dare walk toward it. At least she'd made it into the Academy, whether she survived to take any classes there remained to be seen.

She was still gaping in terrified awe when Diana appeared beside her, standing on nothing and glowing with starlight.

"It is amazing. I never get tired of looking at it," she said. "I came to make sure you were okay."

"Thanks, I'm really glad you did." Molly sighed in relief. The endless space and eerie not-quite-silence weren't so scary now, but she was still afraid to move.

"Don't worry, you're not lost in space. You're safe inside the Academy, which is actually everywhere and all-times. Since we're creatures of time and place, we can't possibly understand what that's like, but I don't think it would look like this," she said, indicating the countless stars with a broad sweep of her arm. "I think this is our instructors' not-so-subtle way of showing us our true insignificance."

"So I can walk around?" Molly asked. She was totally not interested in weird physics theories or psychological statements; she just wanted to know how to get to and from her classes.

"No problem," Diana replied, taking a few steps back and then forward. "But we don't get to our classes by walking, we get there by imagining them. You can't get anywhere at the Academy unless you can visualize it."

Molly took a few nervous steps to the door, reminding herself that all that star-studded blackness was an illusion. Diana reached over and gave her a hug. "You are so brave," she said. "The first time I did this my friends found me curled up and howling, but you're doing fine. Whenever you're ready, just open that door and walk into Greek Mythology."

And she disappeared.

Molly rubbed her sweaty palms on her jeans and pushed open the door.

Brilliant sunlight made her blink, and a warm breeze that smelled of ancient dust and saltwater with the barest hint of pine stroked her face as she stepped over the threshold. She was standing on a hill dotted with evergreens and trees with gray-green leaves and gnarly, twisted trunks. Tiers of stone benches followed the hillside down to a half circle of stone pavement. It looked like the end part of a small football stadium minus the Astroturf. A temple supported on all sides by marble columns spanned the diameter of the half circle. But this didn't look like the pristine marble temples in her history books. The columns were white, but the tops and the sides of the building were painted in intricate patterns of bright greens and blues and reds and yellows, and it actually had a roof made of terra cotta tiles. Behind the temple, brilliant blue water sparkled and danced out to an endless horizon.

This was going to be totally awesome.

Tingling with excitement, she breathed in the hot, tangy air and looked down at the stone semicircle. An old man in a beautifully draped toga was talking with five students in plain white, light blue, or sage green sleeveless tunics. They were all mages, and, somehow, she could hear them perfectly, even from the top of the stadium. But they weren't speaking English. Judging from the outfits, it was probably Latin or Greek. Molly was beginning to feel overdressed and out of place until she noticed another group of five in regular clothes over to her right. They were watching the first group and chattering excitedly among themselves. She couldn't hear what they were saying, but they looked and acted like freshmen. The other students and their toga-draped teacher paid no attention to them or to her.

As Molly ran down the narrow steps next to their section of the stadium, she was relieved to see someone she knew. Ophelia Pettygrove, the tiny mage from Grant, smiled and waved her over.

"I'm so glad you're here," she said. Her brilliant green aura pulsed and jittered. "I don't know anyone and I can't figure out what's going on. We can hear that class over there perfectly, but there's like this invisible wall between us and them and we can't get through it and they can't hear us. And we're not alone," she said, looking around nervously. "Can you hear all those voices?"

Molly noticed that the other students were also looking uneasy and glancing over their shoulders. And then she heard it too—a nearly inaudible murmur, like they were surrounded by hundreds of muted cell phone conversations.

"Welcome to Tesseract Academy. My name is Krios and this is Greek Mythology."

Six heads snapped around, and six pairs of eyes focused on a young man standing one row below them. His sleeveless, full-length white tunic caught in at the waist with a woven leather belt accentuated his muscular torso and slim waist. There was a brief silence as the students assessed this new development.

"I can't believe I'm drooling over a man in a dress," a girl next to Molly whispered.

Then six shrill voices began firing off questions.

The man in the dress grinned. "Silence," he said, raising his hand. "We are strangers, but because we are all members of the Web, we will be working together for the rest of our lives. Let us take a few minutes to get acquainted."

After the introductions, the questions began.

"Where are we?" Alim Rahotep asked. He lived in Cairo, Egypt, and was attending the Academy in Alexandria. His calm, dark eyes gave away nothing and took in everything, and his long, black eyelashes were totally wasted on a guy.

"This is a small Greek amphitheater on the Peloponnese, the large peninsula that forms most of southern Greece. We are looking eastward over the Aegean Sea. The year is 303 CE."

"How did we get here?" Zeno Bonaventura attended the Academy in Rome. He was wiry and bristled with excitement.

"Yes, how? Going back in time is impossible," said Elspeth Pomeroy. This was news to Molly, but everyone else was nodding. Elspeth was from Edinburgh, but her family had moved to London so she and her brother could attend the Academy.

"This is true," Krios replied. His dark eyes sparkled over his hawk nose. "But we are at the Academy now, in a time that is not a time and a place that is not a place. We should be able to travel anywhere and to anytime in the multiverse with just a thought, because every place and every time that is, was, or ever will be exists right here."

The students gaped in confusion.

"However, you will notice that we are not quite here." He pressed against the barrier like a mime trying to get out of an invisible box.

"Well, then where are we?" Molly asked.

"You are in ancient Greece, 303 CE," Krios replied with a sweeping gesture that made his tunic flare gracefully, "but enclosed in a bubble of force that isolates you from everything here."

"So we're here but we're not here," Ophelia said, staring at the long-dead teacher and his long-dead students.

"But why are we separated from them?" asked Jenz Torsteinsen. He was from Norway, but was staying with an aunt in London while he attended the Academy.

"That is a fascinating story," Krios replied, "and one that you will study in great detail in Western Esoteric Civilization, which is the study of history from a mage's point of view. But for now, I will give you the bare bones. Long, long ago, just before the beginning of the Christian era, the Librarian set up Tesseract Academy as a training center for new mages. The mages found that because the Academy was everywhere and everywhen, they could travel not only to any present or future they wanted, but also to any past they wanted just by imagining it. They'd never been able to do that before. Somehow the nature of the multiverse had prevented it, and, of course, it still does.

"'Aha!' they thought. 'Now we can go back into our past and correct the mistakes and accidents of our ancestors and make the world a better place.'

"And so they did this for three hundred years and kept careful notes. During this time, the Roman Empire, despite the mages' best efforts and frequently because of them, slowly disintegrated, and western civilization began its plunge into the Dark Ages. History seemed to have a mind of its own. As a result, they spent too much of their time arguing about how to correct the past and not enough time preparing for the future and taking care of the present. And so, after months of heated debate, they asked the Librarian to make the past inaccessible from the Academy.

"However, the scholars among them recognized a great teaching tool when they saw it and asked the Librarian to make one exception, and allow them go back and watch every class that was ever taught at the Academy. The Librarian complied, but made sure we could only watch them, not interact with them."

"So I'm not going crazy," said Jenz. "Those tiny voices are other students sitting in on this class, ya?"

"Exactly," said Krios. "And those voices come from the past, present, and future."

"What about when I go to the loo?" asked Elspeth. "Am I going to have an audience from the past, present, and future?"

Everyone laughed, but sobered up quickly as they thought about all the implications of that question. Their instructor smiled in understanding and said, "No, you won't. Each lodge has its own dorm, and the only way into a dorm is to picture a specific something in one of its common rooms. Private rooms like bedrooms and bathrooms in the dorms are just that—private, and set completely in linear time and space. The only way into them and out of them is through a physical door, which can be locked. This is not just for the sake of privacy; it also insures that when you sleep you will remain safe in your beds and not get lost in your dreams."

"Gods, that's right. You could!" Zeno looked distinctly uneasy. The class erupted in more exclamations as they realized the implications of getting lost in your dreams.

"And now," Krios said, stepping back and crossing his arms over his chest, "you are going to do a time shift from the Academy."

There was immediate quiet.

"Think of a place you know well. Be sure it's a private place, where no one who isn't a mage will see you appear. Imagine this place one day in the future. When you arrive, explore it briefly. Then imagine this class, and you will return here sometime in the next few minutes. Enjoy the trip, because this is the last unscheduled exit and reentry the Academy will allow."

They all sat motionless on the warm stone benches and stared at each other, eyes wide with wonder. Then Zeno closed his eyes and disappeared.

Molly envisioned Gram's kitchen/family room tomorrow afternoon.

And she was there. So much easier than the jumps she had learned to do in Damia.

A few lunch dishes were piled next to the sink, and *The Wall Street Journal* sprawled on the kitchen table. Golden afternoon sunlight streamed in through the windows and onto the couch, illuminating a blinking Asmodius. The cat looked at her and yawned, exposing a pink tongue curled in the midst of rows of pointy white fangs.

It's too early for you to be home, so you must have come from The Academy. Go back to class.

"Where's Gram?"

She's teaching astrology at the Academy. He curled up and went back to his nap.

Molly stared at the familiar room in wonder and checked the date on *The Wall Street Journal*. It said September 10. Today was the ninth. She walked over to the bookcase and inverted one of the books. If it was upside down when she came home tomorrow afternoon, then she'd know she'd been here. She reached over and stroked Asmodius's silky fur.

Go back to class.

She was the first one to return, but in a moment Elspeth appeared beside her. Her face wore an expression of stunned grief.

"Where did you go?" Molly asked.

Ophelia appeared beside Elspeth. She was smiling, and obviously had a story to tell, but she picked up on the intensity of the girls beside her and just listened.

"My grandmother is sick and I went to see her in hospital." Elspeth stifled a sob and tears rolled down her cheeks. "She was dead. I mean, she will be dead. She'll die tonight. When I asked the nurse about her just now she said Grandmother had died last night."

Molly reached out to the sobbing young mage and shook her gently. "Where's the hospital?"

"Edinburgh."

"Then if you want to talk to your grandmother before she dies you've got to visit her right now, in the present."

"Just remember," Ophelia said, gently patting her weeping classmate's hand, "what you saw just now is only a probable future. My mom says that when you jump, you often wind up in a parallel universe where your life is a little or a lot different. Your grandma may be fine and live many more years here in this universe."

Really? This was also news to Molly. Maybe that book wouldn't be upside down when she looked for it tomorrow afternoon.

"Yeah, maybe she'll be fine." Molly said as her brain scrambled to understand all this new information. "But I'd still go see her. If you're a little late coming back we'll explain."

Elspeth wiped her tears away and smiled gratefully. "You're right. I'll go see her."

She disappeared.

9

Tesseract Academy • A Bit Later

 olly decided that even though she was just a freshman, Ophelia still knew more about time travel than she did. So as they waited for everyone to return, Molly asked about the one thing that still confused her. "So when you jump ahead, why aren't you stuck there? You can't jump back in time, right? And to return to where you started, that's what you'd have to do."

"Yeah, I couldn't figure that out either," Ophelia replied. "But it makes sense if you look at what happens during both the forward and backward jumps. When you jump back, you actually return to a time a few moments ahead of when you jumped forward, so the total jump actually takes you forward in time, which satisfies the multiverse's rule of no backward jumps."

Before Molly could reply, the rest of the students began returning in rapid succession and began talking excitedly about their first attempt at time travel. Alim had tried to travel back in time to his father's office in their bookstore in Cairo and floated in black nothingness. In a panic, he'd imagined the office one day into the future and landed there. Jenz had been missing his family in Norway, so he jumped to his bedroom in Oslo. His mom was home and confirmed that he had, indeed, jumped one day ahead. He got caught up on everyone, inspected the new kitchen remodel, feasted on a bowl of his favorite fish stew, which just happened to be left over from last night's dinner, and returned.

But Elspeth sat closely bracketed by Molly and Ophelia, her porcelain skin devoid of color and brittle with shock. When she had gone to see her grandmother in present time she'd looked to be near death.

"Now that you have a better understanding of the Academy and how your classrooms work, we can begin our study of Greek mythology," Krios said, interrupting their chatter and gesturing to the nearly two-thousand-year-old class framed by the brilliant temple and sparking Aegean.

"The teacher is the Divine Iamblichus. He was a Syrian, and he lived three hundred years into the Christian era. We begin with him because he was the man most responsible for the shape of modern Western paganism and set the stage for Neo-Platonism, which is the basis of most Western magic. By the fourth century CE, paganism had deteriorated into a religion of superstition and rote ritual. The temples were crumbling from neglect and the network of oracles was falling silent, one site at a time. Iamblichus's reweaving of ancient wisdom and philosophy breathed new life into the aging religion and inspired philosophers for centuries to come."

"But I'm not pagan, and I don't want to be," protested Jenz. "I thought this class was going to be about mythology, not religion."

"Not all mages are pagan, but most of the magical symbols and correspondences we use in magic were developed by pagans. To understand these concepts, one must understand paganism. And to understand Greek mythology, one must understand Greek religion; one defines the other. As we listen to Iamblichus, notice that he borrowed some of his ideas from Judaism and the new Christianity, and that many of his ideas also crept into those religions. Even an atheist will find..."

This is so bizarre, thought Molly. Everyone that ever was or ever would be and everything they ever did are hanging out sort of inside each other in this space.

Which is really not a space.

Totally crazy-making.

Her thoughts slid away from the idea the same way she would have slid down an impossibly steep, icy slope...and Micah Ortiz slipped into her mind—his thin curl of a smile, his close cropped black hair...

And there he was, standing right in front of her, his mirrored lenses reflecting a disconcertingly distorted image of her face, eyes wide, mouth hanging open. His expression morphed from surprise to a smirk. He and several other mages were gathered in a summer forest. And they were all grinning at her.

Molly's cheeks flushed with embarrassment, which, she was sure, made every freckle on her face look twice its size.

This place was just wicked.

You couldn't even daydream.

Before the instructor, who had his back to them pointing at a tree, noticed her, she imagined her class and was back in her seat. Everyone was staring at her. Krios's eyes twinkled in a mix of amusement and severity. "I'm sorry if we're boring you, Molly, but do try to keep focused."

The class looked vaguely puzzled, but, one by one, each of them grinned in understanding. Zeno and Alim actually snickered.

"Thanks for the heads up, Molly," Elspeth whispered. "I'm glad it was you instead of me. I would have just died."

And Elspeth only knew this half of it. Just thinking about the look on Micah's face made her insides clench into an embarrassed knot. Being dead would be good right now. Molly's whole body prickled with heat as it tried to melt into the stone bench.

"Since I doubt that any of you understand ancient Greek, the Academy will translate." Krios continued. He touched the barrier and just like that, Iamblichus was speaking English. Molly sagged in relief as the class's attention moved back to Greek mythology.

"The multiverse is neither good nor evil," Iamblichus said. "The multiverse is.

"And it is driven by desire."

Molly forgot all about Micah's mocking grin. And she forgot that her classmates probably thought she was an idiot. Her attention was riveted on the old man in the toga. His face radiated an ethereal power. He was like Jesus and Santa Claus and Abe Lincoln all jammed into one dynamic personality. If he'd been seated, she'd have wanted to sit on his lap and tell him all her problems.

"The first desire was the creator's, the ineffable One's, desire to know itself. This desire is what caused it to create two. It made the one, or *nous* (knowing), and the many. In this way, the *nous* could contemplate the many and the many could strive for *nous*...."

Molly's eyes drifted skyward and her brain struggled to make sense out of nonsense as the lecture continued.

Even Iamblichus couldn't make this easy.

The dude believed that there was this spirit stepladder with the ineffable One at the top, then the gods, then the angels, then these things called daemons, which were lesser spirits. Humans were stuck on the bottom rung, the material world. Getting to the top rung and hanging out with the One was supposed to be the goal of every mage and everyone's true desire. And the way you got there was by honoring only those wants or needs that brought you closer to the One.

By this time even Iamblichus's class was looking confused.

"But Master," said green tunic, "how do we know which desires will bring us closer to the One?"

"Ah yes, that is the difficult part. Some are obviously wise or unwise. But some that we originally thought of as wise eventually prove to be unwise, and vice versa. And the same desire that is wise for one person is unwise for another. We each have a different path to the One," the sage replied, and began pacing.

Green tunic was not content and neither was Molly.

"So how do you tell which is right?" asked green tunic.

The answer sounded like a bunch of mystic psychobabble. You had to know yourself and understand where your desires come from and how they control you. Then you had to get in touch with the daemons, and then the angels, and then the gods, and get their advice and guidance.

"So how do you get to know a god? Take him home for evening meal?" asked blue tunic.

"Essentially, yes," said Iamblichus beaming fondly at the student. "I will teach you to open your hearts to the beings of the upper realms and commune with them by using a process I call theurgy. This is possible because there is no part of us that is not of the gods, and no part of us that is not of the ineffable One, the creator who made us all."

Krios touched the barrier and they were no longer a part of Iamblichus's class. The intensity of the ancient mage was gone, and they were back to simply watching a distant video of his class.

"I know, and I'm sorry I don't have Iamblichus's charisma," Krios said with a sad smile, "But since you can't communicate with Iamblichus, I will be your guide along the path of theurgy and teach you how to invoke and commune with the gods. In this class we will focus on the Greek gods. If you aren't pagan, simply view the gods as facets of the Divine One. If you are an atheist, think of them as archetypes, or powerful ideas. Next class we will learn a ritual to invoke the daemons, which are our personal guardian spirits and the guardians of our physical space. Read the chapter on Iamblichus and the one on daemons."

A thick textbook with a picture of a Greek temple on its cover appeared on Molly's lap.

Thursday, September 8 • 12:55 PM

The intensely beige halls of Grant High School looked drab after the sun-drenched Greek amphitheater. Concentrating on Pre-Calc and Forensics had been a challenge, and Molly was looking forward to running around the soccer field and kicking something that wouldn't kick back. Unfortunately, it was raining. Well, actually it was dripping, but the field would be wet and it was gonna be a slog. She was hurrying to catch up with Shandra when Theo Peregrine fell in beside her.

"Wait up a minute, we need to talk." His thin smile looked totally fake.

In Molly's experience, conversations that began with "We need to talk" never turned out well, but she stopped and gave him her full attention. She figured there was no point in being rude.

"Why do you insist on hanging out with all the wrong people?" he said. "Adam is a loudmouthed, egotistical troublemaker and Diana is a...werewolf." He shuddered delicately, and glared over her shoulder and down the hall at Shandra. "And she isn't even a mage!"

His voice was a furious hiss that knocked her back a step. Four months ago she hadn't been a mage either, and neither had her parents nor any of her friends at Concord Academy. Her shock collapsed into outrage.

"I'm just trying to help you," Theo continued, "The Academy and the Web are no different than any other group. It's not what you know; it's who you know. And even more importantly, it's what you know about who you know." Theo smiled a smile that almost convinced her that he knew every last one of her terrible secrets. "You're a talented mage and you could go far, but not if you keep hanging out with losers."

The threat squatted between them, mean and ugly. A burning desire to smack that smug smile off Theo's face consumed her. Unfortunately, she was pretty sure that it wouldn't bring her any closer to Iamblichus's ineffable One.

It would, however, be most satisfying.

"My friends aren't losers," she said, her voice low and shaking with rage, "but you are."

She turned and stalked down the hall toward Shandra, who was scowling at Theo.

"Mm mm," she said as they pushed out the doors, "that boy is pissed at you. What did you say to him?"

"Nothing, he was bein' a jerk," said Molly.

"He's the other evil whiz kid, y' know."

"Yeah."

10

Saturday, October 1 ♦ 3:00 PM

 soft October sun warmed Molly's shoulders as she headed for Diana's house. Life was good. She had finally managed to push her fear of the Web's demise back into a dark corner of her mind. There wasn't anything she could do about it now besides concentrate on her studies and enjoy life while she could. The only immediate problems she had were tonight's homecoming dance, which she was dreading, and Micah, who had her both spooked and fascinated. The guy was scary. And he was everywhere. She'd lost count of the times that his dark, edgy energy had slammed into her shields and there he'd be, watching her, inscrutable behind those freakin' mirror lenses. His presence sharpened her senses and filled her with fear and longing. "Know your enemy," Tamerlane had said when she'd

complained about Micah. So she'd asked everyone she knew about him and they had all told her he was bad news and probably a gang leader and drug dealer. And he was impossible to follow. It was much easier to watch the jerks he hung out with. Yesterday, she'd seen Zach Jefferson lurking on Alberta and decided to see what he was up to. He slouched down the street, staring at the girls and hi-fiving friends. Molly was getting bored and was about to stop in and get an ice cream when she saw him hand a tiny package to a well-dressed middle-aged woman. She would have missed it if she hadn't been watching closely. So everyone was right. Micah was up to his mirror lenses in the drug trade. But why was he always watching her?

She turned up the sidewalk to the Andruskos's house and rang the doorbell. Sofiya, Diana's mother, threw open the door and pulled Molly into the house. She looked totally freaked.

"I'm so glad you're here. It's Diana. I'm at my wit's end. She's up in her room. Please go talk some sense into her."

Molly ran up the stairs. What could possibly be wrong? She pounded on Diana's door.

No answer.

"Diana, it's me."

"Go away," snarled a distinctly un-Diana like voice.

Molly opened the door and stepped back in shock. Diana's bedroom usually looked like something out of *Homes and Gardens*—sky blue walls hung with intricate botanical prints, chenille bedspread, and maple furniture. Today it looked like a maniac had rampaged through it. The bed was a tangled mess; underwear, jeans, sweaters, and T-shirts littered the floor, and the soft, cream-colored Berber carpet was streaked with mud and something that looked suspiciously like dried blood. The smell of wet dog was overpowering. Diana was pacing—kicking at the heaps of clothes that got in her way. Her sapphire eyes were red-rimmed and haunted. Her once lustrous black hair was matted and streaked with even more white. She really needed a shower.

"What's wrong?"

"I am not feeling well."

"Yeah, and you don't look so good either."

Tears filled Diana's eyes and she threw herself onto her unmade bed and curled into a ball. "Friday was full moon and I changed. Mother drove me out to Forest Park after school, dropped me off at the end of a dirt road, and left. She said to meet her back there at dawn. I hurt so bad and was so scared that I barely heard her. It was like there was this beast tearing its way out of me. As the sun began to set I could no longer stand. I crawled into the bushes and watched my fingernails shoot out into horrid claws and my hands shrink into paws. My face felt like someone was trying to pull it off and I couldn't talk and my teeth grew into long fangs and all I wanted to do was kill something. And I did. I ran down a deer and tore it to pieces.

"I am a monster. I do not belong in human company." She rocked back and forth in the jumble of covers and wailed.

Molly stared in horror at her weeping friend and cursed herself for being an insensitive bitch. Diana had been touchy last week, but Molly had been so absorbed in adjusting to Grant and Tesseract Academy and so excited about having weapons practice with Tamerlane three days a week that she'd just ignored her. And, duh,

Friday had been full moon. But had Molly noticed? You'd think that if your friend was worried about being a werewolf, you'd keep track of full moons.

Molly wrapped her arms around Diana, pulled her up, and shook her gently.

"Stop it! Stop it now! You're not a monster, you're a werewolf."

"What's the difference?" Diana howled, sniffing and wiping her nose with the back of her hand.

Good question.

"Um, well, you're only a werewolf one day a month—not all the time—most of the time you're this wonderful person. And it's time for that wonderful person to get ready for her first home-coming dance. The wolf is gone. Uh, think of it sort of like being on your period—only worse."

Diana stopped crying, stared at Molly, and began laughing hysterically. Molly kept her arm tight around her shoulders.

"You are weird," Diana finally said.

"Look who's talking," Molly replied.

"I am still not going."

"Yes you are." Molly pointed to the open closet door. A tiny, blue, strapless dress that exactly matched Diana's eyes was hanging on it. "You and Shandra and I looked all over the mall for that thing. You've got to wear it."

"No I don't." Diana gazed sadly at the dress.

Molly sensed victory.

"Yes you do. Adam will be so disappointed. And Shandra and I would miss you too. C'mon, get in the shower," Molly said, dragging her friend down the hall and into the bathroom.

"But I'll look horrible. I have never worn makeup, and I don't know what to do with my hair," she whined, pulling at her matted curls.

Molly thought fast.

"I'm not any good at hair and makeup either, but Shandra is. She can make you look fabulous. I'll call her, and we'll all get dressed together in my room. It'll be fun. Adam can pick us all up there. Don't worry, I'll just tell Shandra we need help with makeup and hair—nothing else, 'kay?"

"'Kay."

"And call Adam and tell him about the change. You were so crabby last week. He thinks you're mad at him," Molly said as she headed out of the bathroom.

An unnaturally strong hand grabbed Molly's arm and spun her around. She found herself looking into Diana's terrified eyes.

"But what if he's grossed out and can't stand to be around me anymore?"

"He already knows you're probably a werewolf and he still hangs out with you. And you've gotta tell him sometime, and sooner's always better. I think he'll be alright with it." She tugged her friend's desperate hand off her arm and touched her shoulder. "But if he isn't, the three of us will still go and have a rockin' time. 'Kay?"

"'Kay."

11

Saturday, October 1 ◆ 8:00 PM

 olly felt like a dork masquerading as Cinderella. Her gold lamé dress was way too short, and the neckline plunged way too low. Her pumps were torture, even though she'd bought the lowest heel she could find. Why had she ever let Shandra talk her into this outfit? Diana was elegant in her blue satin dress and pearl necklace and earrings. Shandra had scooped Diana's hair up in a mass of curls and applied just enough makeup to highlight her already exotic features. There were stars in Adam's eyes every time he looked at her. Shandra, of course, was a knockout in her red strapless dress set off with a chunky gold necklace, bracelets, and earrings.

"Quit yanking your dress down, you look like a little kid that has to pee!" Shandra said as they walked down the sidewalk toward the gym.

"It's too short. It makes me look like a hooker," Molly said, letting go of the hem of her skirt and crossing her arms over her chest.

"For the gazillionth time, you look fabulous, and that dress is just the right length for you. Now put your arms down and show some cleavage. Chin up, Tiger, and smile. We're going in."

Adam threw open the door for them and Molly gasped in amazement. The gym had been transformed. Crystal Delaney, one of the Grant cheerleaders, had turned it into a fall fantasy. Thousands of streamers of gold, copper, and red foil leaves cascaded down from the now invisible ceiling trusses. A disco ball hanging just below them cast droplets of light up into their midst making them shimmer and sparkle. The place looked like a magical fairy forest and smelled like one too. So how had one girl found enough money and time to hang all those gorgeous streamers? Molly "looked" a little closer and smirked. Most of the streamers were an illusion, copies of the real ones that were dotted across the space. And if she concentrated, she could almost smell the gym's testosterone-laden, sweaty fug lurking under the crisp woodsy air.

Crystal was a clever, crafty mage.

Students, glammed out to the max, packed the room, filling it with laughter, dancing, and shouted greetings. Over in a corner, a deejay with a gray ponytail was playing golden oldies on a high-end sound system. A huge cut-glass punch bowl, filled with ice and bottles of water and fruit juice, glittered on a white damask tablecloth, and the guys were already decimating the adjacent snack table. Chaperones in black suits and modest dresses held up the walls and chatted. Rathkin was there, stalking the perimeter of the dance floor and glaring up at the streamers. Crystal would pay for her lovely bit of illusion.

Molly's heart pounded and her mouth went dry as she and her friends strolled in and began to mingle. Fire-breathing dragons were nothing compared to this. But as several students smiled and waved or came over to gossip about who was with whom, she began to relax.

A sudden silence at the doors drew her attention. Micah Ortiz was standing there like he owned the place and everyone nearby was suddenly trying to be somewhere else. He was slim and not very tall, but he managed to take up a lot of space. In his tight black jeans, black silk shirt, white fedora, and diamond ear stud he looked like a mafia godfather surveying his domain. Zach Jefferson and another loser were right behind him. After a tense few moments he and his entourage moved as a unit to a corner where he could see everything and everybody. The noise level swelled back to a roar and the dance continued as if nothing had happened.

But for Molly everything had changed. No matter who she was talking to or what she was doing, she was aware of his presence, like a black hole pulling her in. Tense excitement tinged with fear fizzed through her. The second his gaze fell on her, she felt it. Even though she'd been careful never to look in his direction, her traitorous eyes now turned to watch him as he strode toward her. His face was expressionless. Like a mouse waiting for a cobra to strike, she was trapped in the mirror lenses that hid his eyes. As he drew near, Shandra moved in beside her.

"We need to talk," Micah said, grabbing her arm.

Don't let him do that! Molly's brain shrieked. You know how to break that grip. Do it! But his touch sent electric tingles rushing up her arm and ricocheting through her helpless body.

"Chill, Ortiz!" Shandra had stepped between them and knocked his hand off her arm. "This is homecoming. If you want to talk to the lady, ask her to dance. Nicely."

Every conversation around them ceased. Curious eyes watched apprehensively as Micah stared at Shandra. He stood frozen, except for a tiny muscle in his jaw that kept flexing.

Oh gods, Shandra, what are you doing? He's gonna blow and it's not gonna be pretty.

Shandra just crossed her arms and stared him down. Molly spotted Rathkin moving toward them. His face was a thundercloud.

Then Micah, turned to Molly, and bowed gracefully.

Rathkin stopped.

"You are, without a doubt, the most captivating woman in this room," Micah said, but his face remained expressionless, belying the compliment. "Would you give me the honor of the next dance?"

Right on cue, the deejay put on a slow dance. Something about moons and rivers.

Oh shit oh shit oh shit. Shandra, what have you gotten me into.

"Um, okay."

Without a glance at Shandra, or Rathkin, or the dozens of students staring at him, Micah took Molly's hand and led her to the dance floor. Once there, he gathered her in his arms and began to dance.

His hand was hot and hers was icy.

Micah smiled, but it wasn't a nice smile.

Molly had never slow danced with a guy before and here she was staring into Micah's mirror lenses, her heart beating out a rumba. She started to panic.

"Relax, Miss Molly. This is like a waltz. The beat's one-two-three. For once, pay attention and let me lead." He pulled her closer, and Molly came to two terrified realizations. One, she would have a hard time escaping that grip, and two, she didn't really want to escape. "Just feel the way I move and follow. It's easy."

Micah moved like a dream. And once she'd focused on the cues he was giving her she was able to relax into the slow, rhythmic movement. This was like the forms Tamerlane had taught her in weapons practice—only better. Everything blurred, and the only things that existed were Micah and the dance.

"You followed Zach yesterday while he was running an errand," Micah said.

Molly lost a step and tripped on Micah's foot. He caught her, turning her blunder into a deep, graceful dip. Her skin crawled with embarrassment. She was sure everyone was watching. This was gonna be all over school by Monday. Relax, she told herself. Look cool.

"I distinctly remember telling you to stay out of my business," His face was just inches away. She could feel his invisible eyes boring down into hers. "This is the last time I'm going to remind you," he said, pulling her up and continuing the dance without missing a beat.

How had Micah found out? She was sure Zach hadn't noticed her.

Best to change the subject.

"Where did you learn to dance? You're amazing."

It was Micah's turn to be surprised. His eyebrows actually shot up over his glasses.

"My mother taught me," he said. Had his lips actually quirked up into a tiny smile?

Molly lingered over a picture of Micah dancing with his mother in the living room.

"She sounds totally cool. What's she like?"

His face turned to stone once more.

"Weren't we just talking about how it's not good for you to be so nosy?"

The song ended. Micah bowed to her once again and stalked out of the gym, his entourage rushing to catch up.

12

Wednesday, October 26 ◆ 2:05 AM

olly snapped awake and sat up in bed. Panic slammed through her as she reached into the parallel universe and drew her sword.

It was covered with blood.

It was a human's lifeblood, and it glistened black in the moonlight.

"Who did you kill, Flick?"

Oh, Molly, her life tasted so sweet. She shouldn't be dead. It was Shandra.

Molly hissed through clenched teeth, speechless with shock.

This was impossible.

Shandra couldn't be dead.

She grabbed her cell phone and called her friend. The time in the upper right hand corner read 2:06 a.m. Shandra always kept her phone with her, and she'd answer any second now and yell at Molly for waking her up. It rang six times. Each ring vibrated through a vast emptiness. Then came Shandra's voice, "I can't talk now. Leave a message and I'll catch you later."

No, she couldn't.

And no, she wouldn't.

As the darkness began to close in, narrowing her vision to a small circle, her heart exploded with grief and rage. She curled into a tight ball and screamed silently into her pillow. She shook with fierce, angry, helpless sobs and rocked gently, searching for comfort that wouldn't come.

First her parents and now Shandra.

In time, the helpless, gripping grief subsided, replaced by rage. "Who did it?"

I don't know. His hand covered my eyes, and his magic was so strong I couldn't call out to you 'til he let me go.

Molly sprang out of bed and began pacing.

This was her fault.

When Gram had created the opening into the parallel universe to hide her sword she had warned her to pull Flick out and keep it nearby while she slept. The house shields would protect them both.

Tonight she had forgotten. If she hadn't been so careless, Shandra would still be alive. In a few hours she'd be banging on the front door and yelling "C'mon Tiger, move yer lazy butt, we're gonna be late!" On the way to school they'd laugh and joke about the cool guys and the dweebs, the teachers that sucked, and who was fighting with whom, and who had just made up—just like they always did. Hot tears burned her eyes as she shoved Flick back between and began pulling on her jeans.

Where are you going? asked the blue plush, overstuffed chair beside her bed.

"To find Shandra."

Shandra is dead, Molly. Gone from this world. You won't find her.

"I don't care. I can't just sit here. I've gotta do something. At least I can find her body," she whispered and slipped out of the room, shrugging on her jacket.

And then what? And what about the killer? Flick says he's a powerful mage. What if he's there waiting for you? the Chair called after her.

Molly didn't answer and didn't slow down. She was outside and running toward Shandra's house in a matter of seconds. The sidewalk was silver in the light of the near-full moon, and the crisp chilly air turned her tear-streaked face icy cold. Her footsteps were the only sound in the quiet neighborhood.

Minutes later, Molly charged up the sidewalk to her friend's house and skidded to a halt. The front door stood open to the night. There was no way she was going in there without checking the place psychically. But could she do it? Magic was much harder here in her world than it had been in Damia. But weeks ago, when she had decided to join the Academy, the Librarian had somehow boosted her powers a bit. Would it be enough? She went still and reached for the shimmering web-lines that connected everything to everything else and concentrated. Ever so slowly, she felt her awareness expand into the house. She couldn't see, but she could sense feelings and presences.

There was nothing alive in the house.

Molly slipped through the door, careful not to touch it. Moonlight poured in through the windows casting white rectangles and black bars on the floors and walls. Everything was neat and tidy except for Shandra's room. It was a disaster area, but it was always a disaster area. Molly choked back tears when she saw the skirts and tops and jeans that Shandra had worn the last few days scattered over the floor and her forensics text book open on the desk beside a page of half-finished homework.

She was standing in the middle of that familiar room with tears streaming down her cheeks when she heard a measured click click click. It was coming toward her down the hallway, echoing on the hardwood floors. A low, vicious growl rumbled, and the shadow of a huge dog or maybe a wolf appeared in the pool of moonlight just outside the door. Terror gripped at Molly's heart, and she reached for Flick.

There was a soft "woof," and in three quick paces the creature was at the door.

She sagged in relief.

"Kaiser, where is everybody?" The Sheehans' German shepherd must have been outside when she arrived. The big dog whined and buried his muzzle in Molly's outstretched hands. She rubbed his face and ears and scratched his back, grateful for the feel of his rough coat and his solid warmth.

Kaiser clamped gentle teeth around her wrist and tugged her out of the room and down the hall. "Okay, okay, I'm coming," Molly said, reclaiming her wrist. She followed him out of the house and they loped like two restless shadows through the sleeping neighborhood to NE Alberta Street. As they trotted past silent coffeehouses and boutiques, Molly remembered all the good times she and Shandra had had here. But tonight, stark, silver moonlight warped the street into a set right out of a horror flick.

Kaiser stopped at a space between two stores, tucked his tail, and cringed. It was a gaping, black hole; not a trace of light penetrated its depths. When Molly began edging into its chill darkness, the dog whined softly and blocked her way.

He was right.

She really didn't want to go in there.

It reeked of death and magic, but it was still as a tomb. She sent her awareness into the space instead. It was like walking into a nightmare that had already happened—almost, but not quite empty.

Molly patted the trembling dog and slipped around him into the gap. After three shuffling steps into the darkness her toe nudged something soft. The dead streetlight behind her chose that instant to flicker back to life. Shandra's dead face stared up at her, eyes wide with terror. Her body sprawled awkwardly on the pavement. As if in a dream Molly began to reach down to pull her legs together and pull down her tiny black leather skirt. Shandra wouldn't want people to see her like this. She stopped herself just in time. The glistening blood that covered her friend's chest and pooled on the ground reminded her that this was a crime scene. The streetlight changed its mind and flickered off, leaving Molly in merciful darkness.

For one exquisitely painful moment she stood paralyzed with shock and horror. Then, hand pressed hard against her mouth to stifle the scream tearing up out of her lungs, she bolted and ran.

And ran.

And ran.

When she finally slowed to a halt, nausea twisted hard on her stomach and she threw up into a nearby bush. Something furry brushed her leg and she gasped in fear.

It was Kaiser. He'd followed her like a guardian spirit. She sank down beside him, buried her face in his warm fur and wept. Her companion supported her on that dark, moonlit sidewalk and she felt his grief mingle with hers. But soon he shifted, whined gently, and began nudging her to stand up.

With one last gasping sob, Molly rose to her feet and reached for her cell phone.

And stopped.

She couldn't call 911.

She was Shandra's best friend, and it was her own sword that had killed her. And to top it all off, they'd been yelling at each other over some stupid thing on the soccer field yesterday. If she called in the murder she was toast. Bitter anger welled up inside her as she realized she would have to leave her best friend sprawled awkwardly in a pool of blood until someone else found her.

"I'm gonna find the bastard who did this," she whispered, teeth clenched on helpless rage and nausea. "I'm gonna find him and make him pay—big time."

—

Molly sat in the Chair cleaning Shandra's blood off Flick. It had dried on, so she had to use a wet hand-towel. But even so, it wasn't nearly as difficult to remove as the memory of her friend's dead, terrified face.

Kaiser hadn't wanted to return to the dark, empty house, but the sound of kibble falling into his bowl had lured him inside. She'd refilled his water dish, slipped outside, and closed the door. She'd even remembered to pull her jacket sleeve down over her hand whenever she'd touched anything.

"Flick, are you sure the killer is a man?"

Yes, I'm sure. He's a man and his magic is very strong, but that's all I could tell.

Molly, you need to tell Estelle and Asmodius about this, said the Chair.

"But if I tell Gram what happened she'll make me leave Flick here under the house shields, and she'll probably keep me home too. I need to be out looking for Shandra's killer. I owe it to her. She's dead because of me."

Bad idea, Molly. You are nowhere near experienced enough to deal with this. You are in real danger. He knows who you are and how to get your sword. He may even kill again, and it will probably be either you or another one of your friends. Wake up Estelle and tell her about this—now!

That stopped Molly in mid-wipe. She was used to putting herself in danger, she'd done it many times, but the thought of losing another friend made her stomach clench.

"Let me think about this for a while," she said, scratching off the last fleck of dried blood and applying a protective layer of oil to the satiny blade. "I'll be extra careful with Flick. Will you remind me to bring him back when I go to sleep?"

Of course—but I still think you should tell your grandmother...

"No!" Molly glared at the Chair. "I'm the reason Shandra is dead, and I'm the one with the best chance of finding the monster who did this. And I can't do that if Gram keeps me safe at home, which is what she'll do if I tell her." She reached into the parallel universe, and brought back Flick's scabbard.

Yuk! Don't put me back in there.

Molly stared helplessly at the bloody scabbard. This last, small, mean act sliced through her hard won composure and she burst into gut wrenching sobs once more.

Give it to me, Molly. I'll take it to Tor and see if he can clean it, the Chair said.

Tor, Ripple, and Feather were three of the "little people" of Damia. Tor had made Flick's elegant lacquer scabbard to match Molly's auburn hair. Ripple had fashioned the hilt and wrapped it in silk cord that exactly matched the scabbard, and Feather had polished the blade to a satiny sheen that revealed the crisscrossing patterns of the forged steel.

"Thanks," was all Molly could manage as she laid the scabbard across the Chair's seat. Between one breath and the next it was gone, slipping through the universes to Damia.

She wished she was going too.

Things had been simpler in Damia. The only person she'd had to worry about there was herself.

Flick was still singing sad, silvery songs about Shandra's too-short life when Molly tucked it under her pillow, crawled into bed, and stared at the ceiling. Her mouth tasted like metal, and she was still shaking with rage and grief. Tears trickled over her temples and into her ears.

13

Wednesday, October 26 • 6:45 AM

he alarm clock shrilled with a vengeance, and Molly batted the already battered timepiece onto the floor. It gave one last cheeky trill and fell silent. She couldn't believe she'd fallen asleep.

Pulling the covers over her head, she considered her options.

She could pretend she was sick and stay home.

Bad idea. She'd never be able to fool Gram.

She could skip school and wander aimlessly.

Another bad idea. Wandering aimlessly wasn't something she was good at.

That left getting up and going to school.

With a shudder, she curled up in a tight ball and wished she could stay in this warm, safe place just a little bit longer. But Shandra's dead face flashed into her memory every time she closed her eyes.

She threw back the covers with a groan and was greeted by the sight of the Chair. It had returned from its errand, sitting solidly back in its place with Flick's gleaming scabbard on its seat cushion.

"Did you have trouble finding them?"

No, they were still in their summer camp.

"I'm glad he was willing to do it."

Tor wasn't happy about the scabbard. He had to take it completely apart to clean it and it made them late leaving for their winter quarters.

"How long did it take?"

A week, but most of that was waiting around for the glue and lacquer coats to dry—the rains had started.

"He did a great job," Molly said, scooping up the scabbard and running her hands along its satiny surface. "Hey, Flick, it's done," she said as she slid her precious sword into its clean scabbard.

Good, I was afraid I was going to cut you last night. I wish I could have gone with you, Chair. The story of Shandra's death is so dark and sad. It's making me edgy. Feather knows all about stories. Maybe he could've helped me make her story come out right. He tells wonderful stories.

"Oh, Flick, I wasn't letting you anywhere out of my sight last night." Molly said. "And even Feather can't make Shandra's story come out right. But if we find her killer, maybe we can make its ending a little better." Molly gave Flick an affectionate pat and slipped it back between.

She was late. She made a swipe at her face with the washcloth, pulled on the jeans she'd worn yesterday, pulled a clean top out of her drawer, and dragged her fingers through her hair, which only made it look worse. With a snarl of impatience, she headed out the door.

Downstairs in the kitchen, her grandmother was already at the table, reading *The Wall Street Journal* and drinking green tea. In repose, her lovely face wore an expression of distracted benevolence. Asmodius was curled up on the window seat.

They looked so harmless, and the kitchen/family room with its hardwood floors, white cabinets, and spectacular view of the city and West Hills radiated peace and tranquility. But as she walked into the kitchen, two sets of razor sharp eyes focused on her, and began a shrewd assessment that made Molly shiver and snap up her shields.

"You look terrible," Gram said, peering over the top of her reading glasses. "What happened last night? Where did you go? I heard you crying." Gram's bedroom was across the hall from hers. She might be getting a bit farsighted, but her hearing was still excellent—and she was a light sleeper.

"Oh, nothing. I just had a bad dream and went for a walk," she said as she pulled a breakfast burrito out of the freezer and shoved it into the microwave. She poured herself a glass of orange juice and packed her backpack, trying to look calm and relaxed. When the microwave dinged, she collected the burrito and the juice and sat down at the table across from her grandmother. As she was taking her first bite, she saw that those two sets of eyes were still dissecting her.

"What?"

"We don't believe you," Gram said. "Something is terribly wrong. Please let us help." Her grandmother picked up a silk pouch from the table. Reaching into it, she pulled out a fine, gold chain. Suspended from it was a perfectly clear quartz crystal about the size and shape of Molly's little finger. One end was pointed and the other was capped with a plain, gold pendant setting.

It was simple and beautiful.

And the Web-lines around it pulsed with power.

"I made this for you a few hours ago. It's woven through with protection spells. When you are wearing this, no matter where you are, Asmodius and I can find you and communicate with you and help you. If necessary, we can be with you in an instant. Will you wear it?"

For the first time since Shandra's death, Molly smiled.

"Of course I will. And you're right. I'll need it."

With a sigh of relief, Gram fastened the talisman around her granddaughter's neck.

Molly wolfed down the burrito, gulped the last of the juice, and shoved the empty glass into the dishwasher. Shrugging on her jacket and backpack, she said, "Thank you. I love you both. I gotta go."

"Aren't you going to wait for Shandra?" Two pairs of eyes regarded her intently.

"Um, we had a fight."

"So? You two fight all the time."

"This was a really big fight. Look, I gotta go, I'll be late."

She tore herself away from their worried stares and practically ran for the door.

～

It was one of those perfect Portland October mornings. The sky was a dazzling blue and the air smelled of wood smoke. Dry leaves crackled underfoot and skittered around her in the breeze. The rising sun was torching the treetops, igniting their autumn reds and golds. Pumpkins squatted smugly on the occasional doorstep. It was a day for laughing and being glad to be alive. Molly did neither. She stalked down off Alameda Ridge, wrapped in her own personal black cloud. A squirrel foraging for his winter larder eyed her warily and scampered off to be with his friends.

She was just walking past the flagpoles and up to the entrance of the huge red brick high school when a cold understanding slipped into her brain.

Shandra's killer was probably in there.

Molly had arrived in Portland just a few months ago. The only people who knew both her and Shandra and were powerful enough mages to steal her sword were behind those doors.

14

Wednesday, October 26 • 7:54 AM

s Molly headed for her locker she detected a sense of unease around her. It felt like the forests of Damia when a predator was nearby. Then she noticed that people were actively avoiding her. The hall was jammed, but she was surrounded by an arm's length of empty space.

They were afraid of her!

How could that be?

"Hey, Adair! What side of the bed did you get out of this morning? You look scarier than hell."

Slamming her locker shut, she spun around and glared at Adam. She could never figure out how he always managed to sneak up on her.

"Shut up, Aubrey," she said and headed for first-period English.

Passing students cringed and moved even farther away from her, but Adam just shrugged and fell in beside her.

"No, really," he said. "Something's wrong. What is it?"

"It's too complicated; I can't talk about it now. Meet me for lunch, okay?"

Molly strode down the sidewalk toward Broadway and lunch. Adam and Diana were in front of her kicking through drifts of fallen leaves and enjoying the sun. Molly was busy thinking. What was she going to tell them? If she told them everything, she was afraid that they'd want to help find the killer, which would be very bad. She already had one dead friend; she didn't want any more.

Molly tensed as Diana turned back to her. She hoped Diana hadn't noticed. It was almost full moon and her kind, sweet friend who wanted to be a naturopath was going to morph into a were-wolf in a few days. The young mage's blue eyes didn't sparkle any-more; they glowed with the bleak cunning of a predator. A trace of shame and anguish lurked like a trapped animal in the back-ground. Flashing reds and blacks lanced through her calm, blue-green aura.

"We were just talking about Shandra," Diana said. "I'm wor-ried about her. Ophelia Pettygrove works in the attendance office and she mentioned that Shandra is absent today and there is no answer at her home or cell phone. When I reach out for her I find nothing. It is like she's not here. I have a bad feeling about this." Her gaze zoomed in on Molly, making her feel like a rabbit that should be running for its life.

"What's wrong?" Diana asked. "You look like a vampire's sucked all the blood out of you."

"Do they know where her parents are?" Molly asked, ignoring Diana's question and trying without success to look calm and mildly inquisitive.

"When the office called the bank where they both work, the bank told them that they were at a conference in Minneapolis and weren't due back until Friday," Diana replied.

"Hey, wait a minute," said Adam, stopping and turning to face Molly. "How did you know her parents were gone?" Molly clenched her teeth in irritation. Adam's quick mind never missed anything.

"Um, Shandra said something about it yesterday."

"Then she would have told you where they were," said Adam. "I bet you know where Shandra is, and I don't think it's good news. You were super crabby this morning. C'mon, give, Adair. If you tell us, we'll eat lunch at Burger King," he pleaded.

Diana smiled in anticipation. Molly knew she'd be ordering at least two double Whoppers.

Her friends stared at her with unblinking intensity.

Should she tell them?

She couldn't do this alone; she didn't know enough about Grant yet. But here were two people who did.

And they were mages.

And they were her friends.

And she really needed to talk to someone about this.

They'd reached Broadway. Traffic roared by and Molly could smell the Burger King pumping out all those Whoppers and fries for starving students.

"Shandra was murdered last night, and whoever did it used my sword," she whispered, cursing herself for being such a wuss. But this was just too much to handle alone.

They stopped and stared at her in stunned silence. Diana's eyes filled with tears and although Adam's face gave nothing away, his clear, electric blue aura went black.

Then they both hugged Molly tight. She fought back her tears and relaxed into the comfort and support. But in the back of her mind was an ugly image of Adam and Diana, stabbed and bloody on a moonlit sidewalk. Molly shuddered and banished the thought.

"Let's go have lunch," she said, giving her friends a final quick, fierce hug and stepping back from the warmth of their embrace.

They walked in sad silence until Diana said, "Ophelia said that Rathkin was a bear this morning and he looked exhausted. The police must have been around to ask questions. Finding out that one of your students has been murdered is not a good way for a principal to start the day. He was snapping at everyone."

"How did you find out about Shandra?" Adam asked, patting gently at her arm.

"Flick told me."

"Who's Flick?"

"My sword."

"Ah."

"We need to tell the police," Diana said, linking arms with Molly.

"What am I supposed to tell them? That I woke up last night and found that my magic sword, which I'd left in a parallel universe by mistake, was all covered with blood and that it told me that a mage had just used it to kill my friend? They'd make me hand over this 'magic sword' and slap me in juvie quicker than you could say 'nutcase.' "

"It had to have been an adept," said Adam, a worried frown lining his face. "Only an adept could find a sword between the worlds."

"And he was strong enough to keep Flick from calling out to me. All it could tell was that the killer was a man and a strong mage."

"What was your sword doing between the worlds?" Diana asked. Molly sighed. If they were going to help her, she'd have to tell them everything.

"It's where I keep it so I can always reach it. Gram made the pocket and showed me how to reach between. My bond with Flick is so strong that no one could steal it while I'm awake. But I sleep like I'm in a coma and anyone could take it then, so I bring Flick into my bedroom at night and the house shields protect us. Last night I forgot."

"Do you forget to bring Flick in very often?" Diana asked.

"Never! This was the first time."

"Odd that the one night you forget your sword it gets used as a murder weapon. I can't believe that's a coincidence, especially with a mage involved. I think he made you forget so he could use it to kill Shandra," Adam said.

"But why would a mage kill Shandra? And why would he use my sword?" Molly asked, although the fear in the pit of her stomach had already given her the answer.

"I bet he did it to make it look like you're the killer. There can't be many swords like that in Portland. And since you were Shandra's best friend *and* you just happen to have a sword, whose measurements will conveniently match those of Shandra's death wound, you are the prime suspect." Adam replied. "In fact, how do we know you didn't do it?" His expression was unreadable.

"You don't. But I didn't do it. How could I? She was my friend." The cold fear in her belly crept up toward her heart. If Adam and Diana didn't believe her, she was lost.

Diana gripped Molly's arm a bit harder making her wince in pain. "We haven't known you very long, and we don't know much about you. But the one thing we do know is..."

"You're a lousy liar!" Adam finished her sentence triumphantly. "And I can tell you're not lying about this."

Her whole body sagged with relief. They were with her.

"So who knows about the sword?" Diana asked.

"You can bet all the adepts at Grant know. Your grandmother would have had to clear the sword with Rathkin, because if they'd discovered it, you'd have been expelled. And secrets are hard to keep among mages," Adam said.

There was one other person who somehow knew she owned a sword and where it was.

Micah Ortiz.

Molly's stomach flip-flopped between sick dread and denial.

"So why would anyone want to kill Shandra?" she asked, changing the subject.

"She was in your face a lot, but she had a good heart. I can't think of anyone who hated her enough to kill her," Diana said.

"I can't either," Adam said. "This is gonna be impossible to solve if we can't find a motive. I wish we could just jump back in time and see who did it."

Molly stopped suddenly. She could think of someone who probably hated Shandra: Micah Ortiz

By killing her and setting Molly up as the murderer he'd get back at Shandra for embarrassing him at the homecoming dance. And hadn't he warned her to quit snooping? Drug dealing was dangerous, and he'd be rid of her curiosity when they arrested her for Shandra's murder. Lost in these ugly thoughts, she accidentally stepped on Diana's heel. Her friend growled in annoyance.

"Oops, sorry." Molly cringed. It wasn't a good idea to irritate Diana around full moon.

"Come on, I'm starving," Diana said, dragging them toward the Burger King.

They could see the line spilling out the door. Molly used the wait time to write out Shandra's class schedule with her own schedule next to it. When they finally had their food, they carried it to one of the outside tables where they could talk and not be overheard. Before she dove into her Double Whopper, Molly pushed the schedules across the table to her friends. Adam stopped dumping dressing on his salad and studied it.

"You guys realize that it's probably one of the mages at Grant," Molly said between bites.

"Why couldn't it be a mage from somewhere else in the Web?" Diana asked.

"It could be," Adam replied. "But I can't buy it, because Molly just joined the Web and Shandra wasn't even in it. How would the killer have known either one of them? It could even be a magic user from outside the Web, but I really doubt it."

"And we'll never be able to question everyone in the Web, and we have no way of even finding magic users outside the Web," Molly added. "So let's start with the most likely suspects."

"Okay. Grant mages it is," Diana said between bites. She was already halfway through her second Double Whopper.

"How can you two just sit there and devour all that greasy meat?" Adam said. "A friend of ours has been murdered, and the killer is probably right here at Grant. I can't eat a thing."

The two girls looked at each other. Diana's lips were smeared with burger oozings and Molly was sure hers didn't look any better.

"We're hungry," Diana said.

"And we've got to keep our strength up," Molly added.

Adam shuddered and pushed his salad away. "This is so frustrating! We have information that will help the police, and we can't tell them."

"They would just laugh at us and take away Molly's sword and maybe even arrest her," Diana said. "And the police would be helpless against a mage."

"How about if we talked to one of the adepts at Grant?" Adam said.

"We could only tell a woman because all the men are suspects. And how do we know that she isn't somehow an accomplice?" Diana replied.

"A regular teacher?" Adam continued.

"They'd never believe us," Molly said.

"Our parents?" asked Diana

"They'd probably just go to the principal," Molly said.

Diana shuddered. "Rathkin is really scary. Actually, I bet he did it."

Adam summed it all up with brutal precision. "So we have no one to turn to. And there's a murderer walking the halls at Grant."

"*And* he is a mage," whispered Diana. "*And* he may kill again."

Molly watched the fear wash over her friends' faces. Fear could defeat you before you even started—or it could inspire you to do things you never thought you could do. What changed your fear from an enemy into an ally was finding just one thing to do to make things better—and then doing it. That one thing could involve either fighting back or running away. Molly's strength—and her weakness—was that, given any threatening situation, her preference was always to fight.

She slapped her hand down on the table. Her voice pitched low, she said: "So, it's just us. But we've got to get this creep. I think we should focus on just the adepts at Grant, since I doubt any of the students are skillful enough to steal Flick. And we need to start with Mr. Liu and Mr. Thomas," Molly said, pointing to the class schedules, "because Shandra and I sat together in Liu's forensics class and Thomas's history class."

"And we need to include Rathkin," Diana added, wiping her face and hands with a fistful of napkins. "I'm serious. He does not like you, and I'm sure he knows you and Shandra were friends."

Molly was relieved to see the fear in her friends' eyes click into determination as they began planning their investigation.

15

Wednesday, October 26 • 6:00 AM

arcus Aurelius Fox stood on the sidewalk of NE Alberta Street and stared at the body of a seventeen-year-old African American woman. It bothered him to see even a corpse in such a vulnerable pose. The crime scene techs were done, so he tugged down the tiny skirt and pushed the legs together. The medical examiner was long gone. Now it was his turn. The ID's in her tiny black purse said that she was Shandra Sheehan, that she had lived just a few blocks away, and was a junior at Grant High School. Her body said that she had been an athlete, and her well-cut, black leather mini-skirt, in-your-face-red Fallen Angels T-shirt, and black leather boots told him she had been a non-conformist with good fashion sense and well-to-do parents.

But last night had been chilly.

Where was her jacket?

Fifteen years ago, discovering a body here would have been unusual, but not unheard of. Now it was almost unthinkable. Alberta Street was in the throes of intense gentrification, with classy restaurants, galleries, and boutiques attracting well-heeled clientele instead of drive-by gang shootings. Murder seldom happened here. On the rare occasions it did, it was usually done discreetly, behind closed doors.

This was a neighborhood on the edge.

The houses ranged from fastidiously renovated and landscaped craftsman homes to slightly shabby, but well-loved abodes with yards full of bicycles, swings, and ragged hydrangeas. There were still a few with peeling paint, sagging porches, and yards full of weeds. They stood amongst their well-cared-for neighbors as humble reminders of recent times.

Marcus would have bet good money that the house Shandra Sheehan lived in was freshly painted in the latest trendy colors and that there wasn't a weed to be found in its manicured yard.

Ignoring the medics shuffling their feet as they waited for him to finish, he allowed his eyes to go slightly out of focus and relaxed.

Seconds ticked by.

More shuffling and throat clearing.

And then, yes! There it was.

The faint shimmer of the victim's angry spirit floating above her body.

And my, my, what was this? An almost nonexistent whiff of magic?

He touched her cheek—cold, and rigor mortis was just setting in. Death had occurred at least a few hours ago. The stab wound in her chest was the probable cause of death. The medical examiner had pointed out the exit wound in the middle of the back.

He stared glumly up at the angry spirit. *What are you doing here? This is no place for a young lady like you. And where did that magic come from?*

The detective pushed up his gold wire-rim glasses and walked toward his black and white. He moved so silently and quickly that the medics jumped in surprise when they noticed he'd gone. Marcus watched them swoop down on the sad remains. They had the body bagged and were on their way to the morgue by the time Marcus had slipped into the driver's seat. He sat, gazing vacantly out the windshield.

And then he sat some more....

And then some more.

Finally, he took his cell phone and a slip of paper out of his pocket. The crime scene techs had pulled two numbers off the contact list on Shandra's cell phone.

They were the ones labeled Mom and Dad.

16

Damia • Afternoon

hen Molly arrived at Tamerlane's house for weapons practice, panic surged through her for the second time that day. With a gasp of fear she reached between the worlds and pulled out Flick's empty scabbard. Her sight began to narrow to a tiny tunnel and her breath froze in her lungs. Without her sword, she was lost.

Tamerlane, who had been pacing back and forth and puffing furiously on his pipe, looked up as she appeared and began to stagger toward him. In an instant he had caught her up in his arms.

"What's wrong? Are you hurt?" he asked as he guided her over to an easy chair.

"I've lost Flick!" she said, holding up the empty scabbard.

"Hogwash! You most certainly did not lose your sword," Tamerlane said. "It was stolen by that bastard who killed your friend. He snatched it in the midst of your jump when you couldn't protect it."

"How do you know about Shandra? And how do you know she was killed with my sword?"

"And how do you know Shandra's dead?" he asked, and his gaze sharpened.

"How did you find out?" Molly repeated.

"Thaddeus Rathkin was just here," the mage replied, watching her carefully. "The detective in charge of Shandra's murder investigation paid him a visit this morning asking about her and who her friends were. The detective also said Shandra had been stabbed with a sword. Your name came up in both cases."

"I didn't do it!" Fear and grief smashed into her heart once again, and Brigga's meticulously trained fighting machine burst into tears.

"Oh, dear." Tamerlane harrumphed and gently patted her shoulder. "I'll make you a mug of tea."

Her best friend was dead and Flick was gone.

Molly pushed down the tide of panic rising up inside her.

As the mage bustled around his kitchen fixing tea and arranging a few muffins on a plate, Molly managed to pull herself together before she disgraced herself even further in front of her mentor.

When Tamerlane returned with the tea tray, she ignored the muffins but gulped down the strong, sweet milky tea. Only after he'd refilled her mug did he ask her how she'd found out about Shandra's death.

She told him everything, from waking up to Flick's frantic cries to finding Shandra's body. As the horrible story poured out, her strength and confidence returned. "It's got to be one of the adepts at Grant," she concluded.

Tamerlane glared fiercely ahead at nothing in particular and everything in general. The shadows in the room skittered and slipped over each other in their haste to put as much distance between themselves and the smoldering mage as possible. The silence was complete. The flames in the fireplace ceased to crackle and snap and flattened themselves out, flickering darkly around the feebly glowing logs. The Librarian no longer whuffled and snorted in its dreams. It crouched on its shelf, ready and expectant.

"Librarian, check all the Grant mage instructors' whereabouts at two o'clock this morning."

While they were waiting for its reply, Tamerlane pointed to Molly's pendant. "That's new isn't it?"

"Yeah. Gram just made it this morning. It's a protection talisman. She was worried about me."

"She should be," he said and looked over at the Librarian.

"We have our answer. Both Thaddeus Rathkin and Robin Liu were absent from their homes at two o'clock. All the other mages were in bed and asleep."

"Thank you," Tamerlane said to the Librarian, who sniffed and went back to its nap. Then he turned to Molly. "This actually tells us very little. Any of the Grant mages could have killed Shandra by jumping ahead from some previous time to the time of the murder and then jumping back. Bah!" he shouted, slapping the arm of his easy chair. The flames disappeared altogether and the shadows wormed their way farther into their nooks and crannies. "We need more information!"

"Why can't we just jump ahead and see who did it?"

"We can. In fact, a few adepts probably have already, but if the killer is never discovered, jumping ahead won't help. And even if we do jump to a future where a killer is discovered, there is no assurance that he or she is the real killer."

Molly groaned. What was the use of all this time travel if you couldn't use it to solve a murder? It actually made matters worse, with suspects constantly jumping ahead and back again.

"So how am I gonna get Flick back?" Molly asked. Panic and fear began rising up inside her once more.

The sharp tang of fire and steel and green growing things swept in riding on a surge of pure energy, and the goddess Brigga appeared in the middle of the room. Silver blond rays of light radiated from her head for an instant before they materialized into strands of hair and fell gracefully to her shoulders. She stood tall in her leather boots, dove-gray leggings, smudged white shirt, and leather-smithing apron. Even though the goddess was a bit shorter than Tamerlane, her presence made the living room seem suddenly small and crowded. Every object in it glowed, and every hair on Molly's body stuck straight out. With a slight shiver, Molly bowed and said, "My Lady, someone's stolen Flick."

"I know it, lass," she replied, laying a strong, calming hand on Molly's shoulder. "This be the second time today that I have felt the blade's absence, and I doubt that it will be returned this time. I have followed the sword through many times and dimensions, and traced it to a place in your universe, but I could nae bring it to you. The magic in your world be hidden and tricksy and we gods can nae directly affect material things there. All we can do is whisper to those who are able to hear us and hope they heed our message. You must go yourself and find the sword you seek."

"In that case, the Librarian will be able to transport Molly to the site if you will give it the when and the where," Tamerlane said, and bowed deeply.

"Greetings my Lady," said the Librarian.

"Greetings and bright blessings to you as well, mage servant. I require you to transport Molly to this time and place and to bring her back when she be ready." She closed her eyes, no doubt envisioning the destination for the Librarian.

17

Wednesday, October 26 • 10:00 PM

olly's world shifted abruptly. There was a quick, lifting sensation and a gentle drop onto a hard surface. She was standing beside a pile of scrap metal as big as two houses. A full moon peeked demurely over its shoulder, conspiring with a few floodlights to cast eerie patches of brightness and shadow across its face, turning the jumble of metal into a surrealist's crazed vision done in black and white. Refrigerators and stoves and washers and dryers that looked like they had weathered an ogre's temper tantrum lay jumbled with the poignant remains of rusted and bent bicycles, baby strollers, and bed frames. Even though the night around it was still and peaceful, the mountain itself was alive with the raucous voices of each and every one of its metal components—metal that had been forged, molded, or

shaped to perform a myriad of tasks. The bits and pieces came together for a short time to make this huge, hulking entity that sang a thousand snippets from a thousand songs about tasks accomplished and jobs well done. The giant machines used to move the piles of metal from here to there stood nearby like trolls frozen by the moonlight. Their sleepy, deep mutterings and rumblings formed a counterpoint to the vibrant cacophony of the scrap metal. Did they realize that they would one day wind up on those same piles?

Brigga's steadying voice cut through her musings. "Flick be in that pile somewhere and there be a guard over in that trailer." A picture of the trailer formed in her mind. It was on the other side of the pile at the far end of the lot.

But finding Flick in the midst of all this junk would be like trying to find one special piece of hay in a haystack. She began reaching into the pile of metal with her mind. This was still difficult, but easier than it had been a Shandra's house. She had visuals this time. A group of wheel rims sent her spinning off, only to be caught and stabilized by a mangled fence post. A bicycle frame sped her on her way, warmed by the memories of a stack of electric stove burners. But wait—over there a bit further—were those heavy metal dreams of blood she was sensing? She made her way toward them and found a sword. But it wasn't Flick. It was ancient and had been drenched in the blood of hundreds of men, women and children. And it wanted more. An aura of evil menace radiated from it and Molly mentally backed away. She could just see the heirs of the sword's owner going through the estate and finding this sword. It wouldn't have taken a psychic Einstein to feel its nastiness. She was sure they had wasted no time in tossing it into the scrap metal dumpster. She felt sorry for the stuff trapped next to it.

Molly's mind continued to glide and ricochet through the pile like a pinball bouncing back and forth through the dreams of a crowd of sleepers all jammed together.

And then she "heard" it. A very faint, *Molly! Is that you? I'm over here.*

Coming to her senses with a jolt, she mentally zipped toward the voice and found her sword.

Flick! I thought I was gonna die when I found you were missing. Was it the same creep? Did you get a better look at him?

Yes, it was the same guy, and I couldn't see him. He jumped as soon as he let go of me. He grabbed me while you were jumping to Tamerlane's. Where am I? This place is really noisy.

Joy sang through her as she felt the sharp, bright energy of the fabulous sword and heard its feisty, silver voice.

You're stuck somewhere in a pile of scrap metal. Now be still while I figure out exactly where you are.

She "moved" back from the sword and "looked" around. Flick was about three-quarters of the way to the top of the pile and jammed under a twisted tangle of rebar. She couldn't just call the sword into her hand—especially not in this universe. She'd need to climb up and pull the scrap metal off it, which would be noisy. And unfortunately, it was on the side toward the guard's trailer. She'd have to be quick and hope the Librarian could jump her out before she got caught.

She was just about to go around the pile and climb up to Flick, when she heard the scrabble of tiny paws. Something bounced off her ankle. She looked down just in time to see a long rat tail disappear into a hole in the pile.

She hated rats. Stifling an impulse to scream, she forced herself into stillness.

Something had frightened that rat.

She pushed her mind out into the yard and found the guard making his rounds.

And he had a flashlight.

And he was doing a thorough job of it.

He moved slowly, shining the powerful beam methodically back and forth along the ground in front of him and up onto the pile. In just a minute he would find her. She almost called to the Librarian to jump her out, but she didn't want to leave Flick. In Damia she had learned to will herself into her surroundings far enough to become invisible. Would it work here?

She melted back into the pile and imagined she was a piece of scrap metal and simplified and simplified her mind into total stillness—except for the vivid remembering of a single purpose. But she kept a tiny part of it dimly aware of the guard's progress.

Boots scuffed on concrete as the guard came closer. Molly struggled to keep her attention on stillness and remembrance instead of her fear of being caught. She felt the warm light beam move across her body and almost groaned in relief as it moved on.

But then the measured footsteps stopped abruptly and she felt the light sweep back and pin her to the pile. She continued to be scrap metal, releasing her fear and surrendering to stillness.

And she waited...

She waited for what seemed like hours, until the light released her and the footsteps continued on at a slightly faster rate than before. She waited until the footsteps died away and the trailer door slammed shut.

Then and only then did Molly stretch, roll her cramped shoulders, and slip silently around the pile to just below the spot where she sensed Flick. The idiot had the trailer lights on. He wouldn't be able to see her. If she could make it up to Flick without rattling anything, she should be able to grab her sword and jump before the guard even made it out of the trailer.

She stepped up onto the edge of a conveyor belt skeleton. It jingled softly as it shifted with her weight. Molly froze and held her breath.

The trailer door remained closed.

She continued carefully upward, checking each piece before she stood on it.

Molly, something's wrong. Everything just went quiet and I can feel something nasty moving under me.

Hang on, I'm coming!

Molly stopped trying to keep still and scrambled up the rest of the way in a panic. She grabbed the rebar, and tugged it away. Her sword was free and she reached down to grab it.

Molly, watch out!

A dark shape flew out of the cavity below Flick. Pain lanced through her arm and she stifled a scream. A black, segmented-metal claw clamped around her wrist and was trying to drag her down into the pile. A knight's helmet in the shape of a rat's head floated at the bottom of the cavity. There was no head in the helmet, but red points of light gleamed malevolently up at her through its eyeholes, and its muzzle-shaped visor snapped open and shut hungrily as the empty gauntlet pulled her hand toward it. Black mage energy crackled around both pieces of armor. A chittering sound like a thousand angry rats rose up out of the pile as the claw pulled harder.

With a snarl of loathing, Molly grabbed Flick in her left hand, and slammed its hilt into the claw, unraveling the black energy with a jolt of her own power and a lot of help from Flick. The hideous armor fell back into harmless bits of metal and lay still.

Just as she straightened, the guard's flashlight beam stabbed into her and he started yelling, sending her already racing heartbeat into hyperdrive.

Oh, please let the Librarian be paying attention.

She sheathed her sword and called for the jump.

—

Back in his trailer, Pat Finn dropped his flashlight on the desk and flicked on every one of the lights. He grabbed a cold beer from the cooler in the corner and popped it open with shaking hands. He wasn't supposed to have all these lights on—they spoiled his night vision—and, of course, he wasn't supposed to be drinking beer. But this job gave him the creeps. The guy who'd trained him had gone on and on about how nice and peaceful it was here at night. Bullshit, the place was crawling with rats and raccoons, and the piles of trash had freakin' lives of their own. They took on all sorts of grotesque shapes and he could hear them gibbering in his head like a bunch of lost souls partying hearty. And just now, he could swear he'd seen a piece of scrap metal turn into this fantastic chick. But it hadn't moved. And then it had slowly turned back into a sort of human shaped piece of metal. It was enough to drive a dude bonkers. He took another gulp of beer and drained the can. Belching noisily, he fished another cold one out of the cooler and threw himself into the desk chair. He sipped this one more slowly, savoring the cold bitterness as his shattered nerves settled down to simple jitters.

Just as he was reaching for his book, he heard the sound he had been dreading ever since he'd started working here. Metal clanged and scraped against metal. Someone was messing with the pile.

Jesus, Mary, and Joseph!

He'd just made his rounds. How'd the bastard sneak in so quick?

Grabbing his flashlight, he flicked off the lights and crept out of the trailer. His night vision was shot, and even the yard flood-lights didn't help much. Pausing a moment, he allowed his eyes to readjust and cursed silently. Another bout of clanging and banging galvanized him into action. Keeping to the shadows, he crept fearfully toward the noise. He could see movement about three-quarters of the way up the pile.

He aimed his flashlight at the commotion, clicked it on, and screamed, "This is private property. Get out!"

The brilliant beam pierced through the dimness and spot-lighted a young woman just completing the act of drawing a shin-ing sword from the scrap metal pile. She stood tall with the sword raised above her head and her left hand holding the scabbard at her hip. And she glowed. It was as if her strong, lithe body absorbed the light from his flashlight and threw it back to him at twice the intensity. Auburn curls gleamed warmly and fanned out from her face in a halo. But it was the eyes that shook him. They locked straight onto his own with an unnerving intensity and fierceness that sent chills shimmying up his spine. She shouldn't have been able to do that—not with the flashlight aimed at her face.

A woman's voice pulsed through him. It filled the empty, aching places and cleared out all the pain and sadness. It made connections where before there had been only confusion. It shook him from his alcohol-numbed toes to his twitching fingertips.

"This is my servant," it said. "Will ye serve me as well, John Patrick MacFinian?"

The young woman resheathed her sword with a snick that echoed through the silent scrap yard, shimmered briefly, and disappeared.

And then he was alone and staring at a heap of metal has-beens. The temperature had dropped suddenly and his breath smoked out in urgent puffs. It was calm and peaceful, and the murmuring of the scrap metal was a comfort. He stood there for a long time— he wasn't quite sure how long. And then he turned on his heel and walked back to the trailer. He picked up the cooler, and went back out to the aluminum scrap pile. There was the better part of a case of beer in that cooler, and he pitched each can into the pile as hard as he could. Then he pulled a pint bottle of Jameson out of his back pocket and threw it into the pile as well.

With each pitch, he made that voice a promise.

18

Damia ◆ Afternoon

olly sagged with relief as Tamerlane's living room appeared around her. The adept was puttering around the kitchen and looked over at her hopefully.

"I got it!" Molly said, holding up her sword. "You are not gonna believe this. I mean, it's beyond weird, he hid Flick in a pile of scrap metal and booby-trapped it!" Still edgy from her close encounter, Molly paced back and forth as she told her story.

The smell of fire and steel and green growing things swirled into the room once more, and Brigga appeared in a blaze of light. And once again, the room pulsed with the goddess's power.

"You did well, lass," she said, striding over to Molly and touching her cheek. "Not only did you find Flick, but you found me a new servant."

"You mean that security guard? He scared the piss out of me."

"He was as frightened as you. With a bit of help from me, and with you as inspiration, I have nae doubt that he will turn his life around—and be most useful to me as well! He is a bright light that was going to waste. You have fulfilled another task for me and I thank you."

"You're welcome, I guess. I was just getting Flick back. I don't see what was so inspiring about a freaked out girl on a scrap metal heap."

"Ah, but you looked fierce and fabulous. I added a bit of high-lighting that showed you off nicely.

"Mind your sword now. We dinnae want to do this again, amusing as it was. Fare thee well!"

And she disappeared.

Molly stared at the empty space and wondered if she'd ever get used to dealing with a goddess.

"We can begin delving into the mystery of who killed your friend when you return home." Tamerlane said, striding into the living room. "Until then it's time to begin your first three-month."

The fire leaped up from its logs in bright relief and the shadows came dancing out.

The Librarian went back to sleep.

And Molly whirled to face her mentor.

"Why? It doesn't start till next week. I need to get back to Grant and figure this out before someone else gets killed."

"Thaddeus has decided to begin it today. Unfortunately, he thinks you are the most likely suspect." Tamerlane said. "He, of course, hopes he is wrong and that starting your three-month here with me will give you and the other mages some time to recoup from the shock of losing a friend and fellow student. The three-month will also give the adepts at the Academy a chance to investigate. He did ask me to watch you closely."

Molly's gut clenched.

"You won't lose any time," her mentor said and gave her shoulder a reassuring squeeze. "You'll be back by today's sixth period. I suggest you write yourself a note that reminds you about what clothes you're wearing and what you're going to do in your afternoon classes. You can forget quite a bit in three months." Tamerlane headed for the door. "Meet me outside for a practice bout. You need the exercise," he called over his shoulder.

Molly scowled as she sat down to write her reminder. Rathkin would probably be overjoyed if she were convicted of Shandra's murder. He'd be rid of a troublemaker. In fact, now that she thought about it, Rathkin was also rid of Shandra, who could sense mages and was beginning to get suspicious about them. Maybe Diana was right. Maybe he was the murderer.

The thought chilled her to the bone.

But at least she had Flick back.

When Molly reached the practice field, Tamerlane had already drawn Death Dancer and Molly could hear its ominous drone.

"You are uncentered," her mentor said. "We will go through the forms until your balance returns."

They began the first set of the tai chi-like moves that contained every position in swordcraft, but Tamerlane soon called a halt.

"You're not fit to fight," he said. "Come back to the house."

As she stood beside the kitchen table, she felt Tamerlane's gaze skip randomly over her until it came to rest at her solar plexus. "Ah, I see," he said. "Hold still."

And then he wasn't there. His body was there, but he wasn't. A burning log snapped in the fireplace and the shadows danced.

And then he was back.

"Damn! Damn! Damn!" the peaceful room cringed under the wrath of the furious mage. "I'm sorry, but this will be uncomfortable." He reached out and pulled an invisible something from her solar plexus. Molly felt a sharp pain, which left her weak and shaky.

"What happened? What'd you do?" she asked, folding her arms over her belly.

"The bastard had his hooks in you. I followed the psychic cord back as far as I could but I came up with nothing. His defenses are impeccable. There was no way through, so I wasn't able to discover who was on the other end. That would have solved our problem once and for all. The best I have been able to do is pull out the cord. Hopefully, he won't be able to hook into you again. You must keep your shields strong, and ask your grandmother or Asmodius to check you for psychic bonds every time you come home from school."

"I feel like you just unplugged me," Molly said as she sank into a kitchen chair.

"My apologies. But it would have been much worse if I'd left it in. He was probably drawing on your energy and definitely using the bond to keep track of you. That's how he knew exactly when you were going to jump. You will feel better soon. I'm not very good with psychic healing, but I can feed you, and a good meal is a healing thing in itself. Come and eat." He ladled a portion of the hot, delicious-smelling stew that was simmering over the fire into a bowl and set it on the table.

Even though the last thing Molly wanted was food, the first bite of stew was magic indeed. It filled her mouth with warmth and savory goodness and replaced nausea with hunger. Before she knew it she'd emptied the bowl and inhaled two slices of bread and butter.

But there was still a hollowness in her stomach and her arms and legs felt like jelly. The weakness frightened her. She needed her strength.

There was a killer out there doing everything he could to pull down her defenses.

Would he be able to reach her even here in Damia?

19

Wednesday, October 26 • 12:30 PM

t was past noon by the time Marcus finished his calls, paperwork, and initial investigations and arrived at the Multnomah County Medical Examiner's office. He pushed open the door, waved to the receptionist, and walked past a long row of offices. Pausing for just a moment, he steeled himself for the coming ordeal and then headed down the hall to the locker room.

He shuddered as the tortured spirits of the bodies stashed in the cooler flashed into view. They'd all had met violent or unexplained deaths, or they wouldn't be here. This part of the morgue always reeked of terror and angst and always swarmed with spirits—he still couldn't believe no one else saw them. They frightened him and pulled at his heart. Fortunately, all of them left with their corpses—except for the one he called Anxious Annie, who lurked in the intake room, wringing her hands near the door where the bodies were wheeled in.

A woman's spirit ran wispy, imploring fingers over his psychic shields sending shivers down his spine and swarms of goose bumps up his arms. Her throat had been so viciously slashed that her head kept falling backwards, giving Marcus an unwanted anatomy lesson.

A rotting assemblage of arms, legs, head, and torso, arranged in rough anatomical order, glided restlessly up and down the hall as if searching for a way out.

Another spirit hung in a corner of the hall. His head was bent over at an unnatural angle, his eyes bulged, and his tongue protruded stiffly from his mouth. He swayed gently back and forth on the end of a nonexistent rope.

He shuddered, walked around the woman, avoided the pacer, pushed open the locker room door and wrinkled his nose at the faint smell of death and disinfectant. Grabbing a lab suit, he pulled it on over his clothes, slipped on the mask, hat, and booties, walked into the prep room and knocked on the door to the intake room. There was a quick click of a key as Miguel, one of the lab assistants, opened the cycle lock for him. The smell intensified and Marcus was glad he'd remembered not to eat breakfast.

"Hey, Marcus!" Miguel smiled a nightmare of a smile. He probably hadn't been real pretty to begin with, but his face was more pucker and scar tissue than skin. But in spite of this and in spite of his occupation, he was always in a cheerful mood, which more than made up for his looks. "You're late. We're almost done. Come in."

Marcus flinched as a frantic ghost zipped through the closed cooler door on the right. His eyes were wide with terror, his clothes were in shreds, and blood streamed from deep scratches on his face and torso. He didn't even slow down as he plunged around Marcus' shields, and then through the closed autopsy suite door.

"Why are you always so jumpy? You'd think that after all the autopsies you've seen, you'd be used to them." Miguel opened the door to the autopsy suite. The all-pervasive, metallic reek of blood, bleach, and old fear smacked into his gut.

Marcus gagged.

The white-tiled room contained three stainless steel autopsy tables. A light stabbed down onto the middle one, illuminating a figure in hospital greens hunched over a body that was red with gore. The only sound was water gurgling down a drain inside the table, sluicing away the blood.

The ghost had wisely decided that it didn't like it in here either and came zipping back out the now open door, and into the cooler. Miguel was headed back to the table and didn't see Marcus shudder as its clammy presence brushed past his shields.

"Hey, Dr. T. Look who finally showed up!"

Dr. Thanaphoros looked up from his grisly work. Brown eyes that snapped with curiosity and intelligence regarded Marcus over his light green facemask. His lab suit was crumpled and streaked with blood, and his hair had somehow managed to work itself out from under the edges of his cap, protruding every which way like black, curly antennae. The effect was slightly manic.

"Ah, Marcus. One moment please. I'm nearly finished, and then I can give you my undivided attention."

He had opened up the body from chin to crotch and cut open the skull and removed the brain. The ribcage was gone and the organs lay like so many chunks of meat on a side table. But Marcus only had eyes for the apparition that floated at the head of the table. This spirit was neither terrified nor disoriented. Her nearly palpable presence shone with pure, incandescent anger. Shandra nodded at him, crossed her arms across her chest, and turned back to glare at the burly pathologist whose short, stubby fingers were busy probing through her body. He muttered "Microphone on" into his headset and finished his report.

"Associated with the wound path are perforation of the heart and left lung producing six hundred milliliters of fresh red blood in the left hemithorax.

"Situated on the back, forty-four point five centimeters from the top of the head and five centimeters left of the midline is a sharp force wound of exit. Its contour is less defined than that described on the front of the chest. With the edges re-approximated, the wound is two centimeters long.

"The trajectory of the wound is the decedent's front to back directly. The wound is suggestive of a long sharp instrument of virtually the same dimensions throughout its length. This wound was the probable cause of death. Microphone off."

Marcus looked up to see Shandra vigorously shaking her head "No!"

He stared in disbelief. How could that wound not have killed her?

Shandra continued to scowl and shake her head.

Miguel began cleaning up and packaging tissue samples. Dr. Thanophoros walked around the table, leaned back on it and studied the white-faced detective.

"Marcus, why don't you just read the reports and skip the autopsies? It's not that Miguel and I don't enjoy your company, but you obviously don't like it here."

So true.

The first time he had come to witness an autopsy, he had only gotten three steps into the hallway to the locker room before he had to leave the building. As he had sat shaking in his vehicle, he realized that his terrifying ability might prove useful. Fortifying his shields, he forced himself back into the morgue to attend the autopsy of a woman who had been found strangled in Irvington Park. As the pathologist sliced through her flesh, Marcus watched her spirit. She'd held his gaze and started to reenact her death. Assuming a sitting position, she floated above her corpse and went through the motions of calmly brushing her hair and talking to someone over her shoulder.

Then, she started struggling and trying to pull something from her throat. Her eyes bulged, her tongue stuck out, and she went limp. However, she didn't fall, she sagged against invisible arms that lifted her up and carried her across the lab.

All through the autopsy, he had watched as she died for him.

Over and over again.

Because Marcus knew that she had been killed in her bedroom and because he'd actually found the hairbrush on the floor where she'd dropped it, he'd concentrated on breaking her husband's seemingly perfect alibi and gotten him convicted as her murderer.

He smiled at the concerned pathologist and said, "It must be your sweet personality and Miguel's good looks that keep bringing me back."

Dr. Thanophoros snorted his disbelief and said, "Do you have any questions? The cause of death was that stab wound."

Marcus glanced at Shandra, who continued to shake her head and said, "Could it be anything else?"

"Well, she shows no signs of asphyxiation, no bumps on the head, or puncture marks. What else could it be? If you're in Montana and you see hoof prints, you don't look for zebras. However, you seem to have a sixth sense about these things, so I'll have them run an extra-thorough blood chemistry and toxicology work up. If anything shows, I'll let you know."

Shandra shook her head even more vehemently.

"Thanks, Doc," he said. "How long has she been dead?"

"She died sometime early this morning."

Marcus sighed. He had learned not to press for a more exact time of death. If he did, the pathologist would just glare at him and start muttering about not having brought his crystal ball in that day.

Shandra held up two fingers.

"What can you tell me about the murder weapon?"

"It was a sword-like implement, it had to be at least twenty centimeters long, it was probably only sharpened on one side, and was one point five to two centimeters throughout its length." Shandra nodded once and then started shaking her head again.

"So, since the path of the blade went straight through from front to back, could you say the attacker was probably about her height?"

"Maybe, maybe not."

Shandra shrugged her shoulders.

"I didn't notice any signs of struggle, did you?"

"Not a one. That's unusual. She was attacked from the front, so she had to have seen it coming. She was a big, strong, healthy young woman—you'd think she would at least have put up her hands to stop the blade."

Marcus glanced at Shandra, who just stared at him helplessly.

"Anything else?"

Marcus shook his head.

"Good. It's been a slow week. You should get the report by tomorrow afternoon. You know where to find me if you have any questions." And Dr. Thanophoros headed for the door.

"Thanks, Doc," Marcus said to the retreating back. Miguel was still occupied with his snippets of gore, so Marcus took the opportunity to acknowledge Shandra with a nod. The angry spirit crossed her arms and nodded back.

Marcus said good bye to Miguel, followed the doctor out of the autopsy suite, stripped off his protective clothing and hurried out of the building. He collapsed into his car, and, with shaking hands, poured himself a cup of sweet black coffee from the thermos that he had learned to bring with him when he visited the morgue. He opened the Honda's sunroof, relaxed back in the driver's seat and let the sun, sugar, and hot caffeine warm the chill of death from his bones.

Marcus was not a particularly religious person. He knew from his encounters with the recently slain that there was life after death—of a sort, but nothing he was looking forward to. And, yes, he knew there were gods, and that was fine; he would leave them alone if they left him alone. But he possessed a well-developed sense of right and wrong—and as far as he was concerned, murder was unforgivable—permanent and unredeemable. It also put things out of kilter in the world and filled it with tortured spirits.

And most of those tortured spirits belonged to living human beings.

The spirit he'd just met had touched him. She'd been a vibrant, intelligent girl, on her way to doing great things.

She shouldn't be dead.

She had also been more communicative than most, and had managed to follow their conversation well enough to comment on it with signs.

So what had she told him?

She had been run through with a sword, but she insisted that it hadn't been the real cause of her death.

But what was?

So far there were no other candidates. Perhaps something would show up in the blood chemistry report. But Shandra had seemed positive that nothing would.

She had raised two fingers when they were discussing her time of death. So, if the evidence supported it, and so far it did, he would assume she had been killed around 2 a.m.

The description of the "murder weapon" had been interesting. The blade had to have been at least a foot long, three quarters to maybe one inch wide, with no taper. It had a sharp point and one sharp edge. Only a few sword types fit that description. The sword, or katana, in the dojo where he practiced Aikido certainly did. And how many other martial arts studios were there in Portland?

And then there was that faint whiff of magic he had sensed at the crime scene.

Or had he imagined it?

If Shandra was to be believed, all he knew for certain was the time of death and the description of the murder weapon that wasn't really the murder weapon.

20

Damia ◆ Morning

fter weapons practice the next morning, Molly stumbled down to the River Selene to bathe. The air was cool, and golden alder leaves floated by on the rushing water. The river's chilly embrace rinsed the sweat, grime, and tension from her body, but as she tugged on fresh jeans and a red polar fleece, she wondered if she'd ever feel really clean again. She was still weak, and she could feel a presence lurking just outside her shields, waiting for an opportunity to insinuate itself further.

Shandra's terrified death mask flashed into her mind.

It had become her brain's screensaver. Whenever it wasn't busy thinking, it reverted to that horrible image. She banished it impatiently. Who had killed Shandra? And why? She was so not gonna waste these three months just studying. She focused instead on Gram's talisman, feeling it weave web-lines into her shields, strengthening them and comforting her.

Back at the house, they sat down to bowls full of oatmeal with raisins and honey and plates of eggs scrambled with forest mushrooms and herbs from Tamerlane's garden. When they'd finished, he leaned back in his chair.

"You're still looking peaked and you fought like a novice this morning," he said. "You need some rest. Why don't you relax and go for a walk? You were supposed to attend your healing classes today, but I told the Academy you weren't feeling well, and it said it wouldn't be a problem if you missed a day. Your instructors will catch you up."

Molly headed down to the trail that ran beside the river, settling into a steady, distance-eating pace. The gentle exercise eased her tight muscles, and the whispering, golden forest soothed her. She was striding along, humming tunelessly to herself when she came upon a trail leading down toward the river. It hadn't been there the last time she'd walked this way, so, of course, she had to check it out.

Madam Rue's caravan was parked around the first bend in the trail.

It was just as gaudy and strange as it had been last summer.

Each side of the caravan was painted midnight blue with two silver crescent moons bracketing a golden-white full moon. Multicolored magical and astrological glyphs formed borders around the moons. The door to the caravan was open, but draped with a fantastical tapestry of palm trees and pomegranates. Molly knew better than to stare at it for too long—the design did nothing for her equilibrium and sense of well-being.

Madam Rue, however, was nowhere to be seen.

Maybe she's not in, she thought hopefully.

But a smoky voice from inside the caravan said, "Ah, there you are, dearie, top o' the mornin' to you. Come in, come in."

Molly managed to walk up the steps and into the caravan with much more assurance than she actually felt. What she really wanted to do was run away and pretend she'd never seen it. On her last visit to Madam Rue, she had been glad that she could remain outside and that the whatever they were—shades, memories, spooks or spirits—were on the inside, trapped behind the curtain. And now here she was, walking into it like a total idiot. She could almost hear a voice in the audience yelling, "No, don't go in there!"

"I've made tea," said the mad gypsy. "Come. Sit and have a cup."

As her eyes adjusted to the gloom, a tidy living space came into focus. There was a small bed/couch that could be folded up into the wall, a tiny one-burner stove, a cupboard, a table set for two that could also be folded up into the wall, and two comfortable chairs that were drawn up to the table. Three of the walls were covered with mirrors of all different sizes and shapes, and the short wall opposite the door was completely papered with the fronts of old Camel cigarette packs. The camels plodded a patient spiral into the center of the wall.

Where had she found those?

The space was alive with unseen movement and unheard voices. Vividly painted scarlet pomegranates, emerald palm trees, golden pyramids, kaleidoscope camels, silver stars, and white moons romped and writhed around the walls, floor, and ceiling in a way that made Molly blush. As she was stepping gingerly across a gorgeous hand-knotted rug covered with cavorting camels, pomegranates, and palm trees she saw a shape flit across the surface of one of the mirrors. When she stopped to look more closely, another face materialized in the mirror and winked at her—only to be nudged aside by another. Both faces looked vaguely familiar. The second one scowled at her and moved out of the mirror to become a shadow skimming across the wall. And then every mirror held a face, and they all looked in curiously as if she were a rare and exotic fish in an aquarium. They all stirred memories that remained just out of reach. One by one, each face gave way to another face that became a shadow that flickered and soared around the caravan. The space seethed with movement and echoed with sibilant whispers. Even the whispers were familiar.

Oh jeez, this is creeping me out. Maybe if I just pretend they aren't there, they'll go away.

And as suddenly as they had come, the apparitions disappeared, but the caravan still echoed and pulsed with their presence.

"That's a bit more comfy, in'nit? But they're not really gone just 'cuz you've decided to pretend they are. An' they are only a smidgen o' what's *really* there—now that's a sight that would truly curl your toes!" The gypsy threw back her head and cackled gleefully.

It sent shivers up and down Molly's spine and set her heart racing. It was all she could do to keep from bolting out of Madam Rue's little house of horrors and back to Tamerlane's comfortable home. Instead, she pulled back the other chair and seated herself at the table across from her hostess, who was gazing not quite exactly at her. Sharp eyes searched and poked and nudged and prodded. When she turned her attention to the teapot, Molly sagged in relief. The gypsy's hands moved gracefully over a white porcelain pot and matching cup and saucer. Her ageless face, framed in a tangle of long ebony hair that twisted and writhed with a mind of its own, was a mask of focused concentration.

Molly shivered and looked away from the serpentine tresses. Her deep blue cloak was no comfort either. It tended to sparkle and glint at inappropriate times, and she could never find the end of it—it flowed off her shoulders and continued on out the caravan. She decided that it was best to concentrate on those lovely hands, which had just finished pouring a straw-colored clear liquid into her cup through an ornate tea strainer. A few pieces of leaves, seed pods, and tiny flower heads lay trapped in its mesh.

"That's not regular tea." Molly said suspiciously. "What is it?"

"I'm doin' well, so kind of you to ask. An' it's nice to see you too!"

Molly rolled her eyes to cover her embarrassment. This woman might be terrifying, but she had helped Molly start her journey last summer and begin weaving a new life for herself. And she had been midwife to no less than Queen Flora of Damia. "I'm sorry, ma'am. Good morning. It's nice to see you again and I'm glad you're doing well."

Madam Rue smiled and a gold-capped canine flashed wickedly. "Apology accepted. My little home can be a bit... distracting. Kings and princes and even mighty warriors have run screaming from this room. You are made of stern stuff. But 'tis always best to observe the niceties no matter where you happen to be. It helps smooth the way, so to speak."

Molly did feel more comfortable after this simple, yet backward, greeting ritual, and she relaxed into her chair and contemplated the liquid in her cup. A wisp of steam curled up from it carrying an ethereal, herby scent.

"And that is a tea of mugwort, poppy, and chamomile. It will calm you and help you do the work you need to do. Drink up."

Molly's head jerked up and she eyed the gypsy uneasily. "What work?"

"That crystal," she he said, pointing to Gram's talisman, "informed me that you needed a healing and there's a spirit with a memory for you. Drink up."

Molly suddenly felt thirsty, and gratefully downed the slightly aromatic, bitter brew. Its warmth soothed and relaxed her tight stomach.

Madam Rue was watching her closely. "There, that's better, in'nit? Some ham-fisted numbskull has torn open your power center. You're bleedin' life force out into the multiverse like a stuck pig. Tell me how this came to be."

Molly smiled in spite of herself to hear Tamerlane described as a ham-fisted numbskull. She settled back in the cocoon of warmth and safety spun by the tea and Madam Rue's art and told the gypsy the whole story. She finished by explaining how Tamerlane had discovered the invasive cord in her solar plexus and removed it. "I feel like I'll never be safe or clean again."

Madam Rue regarded her sadly and replied, "Ah, dearie, all will be well soon. Last summer's adventures left you tough and well balanced. It will be a simple matter to reweave your light body. But first, I have that memory for you. I am not a delivery service, but this spirit was most insistent. Have another cup of tea."

As Madam Rue reached out for the teapot, it started to shimmer. Then it began to shift and fold as if an invisible hand were reshaping it. Color washed over it as it gradually morphed into a human head and face. The eyes snapped opened and looked straight at Molly. They were Shandra's eyes. The handle had transformed into one of her dreadlocks and her mouth and protruding tongue formed the spout. The tea streamed out of her mouth and into the cup that had morphed into a replica of Molly's head. Only the head was dead—very dead. The glazed eyes were wide with pain and terror and a trickle of blood ran out of its screaming mouth. It was a thin, panicky, thread of sound that went on and on.

No, wait.

That wasn't quite right.

The head wasn't screaming, she was.

"Hush, dearie," said Madame Rue. "Drink your tea and attend Shandra's memory."

Molly drew a shuddering breath, reached for the ghastly teacup, and drank. The room spun. Dark shadows twisted and turned and vanished as new ones swooped in and exploded in tiny multicolored lights. A high-speed gibbering sang in her ears. She was going nowhere fast. There was no up nor down, nor front nor back, nor in nor out, nor left nor right, nor now nor then.

"Here it comes, dearie, grab it."

Shadows out of everywhere began whizzing by. Molly reached out and grabbed one that sparkled and gleamed.

And landed with a jolt.

—

It was a clear chilly night, and she was walking along Alberta Street. It was deserted and deathly still. A full moon washed the streets and shops with silver and cast black shadows that looked like openings into another, darker world. Her boot-heels made a staccato click with each step.

Wait! She didn't own a pair of boots with heels this high. And these weren't her clothes. And she'd never been able to see that far into this shop. She was too tall.

No, she was Shandra.

And she was walking to her death.

Shandra's mind was mostly blank, but Molly could hear a small part of it screaming in outrage, as her unresisting body walked into danger.

She turned into a gap between two buildings.

A hand grabbed the back of her neck.

She tried to turn and fight back, but searing pain lanced through her.

She was paralyzed and her vitality was pouring out like water down a drain. She watched in helpless horror as each cell and then each organ screamed away its life.

A sword materialized in front of her, held by a black gloved hand.

It was Flick. The wicked sharp blade plunged between her ribs and straight into her heart.

And she hadn't been able to do a thing about it.

Molly was floating in warm soothing blackness, raging with anger.

—

"Drink up, dearie, three's a charm!"

The tea service was pristine white porcelain again. A soft breeze ruffled the pomegranate print tablecloth. Molly shivered and looked into Madam Rue's deep wild eyes. "Are there people out there who can just suck the life out of you?"

"Aye, dearie, that there are. Fortunately, they are rare—it takes a keen, clever mind and strong, cruel will to draw the life from a living thing. Drink up!"

The last thing Molly wanted was another cup of that tea. But she wasn't feeling up to telling Madam Rue "No thank you, I'd rather ask you some more questions," either.

She downed her third cup.

No sooner had she settled back in her chair than the room around her disappeared once more. As she looked around, trying to orient herself in the black nothingness, a faint glow caught her attention and she latched onto it like a drowning swimmer. It grew larger and brighter and became an oval shape of brilliant lines that formed a web of light and that radiated out into the darkness. It sparkled and vibrated in every color of the rainbow. Embedded in the web was a column of flower-shaped whirlpools with glittering ribbons of light spiraling in and out of them.

"Pretty, in'nit?" Madam Rue said from beside her.

"It's totally awesome. What is it?"

"That is you."

"No way!"

"It's your light body. What your aura *really* looks like. It exists in exactly the same space and time as your flesh and blood body, but in different dimensions. If it's damaged, it has trouble repairing your flesh and blood body. If the damage is bad enough, your light body and then your physical body begin to break down. Your light body is badly damaged. I've taken a part of you out of yourself so you can see the problems in it and learn to fix them.

"But first, I'm going to put you back into your body. Attend to the process carefully, for once you're back, I want you to return here. Then we will both know that you know how to get here—because this is where you need to be when your body and spirit are in need of healing."

Molly felt a gentle shift and a series of openings and closings and reachings and weavings in the web of light and she was back in her body gazing across the table at Madam Rue, who smiled what she probably thought was an encouraging smile.

It wasn't.

"I'll see you back there then," the gypsy said, and closed her eyes.

Molly closed her eyes as well. She pictured her light body and the vast darkness around it clearly in her mind and repeated the series of openings and closings and reachings and weavings that she'd just felt.

"There! Not so hard, then, was it, dearie? Now, attend. Your light body is, indeed, a lovely thing—most are. But if you look carefully, you will be able to see where it is hurting."

She gazed in wonder at herself. It was so beautiful, how could anything about it be wrong? But then she saw it. A hole in the yellow vortex located about where her solar plexus would be. As fast as the other vortices pulled energy in, this one was spewing it out.

"Aye, that is the biggest, and naught else will mend 'til that one's healed.

"Now, none of us can do a healing by ourselves. That's the secret—you cannot do it by yourself. You must ask, kindly and humbly, for help from the multiverse. It will be overjoyed to help you and will show you what you must do."

Tentatively, Molly addressed the multiverse. "Hello, multiverse." She paused. This was really dumb. The multiverse was more gigantic than gigantic. Why would it bother to listen to her?

"Nice start, dearie, now you must tell it what you want."

She gazed hopelessly into the infinite, uncaring blackness and said, "I've been hurt. Would you help me heal myself?"

Nothing.

The vast blackness just sat there looking black and empty.

Now what was she supposed to do?

The image of Tracy Bliss, the strange dude who had literally fallen in out of nowhere and sent her screaming into the kingdom of Damia, slowly materialized, suspended upside down between her and her light body. He'd shown up several times in Damia to help her, right when she'd needed it most, and here he was again.

Totally awesome!

The multiverse had actually listened to her.

His shaggy, ash blond hair flowed down away from his peaceful face. He was wearing the same blue earth T-shirt, khaki hiking shorts, and day-glo-orange high-tops he always wore. But why were his eyes closed, and why was he ignoring her? And why was he upside down? She took another look at his screaming orange shoes. One was up and one was down. He looked like he was hanging by one leg.

The same position she'd been in when that ghastly corpse tree had nabbed her.

The only way out of its clutches had been to empty her mind and be still.

Be still.

"That's it! Thanks, Tracy. I've got it."

Tracy opened his eyes, grinned, and disappeared.

Molly relaxed, and let go of her thoughts.

She was much better at it now than she had been, but it still wasn't easy.

Finally her mind stilled.

Time passed...

The empty blackness began to hum.

It was an ethereal sound that vibrated every part of her.

At the first tone, her light body stopped pulsing and flickering and became still. As the song continued, every tiny glimmer and vortex began pulsing in a single, simple rhythm, and Molly's hands moved of their own accord toward her solar plexus.

She studied the gaping wound and immediately "knew" how to reweave its fabric. Humming along with the multiverse, she picked up her first strand of light, one that was deep inside, and began weaving her way to her surface until she was finished.

Where there had been chaos, there was now a beautiful golden vortex pulling energy into her body and revitalizing it.

"Well done, dearie, but there are other places that need tending to."

Yes, there was a dark spot in her base vortex, and the flower at her heart was a bit misshapen, and there was emptiness around the one at her throat... As quickly as she spotted the problem areas, her hands flew in to make the corrections.

And then she stepped back to check her work.

"Excellent! Now thank the multiverse and return. You need to rest."

—◆—

Molly awoke to the sound of clinking china. She was on the couch, and, judging from the lazy torpor of her body, she'd been there some time. A warm breeze was blowing afternoon sunshine and glittering dust motes into the open door of the caravan. The mirrors were just mirrors. No ominous shadows flitted over them, and the camels and palm trees and pomegranates seemed to be done romping.

As she got up to sit at the table across from Madam Rue, she noticed that she felt lighter and movement was easier. But most importantly of all, that helpless, toxic feeling in the pit of her stomach was gone.

The gypsy gazed at a spot just over Molly's shoulder and said, "Ah, much better, dearie. Have a cuppa tea."

Molly looked suspiciously at the teapot and cups on the table. They were a cheerful, safe-looking, floral pattern, and what Madam Rue poured out of the pot and into the cups looked and smelled like plain black tea.

The gypsy grinned her wolfish grin, flashed her gold tooth, and said, "Relax, dearie, and drink up. This tea is just to help you get movin' again and set the healin' in your body." She added a splash of milk and a spoonful of brown sugar crystals to Molly's cup. "You've finished your work here. Feelin' better?"

"Much better, thank you."

"And you remember how you did it? Next time you're injured, can you heal yourself? This is only the beginnin' of a lifetime of hurt, you know. The path you have chosen isn't safe, nor is it comfortable."

"Yes Ma'am."

Molly downed her cup of tea and felt its warmth work its way through her body. She actually managed to relax and smile at Madam Rue. "I never thought I'd feel like this again. Thank you."

"Don't be thankin' me, dearie. It was the multiverse that sent you the help. I just showed you how to ask. It will always be there for you. The trick is knowin' how to ask. Now, off with you. I've a busy evening ahead."

Molly walked out of the caravan and into the golden fall afternoon.

When she returned to Tamerlane's house, he took one look at her and raised his bushy white eyebrows in surprise. "That must have been some walk. You look wonderful!"

"I feel so much better. I met a gypsy and she gave me a healing."

"I've never seen a gypsy in the Wildwood before."

Molly decided she wasn't quite up to explaining Madam Rue to the practical mage.

"How much did you pay her?" Tamerlane asked, and she realized that Madam Rue hadn't asked to have her palms crossed with silver like she had the first time they'd met.

"Nothing."

"Ah, then you haven't seen the last of her. Gypsies don't work for free."

21

dam, wake up," Diana said. Her voice was sexy and full of sleep.

Adam yawned, stretched, and blinked in the sunlight streaming through his bedroom window.

"Adam, wake up," Diana repeated.

He snuggled under his blankets and snoozed for a few minutes.

"Adam, get your butt out of ..."

He grinned as he touched the off button on his alarm clock. Within seconds he'd made his bed, collected his stuff, and was padding down the red-carpeted hall lined with fabulous oil paintings. If you stared at one for too long, the painting dissolved and you were looking into the time in this universe that the painting was about. The handsome portrait of Christopher Columbus was especially awful. It became an up-close and in-your-face replay of quick, annotated, segments of Columbus's four voyages to the New World, and the torture, massacre, and enslavement of its inhabitants. Dragon Lodge was big on history, and it was able to show its mages the real thing.

Moist, green-smelling air billowed out of the men's room door, and he walked into a lush jungle. The sinks were rustic stone basins set on a tree stumps. Adam jumped as an extremely large tiger leaped over one of them and froze in midair. It held a gaudy gold framed mirror in its gaping jaws. Merriwether Orpington was belting out the Hallelujah Chorus as he showered under a steaming waterfall. Discreetly placed tropical flowers mercifully shielded him from view. Even fully clothed, Merriwether Orping-ton was not easy on the eyes. Adam wandered off in search of a toilet, which was probably behind another bunch of flowers.

This happened every year.

The freshmen couldn't resist messing with the décor.

Things would settle down in a few weeks.

⁓

Adam took a minute to enjoy the stars. There were only a few this time, and a thin crescent moon floated just above him, so close he might have touched it. But he knew from past experience that no matter how far he reached, the moon would always be just an inch or so away from his fingertips. All his friends dreaded this starry threshold into their classes, but for him it was a mystical time when he could relax, suspended in the infinite and eternal, and contemplate making the impossible possible.

After a few precious minutes, Adam opened the door to the alchemy lab. Tense with excitement and maybe just a little apprehension, he stepped onto a narrow stone stairway that spiraled up and down as far as he could see. The door closed softly behind him. Stygian darkness descended, and the aroma of burnt farts curled around him. A very faint light glimmered on the stairs high above him. Below him was only blackness. He climbed toward the light, and, much sooner than he expected, stepped into a large circular laboratory.

The origin of the stench became immediately obvious. Percy Pomeroy had got there early and was dumping thick black goo out of a beaker and into a wide, round-bottomed glass cylinder. Fumes poured out, so intense you could see them. Even though Percy had woven a web of light around the glassware to contain the fumes and channel them up to the lab's large, open clerestory windows, the room still smelled like an overfilled porta potty. Percy set down the empty beaker, waved cheerfully at Adam, and pointed to the lab stool beside him. As Adam made his way past a few other busy students, Percy grabbed an open-ended cylinder, fit it over the top of the one with the goo, and clapped a dome-shaped, copper lid over the open end. The stench dissipated in seconds.

"How's it goin'?" Adam asked, setting his pack on the stone floor and perching on the five-legged wooden stool that was black from ages of use. Trying for just the right amount of coolness, he pulled out his alchemy lab text and dropped it on the lab bench's slate countertop. But he was so glad to see his friend and so ecstatic to actually be in the alchemy lab, that he could have whooped with joy and hugged the bespectacled, redheaded young Scotsman until his freckles popped. But that sort of thing just wasn't done when Ouroboros Lodge members were working.

He had desperately wanted to be an Ouroboros, but the Academy had placed him with the Dragons and their silly performance classes. Juggling and gymnastics had been sheer torture and divination was going to be a bitch, but he was surprised to discover how much he enjoyed acting and singing. Fortunately, the Academy had allowed him to take all four of his outside-the-lodge classes in the Ouroboros Lodge. After two years he was beginning to appreciate the Academy's decision. Ouroboros Lodge took itself way too seriously.

"I'll let you know in a bit," Percy replied, his voice tense with excitement. "This has been fermenting since last three-month."

"Yuk! It smells like it's been fermenting forever."

Percy ignored the comment and pointed to a beehive-shaped pile of bricks sitting on a large stone block. "Lemme show you how to light our athanor," he said. "It's easy, they're gas fired." He opened a small arched doorway in the dome of bricks, revealing a black tube sticking up inside. Turning what looked like a faucet handle beside the furnace he said, "Just turn on the gas and light it."

There was a hiss and a loud "whoof" as a spark leapt from Percy's middle finger and ignited the gas. The athanor burned with a soft, earnest roar. Other students had arrived, and one by one the roars of their alchemical furnaces joined Adam and Percy's. And one by one orange cyclopean eyes glared balefully out at the lab.

Thomas Nicodemus, their alchemy instructor, appeared in a dramatic puff of smoke at the front of the room. His long white hair flowed over his full-length black robe, and his vivid blue eyes searched out the eyes of each of his students. Every conversation stopped.

"Welcome to Alchemy 101 and 202. I would like to remind the new students that, if at all possible, your lab partner should be a second-year alchemy student and someone of the opposite sex." He looked out over the class and nodded. "I see you've managed that fairly well. Unfortunately, alchemy seems to attract more men than women.

"You all should have your alchemy lab book and notes for the work we'll be doing for the next two years. The 202 students have already done the part that the 101 students will begin today. Help each other and your work will go more smoothly." He pointed to a glass canister filled with a black substance. "101 students, this is *nigredo*, the beginning of this and most other alchemical processes. Your first task is to separate it into masculine and feminine, sulfur and mercury." He then began a slow perambulation of the lab, checking on the second year students' progress and answering questions.

Percy held up his apparatus. The black liquid inside it was writhing with ghostly worms and creepy-crawly things with dozens of legs. He placed the glass column in a holder on the athanor and read out loud from his lab notes, "The repeated action of fire upon water forces water to defend its specific qualities while abandoning its superfluities." The goo began bubbling almost immediately, and Percy began weaving strands of rainbow light and sending them in to dance in the boiling blackness and even blacker vapor emerging from it. The black vapor hit the copper dome, cooled, and turned into black streaks of liquid running down the sides of the cylinder.

Adam enjoyed watching other mages work. Each had a unique style, their own way of moving the web of luminous lines around them to make things happen. Tamerlane was so strong that he simply blasted the lines in the direction he wanted them to go and it was a done deal. When Adam had taken Spellcasting 101 from him last year, the adept had had to curb his power and slow down so his students could see how each spell worked. But Percy gently nudged, coaxed, and cajoled the lines into place. His work resulted in a subtle, unforced process that looked like it had made up its own mind to happen.

"*Lac virginis*!" Percy said, making a soft, sweeping gesture. The streaks of black condensate slowly became pearly white droplets.

"Virgin's milk. That is so cool."

"Yes, it's way cool. Now it has to continue purifying and separating into body and spirit. Let's get you started while it's working."

As Percy helped Adam set up, the black vapors at the top of the column coalesced into a shadowy raven's head with fiercely gleaming amber eyes. The ghost of a white dragon shimmered above the liquid at the bottom, which the condensate was slowly turning white.

Eventually Percy turned back to his apparatus and began a series of gestures. "*Separatio animae a corpore,*" he said. The raven and the dragon leapt into sharp focus, the raven at the top of the column, the white dragon below.

Adam shifted his brain into Latin mode and translated: "Separation of spirit and body."

The dragon disappeared, leaving behind a white powder.

"*Corvi de capite peribit*," Percy murmured and closed the valve in the center of the column.

"Cut off the raven's head," Adam translated.

"*Totalis separatio*!" Percy cried.

The white powder at the bottom of the column shifted and stirred and formed into a perfect white rose. Even though the rose was hermetically sealed behind glass, its heady, heartlifting perfume filled the air.

"Yes! Oh yes!" Percy chortled, doing a happy dance. His golden-yellow aura gleamed even brighter than before.

Adam was grinning at his ecstatic friend when he sensed movement. He looked over at the rose just in time to see a tiny spark of light zoom in and strike one of its petals in exactly the wrong place. The beautiful rose exploded, turning into black gunk, and the raven's head disappeared from the top of the column. Adam followed the spark's trajectory back to Theo Peregrine, who smiled and turned away. Adam grabbed Percy's arm to get his attention and pointed to the apparatus.

"Bugger!" said Percy, pounding the lab bench, "Back to *nigredo*!"

Several Ouroboroses shot him scandalized looks.

"What did I do wrong?" Percy wailed.

"You didn't do anything wrong. A spark from outside hit the rose and ruined it. Why didn't you put up shields?" Adam asked, glaring at Theo's back.

"I've never needed them."

"Well, you do now. That was no accident."

"Let me guess. Theo?"

Adam nodded.

"Bloody bastard! He totally sucks at alchemy and can't stand it when someone else is making progress."

"You're totally screwed. You'll never have time to finish."

"Don't worry," Percy said as they began tidying up, "it won't take me long to re-create the *rosa alba*. Figuring out the process and making it happen changed me and became part of me, which was actually the whole point of doing it in the first place. I'll have an even better white rose in no time."

Percy carefully wiped down the battered slate counter and repeatedly rinsed the sponge under a copper gooseneck faucet in the countertop sink. His shoulders were slouched and his brow furrowed as if he were trying to make up his mind about something. Finally he quit rinsing the sponge, wrung it out and tossed it behind the faucet. Squaring his shoulders, he turned to Adam. "I'm sorry about Molly; I know she was your friend," he said, touching Adam's arm and looking miserable.

Shock surged through Adam. Had the killer gotten her too?

"What happened?" he asked, grabbing the lab bench to steady himself.

"You know what happened," Percy replied, patting Adam's shoulder. "She killed her best friend."

Anger and relief replaced shock.

"She did not!" he said, backing away.

The Ouroboroses were staring at him like he was some stinky fermentation product. Adam glared at them and shouted, "She didn't do it. Anyone who says different is lying!"

Percy pulled him down onto his lab stool and whispered, "Put a cork in it. Yelling at my lodge-mates won't help, it'll only piss them off. For what it's worth, I'm willing to believe you. Molly is taking Greek Mythology with my little sister, and she helped Elspeth over a rough patch on the first day. She can't believe Molly did it either."

"Thanks, Percy," Adam said with a sad smile. "Who told you about Molly?"

"Theo."

"He's had it in for Molly since her first day at Grant. I think it's because she hangs out with me and Diana. He's lying."

"Don't think so. I can read Theo pretty well and he seemed quite sure of this."

They looked up to find Theo smiling at them from across the lab.

It wasn't a nice smile.

"Molly told Diana and me what happened that night," Adam said, "and if she's telling the truth, the person who killed Shandra is a powerful male mage. And the only people who fit that description and knew both Molly and Shandra are the adepts at Grant."

"Shit," said Percy, "this is awful," The blood drained from his face, making his freckles even more prominent. "If Molly's telling the truth, the killer is one of us!"

"So is Molly!"

"Not yet. She's new, an unknown."

Adam was about to argue, but then realized Percy was correct. He and Diana liked Molly and knew her well enough to know that she would never have killed Shandra. But she was a dangerous stranger to the rest of the Web. And mages were only human. They would be quicker to accuse a stranger of the awful crime of murder than one of their own. Fear and anger shook him as he realized that his friend was in mortal danger. And the threat came from his fellow mages, people he trusted and admired.

"But, even if she is an unknown," Percy continued, "we can't just accuse her because it's convenient. Because if we do, and if we're wrong, that leaves a killer running free in the Web."

Relief rushed through Adam. Thank the gods that Percy was willing to look beyond the end of his freckled nose. Hopefully the Webmasters would be as logical and far sighted.

"We have a short list of suspects," he said. "If I could just find out more about them, I might be able to figure out who it is."

Percy sighed and pulled distractedly on his ear lobe.

"I may regret this," he whispered. "But I think I can help you. Meet me in the library after dinner."

⌒

The first dinner of each three-month was always a grand party—special decorations, tons of desserts, and a chance to catch up with friends you hadn't seen since the last three-month. Since All Hallows' Eve was coming up, cobwebs, candelabras, skulls, and pumpkins decorated the tables, and ghosts floated by with trays of food. Adam grabbed a dish of worms squirming in yellow goo, broke the mesmerizing lines of illusion dancing around it, and said "mac-and-cheese." The writhing mass immediately became a normal entree. Diana snagged not one but two plates of dead rats and immediately gobbled the first rat.

"Yuk, that's totally gross," he said. And then he noticed that his friend looked terrible. Her hair was a mess and dark circles framed her eyes. "What's wrong?"

"I'm starting the change," Diana growled irritably, "My skin is crawling, everything hurts, and I can't think straight, so I'm going to fail all my classes."

"Gods! I totally lost track. It's almost full moon. This is terrible. Last time you had enough trouble dealing with the change for a few days. Three months are gonna be torture, and we'll be lucky if you don't kill someone."

"But what can I do?" Diana gazed at him desperately.

A multi-headed monster crouched in the middle of the table spitting water, juices, and milk out of its many mouths. The streams of beverages disappeared in midair. Adam thought fast as he filled his glass part full with cranberry juice, added some water, pointed at the mixture and said "Spritz!" He filled a glass with plain water for Diana because he'd noticed she was having trouble making her hands work right.

"Go talk to Dr. Lovelace and tell him what's happening," he said, setting the glass next to her plate. "Maybe he can think of something. You can't go on like this."

"I'll do that." Diana glared at her second plate of dead rats and said, "Pot roast."

———

After dinner Adam hurried to the small alcove in the library where he always met Percy. The Librarian had insisted that the Academy library be an exact replica of the main hall of the Royal Library of Alexandria, but instead of cedar and sandalwood pigeonholes it had cedar and sandalwood bookshelves. The Librarian snored and whuffled on an ornate ebony bookstand in its center, waiting for someone to order a book and busy, no doubt, at several other locations around the world. During the day, sunlight flooded in through dozens of skylights, but at night the only light came from small reading lamps perched on each table. Their dim light made the darkness even darker and the shadows even more shadowy. Adam relaxed back in his chair savoring the haunted quiet and the wonderful scent of aromatic woods and paper. This was his favorite place in the Academy, and he was almost disappointed when Percy appeared and disturbed his solitude.

"I know how to get to the Records Room," his friend said, getting right to the point. "My dad was the Web secretary when I was little, and he had to go there once while he was watching me. He couldn't leave me alone, so he took me with him. The room was so totally awesome that I remembered everything about it. When I found out about how to get places in the Academy, I started picturing all the stuff I'd seen there, and finally one of the images worked."

"What's the Records Room?"

"It's a combination library, attic, and museum, and it's all about the Web. Everything the Web knows about your suspects will be in there."

"Yes!" Adam whispered, punching air. Good thing Percy had a mind like Velcro. "Let's go!" he said, grabbing his friend's arm.

—

Glowing yellow eyes the size of headlights glared at him over a pair of jaws lined with what looked like ivory chopping knives. Adam screamed and leaped away from the scaly, green nightmare.

Percy laughed.

"Calm down, it's not alive," he said. "Touch it if you want to know what it is."

Adam waited until his heart stopped trying to leap out of his chest and began to examine the monster, which floated placidly in the space in front of him. A spiny dorsal fin stood atop its serpentine body, which meandered back into the gloom, and two deep purple pectoral fins fanned out just behind its reptilian head. He reached out and touched a fin with a finger that hardly shook at all.

"Replica of the only specimen of *Megasaurus marinus* ever encountered. It washed ashore on Horta, the westernmost Azores Island, in 1412," a feminine voice said in soft, cultured tones. Adam jumped and looked around, but he and Percy were alone in a room the size of an airplane hangar. It had a dry, dusty, papery, attic-y smell even though there wasn't a speck of dust anywhere.

"Who said that?" Adam whispered, looking fearfully around the room.

"The Academy," said Percy. "You don't have to whisper, it won't kick us out. In fact, it seems to like it when I poke around in here. But the adepts would have a bloody fit. Access to this place is strictly limited."

"The Academy's a she?" The voice had been smoky and seductive, which was totally not the way he pictured his school.

"Who knows what the Academy is, that's just the voice it always uses."

A suit of armor stood next to them. Beside it slumped a pile of ancient looking carpets crawling with fantastic designs. A tangle of silver candelabras glinted in the half-light. The air teemed with strange birds and fish, and fabulous beasts peeked around countless piles of amazing stuff. Tall banks of filing cabinets, pigeonholes stuffed with scrolls, and shelves crammed with books lined the walls and jutted out into the room.

"Come on," Percy said, pulling Adam toward a wall of filing cabinets. "The Finch comes in and out of here all the time. I'll get you started and then I'm leaving. If you get caught, it's your problem."

They passed a small, beautifully crafted harp made of reddish wood hanging from a peg at the end of the wall of bookcases. Adam reached out and touched it, just so he could hear that voice once more. "This harp was beloved of Taliesin," the Academy confided in intimate tones. "He was the greatest of the Celtic bards and a distinguished member of the Web. He was born in Wales in 536 CE..."

"Cut it out and pay attention," Percy said, giving him a shake and pushing him over to a library table and chair sitting in front of the wall. "Sit in that chair and say the name of the person or thing you want to know about."

Adam sat down and said, "Robin Liu." All the filing cabinets blurred and came back into focus and the one directly in front of him, which was now labeled "Robin Liu," opened. The sudden movement in the perfectly still room lifted the hairs on the back of his neck. "This is so awesome," he said. His inner hacker practically drooled in anticipation as he reached for the drawer full of information.

"When you're done with that lot," Percy said, "Close the drawer and say the name of your next subject. Make sure you close the drawer you were working with before you leave, or the Finch will go ballistic. I'm outta here."

"Wait," said Adam, grabbing his friend's arm. He was in hacker's heaven and he needed to know how to get back again. "What's the pass-image?"

"There is no way in Hades that I'd give you the pass image, Adam Aubrey. No one's secrets would be safe. I never look in people's files when I come here, I just poke around and explore all the stuff. I don't figure there's any harm in that. But giving you unlimited access to all this," he said, making a sweeping gesture that took in all the filing cabinets, bookcases, and pigeon holes, "would be almost as bad as letting a dragon into the Tower of London to see the Crown Jewels."

"Aw, come on, Percy, you're breakin' my heart. This is the coolest place in the multiverse. Knowing it's here, but never being able to come back is gonna be torture. Please, I'll never use the information to hurt anyone. I promise!"

"Don't be making promises you know you can't keep," Percy said and gave Adam as stern a look as his boyish, freckled face could manage. "I'm only letting you have these few hours because I want to help Molly."

And he disappeared.

Adam sighed in frustration and began selecting files from the drawer and arranging them on the polished oak tabletop. He had two-and-a-half hours before curfew, and he was going to make the most of his stay in paradise. Settling down at the table he started flipping through the first file.

Minutes later, a triumphant smile spread across his face.

22

Tesseract Academy ◆ 12:35 PM ◆ Three-Month, Day 2

unlight streamed in through open clerestory windows spaced between stone columns in the monastery refectory. The barrel-vaulted cream-colored ceiling reflected the light down onto two rows of heavy oak tables and benches that ran the length of the huge room. The wall behind the empty reader's pulpit where the crucifix would have hung was blank, and but for an empty space, it felt quite crowded. It was lunchtime at Tesseract Academy and the room was filled with students from all over the world. They chattered at each other between bites or ate quietly with their noses buried in books.

Diana sat with her back to the wall and inhaled her second blood-rare hamburger. She had a table to herself. Who wanted to eat with a werewolf?

She wiped her greasy chin clean, and growled.

This three-month couldn't have come at a worse time. Her body felt like it belonged to somebody else. Things were never quite where she thought they'd be when she reached for them or took a step, and she was constantly tripping and knocking stuff over. Sometimes her face felt like it was stretching out into a muzzle, and like her toes and fingers were sprouting phantom claws. Last month, during her first change, she had panicked when this happened, certain that she was morphing. Many terrified trips to the mirror had convinced her that her face and hands still looked completely normal, even though they felt like silly putty being mashed and pulled into a new shape. She was irritable and flared into rages over nothing, which was scary because when she was angry, biting people's heads off seemed like a viable option. She was always hungry, and a salad wouldn't do. It had to be meat, the bloodier the better.

Fortunately, she had taken Adam's advice and gone to see Dr. Lovelace right after dinner. The good doctor had been horrified at Diana's plight and immediately began going through all his werewolf anatomy and physiology reference books.

"Yes!" he said, tapping a page, "This should do it. Unfortunately it's not something the infirmary keeps on hand." He turned to his copy of the Librarian.

"I need a three-month supply of an infusion of *Aconitum columbianum* flowers immediately." Since the Librarian was speaking just to Dr. Lovelace, Diana only heard the doctor's half of the conversation.

"Yes, I know they're out of season."

"Jump ahead a year or find some that's already been made. I don't care. Just do it. Now."

"Yes, damn it, it's an emergency."

A moment later three small clear-glass dropper bottles appeared on the doctor's desk.

"Thank you," he said snarkily, and, handing the bottles to Diana, he said, "This stuff is toxic, so only take one dropperful three times a day, no matter how bad it gets."

"What is it?"

"Wolf's bane," he replied with a wicked grin.

The infusion had taken the edge off. She would survive the three-month without failing all her classes or killing anyone.

Firmly resisting the urge to use her fingers, she forked her third burger out of its bun and cut it into four bites, which disappeared instantly. She was going to be a blimp when she got back to Grant, and everyone would wonder how she'd managed to gain all that weight in just a few minutes.

And as if things weren't bad enough, Molly was a murder suspect and nowhere to be found, and Adam, her only other friend at the Academy, was ignoring her. He wasn't at lunch, and at dinner yesterday evening he disappeared as soon as he possibly could, like he was embarrassed to be seen with her.

She growled forlornly and eased further into her self-pity party.

It was probably just as well. She shuddered with shame and loathing as she remembered the last full moon, running naked through Forest Park with the scent of a frightened buck flaming through her brain. She'd heard him slipping through the underbrush a football field's length away. Desire had gripped her strong, furry body and sent saliva dripping down her fangs. Her claws dug into the soft Doug-fir duff as she bounded after him. Moments later she leaped onto his back, snarled in ecstasy, and sank her teeth into his shoulder. The buck's terrified scream and salty blood drove her to madness as she shredded his hot, pulsing flesh, devouring him alive. He shrieked until she tore out his throat. She shuddered again and vowed that at least this full moon she would make a quick kill.

She sighed and scrubbed her face, which felt like a muzzle, with hands that felt like they had claws.

Oh, come on, who did she think she was kidding? It had been the most wonderful night of her life. She had never felt so alive. As she was ripping out the buck's throat, his spirit flew free and a part of her had leaped up to join it. For one, marvelous moment she felt herself click into the multiverse like a missing puzzle piece. And everything had been totally and absolutely perfect.

But how could she have done all those horrid things, and how could she possibly have enjoyed them? She'd always thought of herself as logical and even-tempered, and kind. But as full moon approached and terrifying rages and bloodlust racked her body, she began to wonder if Molly had got it wrong and maybe she really was a horrid monster and the other Diana was just a story she'd made up about herself.

She was going to have to make sure Adam remained just a friend.

It would be safer that way.

She sent her dishes back to the kitchen with a flick of her hand and reached for her astrology notes. She dreaded going to class. How were you supposed to act with someone whose granddaughter was a murder suspect? Estelle seemed to be doing okay. She acted like she didn't have a care in the world, but Diana could smell the fear and worry on her and it made the beast inside her edgy. And besides, astrology was really hard and Estelle insisted on nothing less than perfection. At least she'd probably see Adam there, since it wasn't a good idea to skip an astrology class.

The skin between her eyebrows began to crawl and she looked up to see Theo and Jeb Dorfman amble over and stand across the table from her.

"Hey, Diana," Jeb said, "You're lookin' pretty mean—like mean enough to bite someone. Whatsa matter? Wrong time of the month?"

Diana shook with anger. Her mouth watered as she caught Jeb's scent and watched the pulse in his throat. It took every ounce of self-control she had to keep from lunging over the table and sinking her teeth into him.

"Now, Jeb," Theo said, "That wasn't nice. Diana's a good little werewolf, wouldn't hurt anyone. But her friend, Molly, is a murderer!"

The beast inside her snarled in fury and Diana jumped up, knocking over the bench.

"She is not!"

She'd said it way too loud. Every conversation in the refectory stopped and every student turned to stare at her. Theo smiled in triumph and gathered up the silence. When he felt that he had just the right amount he dropped his words into it.

"Ah, but she is," he said.

And he wasn't lying.

She would have smelled it.

23

Damia ◆ Midmorning

ave you read any of your esoteric western civ text?" Tamerlane asked.

"I sort of got through the first chapter last night," Molly replied, sitting down at the kitchen table and opening her notebook.

"Then you have probably noticed that esoteric civ reads a bit differently than the regular history texts. Mages are a secretive lot, and much of what they do goes unnoticed or gets misinterpreted. It is those discrepancies that we will be studying in this class..."

And so began a morning of intense lecture and discussion that was even more exhausting than weapons practice. There was a break for lunch and a quick run. In the afternoon she had her basics of magic, magical ethics and etiquette, and philosophy classes. Then there was time out to prepare and eat a simple dinner, and after dinner there was reading for her next classes. Bedtime was at nine thirty.

⸺

The next morning after weapons practice and breakfast, Tamerlane announced that her who's who class was this morning and that the Librarian would transport her to the Academy.

"So who's the Who's Who in the Magical Realms teacher?" Molly asked with a grin.

"Her name is Philadelphia, and she will also be your divination instructor."

"What's she like?" A teacher named after a cream cheese brand didn't sound promising.

"You'll find out soon enough. You'll be back for lunch and then afternoon classes. You don't need to take anything with you. Are you ready?"

"Yeah, I guess."

"Remember to keep your hand on your sword," he reminded her.

⸺

Almost immediately she felt the familiar lifting sensation and then her feet touched down on nothingness, and the planet Saturn hung suspended in front of her, filling the black silence, its rings circling it gracefully.

Beautiful.

She took a moment to watch.

Returning Flick to its pocket, she opened the door to her Who's Who class.

The blare of dozens of cranky car horns crashed into her ears. The smell of exhaust fumes was nauseating after the pure air of the Wildwood. Brick walls surrounded her on three sides. Concrete stairs with a fancy wrought iron railing led up to a sidewalk bustling with the feet and lower legs of pedestrians. The door behind her was locked, so she climbed the steps to the sidewalk. A shiny black BMW motorcycle was double-parked next to a powder-blue Lexus.

Where was she?

"You're in New York City."

Molly spun around. A tall redhead dressed in skintight, black riding leathers looked down on her from the steps of a four-story row house. "I'm Philadelphia." Shifting her helmet over to her left hand, she glided down the steps and gripped Molly's shoulder gently. Green eyes flicked over her. "I always have my students meet the vampire first and get it over with. Otherwise every class begins with some silly girl asking when she's going to meet one. The vampire that usually instructs our students is people-friendly and unlikely to give a young mage any romantic ideas about his kind. But last night I had a visit from what looked like the tarot High Priestess on LSD." Molly suppressed a grin at this perfect description of Madame Rue. "She informed me that you needed to talk to Iskander, not Joseph," Philadelphia continued. "I tried to tell her that Iskander is dangerous, but she insisted, and hinted that things would not go well with me or with you if I ignored her instructions."

"So how did I get so lucky?" Molly asked as she moved out of her instructor's grasp. She could almost feel all her secrets being sucked into those red lacquered fingertips.

"Lucky isn't the word I would use. She says you are in danger, and only Iskander can give you the information you need to save yourself."

"Who killed my friend? That's what I really need to know."

"She didn't say." Philadelphia glanced over her shoulder, and Molly looked up just in time to see the second floor bay window curtain twitch. "He's ready. Convincing him to see you on such short notice wasn't easy. Go up and knock on the door."

"Aren't you coming in with me?"

"I wish I could, but my visitor insisted that you go alone. Whatever you do, don't get him angry. He's not a pretty sight when he's mad." She headed for the BMW. "See that coffee shop down the street? Meet me there in an hour and we'll go over what you've learned, and I can make sure he gave you correct information." Mounting the bike, she pulled her helmet on over her short, smooth cap of hair. "Good luck, and be careful." Philadelphia rocked the bike off the kickstand, touched the starter button, and zoomed off into the crowded street.

Molly stared after her and then walked up the steps. A hideous gargoyle leered down at her from the intricately carved stone railing of the third-floor balcony. An upside-down iron bat with folded wings hung on the massive, black front door. Its two garnet eyes glared at her as she grabbed its head and knocked.

The door creaked open, revealing a long, empty hallway tiled in black and white marble squares set in a checkerboard pattern.

The alabaster bowl lamp that hung at the center of the high ceiling somehow managed to cast more shadows than light. The walls were oxblood red.

A deep, slightly accented voice purred, "Good afternoon. Please. Come in."

A young man just a slight bit taller than Molly stepped out from behind the door and bowed. The movement was calculated to show just the proper amount of respect and no more, but it was sheer poetry. Her trained eye noticed with awe and perhaps a touch of jealousy the controlled, effortless power that moved each muscle precisely and in perfect harmony with all the others.

He was heart-stoppingly beautiful.

And he sizzled with magic.

Molly felt his glittering black eyes dance over her entire body before coming to rest on her face. "I am Iskander. A pleasure to meet you, young mage." Everything about him was black, from his designer jeans to his sleek, perfectly cut hair, but the hand he extended toward her glowed white, like the alabaster lamp above them.

When Molly touched it, it was all she could do to keep from jerking her hand away. It was so cold it sucked the heat right out of her. Remembering that she wasn't supposed to piss this guy off, she suppressed a shiver and broke the handshake as soon as politely possible. "Nice to meet you, sir. I'm Molly."

The vampire smiled. She had seen Asmodius smile that same smile as he played with his unfortunate dinner. "My hand is cold. I am sorry. It has been too long since I have had any...sustenance. Come into my sitting room, we can talk there." He motioned her through a door on her left. The last thing she wanted to do was turn her back on this dangerous creature, but it would be awkward to do anything else, so she entered the room ahead of her host. The skin between her shoulder blades twitched and prickled.

Any light that might have entered through the bay windows was cut off by shrouds of floor-to-ceiling drapes. Across from them, flames flickered franticly over the fake logs in a gas fireplace, trying to heat a room that was cold as a crypt. The wall that the brownstone shared with its neighbor was graced by a *trompe l'oeil* mural of a window looking out over a moonlit stormy sea. Lamplight and firelight gleamed on the dark hardwood floor, and a taupe carpet decorated with an intricate design of ivory circles and diamonds floated in its center. Molly sat in a brown leather easy chair with her back to the bay window and stared at the bookcases that surrounded the fireplace. They were packed with books of all different sizes and shapes bound in a subdued rainbow of gleaming leathers. They were as old and steeped in magic as the tomes in her grandmother's and Tamerlane's libraries. But there was no Librarian here. The vampire had collected all these himself. It must have taken a ton of money and many lifetimes, and she had no doubt that he'd read each and every one.

Iskander seated himself across from her and regarded her over steepled fingers. "The mages never send me their young ones. I think they are afraid I would talk them into becoming vampires. Why are you here?"

"To learn about vampires, I guess. Why would I want to be a vampire?"

"Power."

He had her attention.

"Vampires are the most powerful creatures on earth. Our long lives allow us to amass great wealth and master many professions. We are also quicker and stronger than any human."

His chair was suddenly empty.

"I am behind you."

Before Molly could even think about turning around, her chair levitated up toward the ceiling.

"I am under you."

And then her chair was back on the floor and Iskander was seated in front of her. "I can hear the woman next door whispering to her lover and I can smell his lust."

"Awesome," she said, shifting uneasily as her traitorous but inexperienced mind conjured up an image of just what the couple next door might be doing, "But I don't think I could get into drinking blood."

"Ah, but the taste of blood is marvelous! Think of your favorite food."

The image of a cheeseburger popped into her head.

"Now imagine that with every bite you experienced the most intense orgasm you can imagine. Oh, don't look at me like that. A lovely young thing like you certainly knows what an orgasm feels like."

Molly felt her cheeks redden. All her orgasms had been self-induced.

Iskander's eyes gleamed.

"Really?"

Molly gasped. "You can read minds!"

"Yet another power. Although most people's minds are so bor-ing and predictable that I usually don't bother."

Fear blossomed in her belly and set her heart racing. She was fast, but not as fast as the vampire. She was trapped in this room with a powerful, dangerous, and unpredictable creature.

Iskander smiled as he read her thoughts.

Was it her imagination or had his canines lengthened just a tiny bit?

"So I'd never die?' she asked, gaining control of her fear and changing the subject.

"A creature who is already dead cannot be killed, but he can be terminated."

"How?"

"Oh, the usual things. Garlic, holy water, sunlight." His eyes danced with mischief.

Liar, she thought before she could stop herself.

Iskander smiled once more.

Those teeth were definitely longer.

"All right. I will tell you. It is no secret to the mages. The only way you could ever die would be if someone were able to either cut off your head, or set you afire and burn you to a crisp."

Unlikely, she thought.

The vampire's eyes twinkled.

Maybe this was working.

"So could I walk around in the sun?"

"Yes, of course, but you would prefer darkness. And, before you ask, garlic wouldn't bother you and you could take a bath in holy water."

"But I'd have to kill people."

"Not necessarily. I visit a slaughter house every week or so and pay the foreman to look the other way when a pig gets drained a bit earlier than usual."

"That is so gross."

"Not any more gross than bacon and burned pork chops."

"So, you never kill people?"

"Never."

Liar—oops, big mistake.

The vampire transfixed her with a glare and her stomach clenched with fear. "And what if I do occasionally take the life of one of the homeless people that swarm in the back alleys of the city? I am doing humanity a service."

Service? Are you kidding? Those people have just as much right to life as you do!

Iskander glared at her and hissed.

Even bigger mistake.

Molly jammed her fury back in a dark corner of her mind, hid it with her fear, and decided she'd better change the subject again. "So, how do you drink blood? I mean, you don't have fangs or anything."

"Ah, but I do. Observe." His handsome face went from white to dead white, and its bone structure jutted into gruesome relief. His eyes emptied into bottomless, smoldering, black holes, and his canines extended into cruel fangs. His manicured hands warped into claws. A demon from the blackest pits of hell snarled at her.

Molly barely managed to stifle a scream, but before she had drawn her next breath, the demon became a man. "So what am I,

Molly Adair, an evil ghoul or a prosperous New Yorker? Is a lion evil because it has fangs and claws and kills for a living? And is everything that looks human really human?"

Molly had no interest in debating good and evil with a vampire. The monster in front of her was the most wicked thing she had ever seen. Creatures like this should never be allowed to exist among humans, like so many ravenous wolves in a flock of sheep. But she kept her disgust deep inside, and showed only helpless fear. Why had Madam Rue sent her here? This was useful information that might one day save her life, but what did this creature have to tell her that a kinder, gentler vampire couldn't?

She gazed into the vampire's keen, black eyes and said, "You are truly amazing. It would be totally awesome to have your powers, but I'm still stuck on the blood thing. Is there a way to suck the life out of a person without drinking their blood?"

"How do you know about that?" Iskander leaned forward and Molly could tell he was moments away from grabbing her—or worse.

"I don't. I know this girl that died that way. That's all," she replied quickly.

"Ah." To Molly's relief, the vampire settled back into his chair and regarded her speculatively. "Perhaps we can trade information. Tell me about this girl—Where did she live? When did she die? Was she a mage? And I will tell you about eternals; because it was one of those that killed her."

Yes! Thank you Madam Rue.

Molly tried to keep her thoughts calm and her feelings sad and helpless, but her voice shook with anger as she said, "Her name was Shandra Sheehan, she lived in Portland, Oregon, and she was killed a few days ago. She wasn't a mage."

"Did she attend your high school?"

"Yes."

"Then the mages have a problem. One of them is an eternal!" The vampire grinned wickedly. "Since he—or maybe she?—managed to infiltrate the Web, he is quite capable of completely hiding his power and his appetites. They will never find him. And if, somehow, they did, he could just switch bodies before they got to him, leaving only his corpse behind." Iskander threw back his head and laughed.

It wasn't a pleasant sound.

Then his face took on a dreamy, almost wistful expression. "An eternal who is also a mage would be invincible. He could rule the world if he wanted to."

Molly's gut clenched in terror. Shandra's killer was not only as remorseless, powerful, and evil as the monster in front of her, but he was also an adept. Which meant, among other things, that he could travel ahead in time and jump to anywhere he'd already been in the multiverse. And he could move from identity to identity. How was she ever gonna find him? And if she did, would she survive?

She was surfing an adrenaline rush of pure terror, which was okay. She was still in control, sort of, and the fear masked the hot anger bubbling away inside her. And Iskander seemed to enjoy her fear, which distracted him from her anger, which was good.

"So what, exactly, is an eternal?"

"It is a type of psychic vampire, someone who feeds off the energy of his friends and associates. Most psychic vampires do it unconsciously, but some are well aware of what they are doing. They are usually harmless. People with strong psychic bodies automatically resist them and the vamps are only able to draw a non-lethal amount from the weak. And some even have groupies, people who, as you say, get off, on the feeling of being drained."

"No way!"

"Yes way."

"But that's sick!"

"It's not. Some people have too much energy. It makes them nervous and edgy. Being around a psychic vampire calms them. Other vampire groupies either want to become vampires or just want to be needed. Giving blood to a vampire is not much different than donating blood to a blood bank."

Molly could think of several reasons why giving blood to a blood bank was different from allowing a greedy monster to suck it out of you, but she stifled her thoughts, and replied, "Yuk! So tell me about the psychic vampires that kill people."

"Patience. I will tell you in good time. It is part of the story of how I became a vampire."

The last thing Molly wanted to do was listen to this evil ego-maniac talk about himself, but she needed information about vampires and especially about eternals. So she settled back in her chair and gave Iskander her full attention.

"I was born in 1823 in Sevastopol, the beautiful, white jewel of the Black Sea. Our home was surrounded by water. From my bedroom windows I could watch the sparkling length of The

Roadstead, dotted with the Czar's warships, flow into the broad expanse of the Black Sea. I remember my childhood as a blur of bright sunshine, blue water, and laughter. When I came of age I traveled to St. Petersburg to become a physician. But my medical studies soon became merely an excuse to spend time in the occult section of the library. Its musty, electric aroma made my skin tingle, and I became fascinated with its volumes of folklore, alchemy, and magic filled with promises of power. One day as I was searching for a book, I noticed a parchment scroll wedged in amongst its neighbors on a bottom shelf. When I realized what it was, I hid it in my coat, smuggled it out of the library, and spent the next few days committing it to memory. When I burned the scroll, black, foul-smelling smoke billowed up the chimney. It described how a sorcerer could draw the life force completely out of another human being and use it for himself. It promised that anyone who mastered this technique and managed to devour ten strong lives in rapid succession would possess not only superhuman powers, but also eternal life. Of course, it would still be necessary to feed on the occasional life and take on new bodies when the old ones wore out, but these were minor inconveniences."

In the secret corner of her mind Molly's temper threatened to blow. Minor inconveniences!? These were people he was talking about. People with families that loved them and depended on them.

"And so I practiced and practiced and became adept at drawing energy from people on the street or in the library or in restaurants. I dressed in rags and began walking the slums of St. Petersburg and feeding on the inhabitants. After a few disastrous mistakes, I learned how to draw the life completely out of a body. It is even more intoxicating than drinking lifeblood—much purer and more exhilarating. After taking a life I could go for days without sleep or sustenance. It was addictive. I craved the intense rush of another's life flowing through me more than food and drink."

Molly struggled to hide her fury and show only her horror and fascination. As far as she was concerned, the thing before her had quit being human even before it became a blood vampire. Iskander's eyes sharpened and she felt his mind, soft and deadly as a cat's paw, begin to push a bit deeper into hers. She stiffened in panic.

"Then why did you become a blood vampire?" she asked, perhaps a bit too quickly.

"Patience, patience. I am getting there."

Molly sat back, praying that her face showed only her honest fascination with Iskander's story.

"Of course I would have much preferred to be an eternal and enjoy the singing sweetness of stolen life as well as food and wine and the sun and all the joys of being alive and human, but that was not meant to be. I bided my time in St. Petersburg, finishing my studies and trying to figure out how I would ever be able to take ten strong lives in quick succession.

"And then the Crimean War began, and I saw my chance. I was a physician, so I did the patriotic thing and volunteered to work in a field hospital. They were death traps, because in those days, we knew next to nothing about how infection was spread. No one would think twice if ten slightly wounded men suddenly took sick and died in a field hospital.

"But before I left for the front in the summer of 1854, I went home to Sevastopol to visit my family. Late one night as I was heading home from a night of hunting across South Harbor, I became aware of someone following me. A psychic vampire who can take lives, even if he hasn't managed to become an eternal, is much quicker and stronger than any man; so I had no fear of my pursuer. I just kept my hand on my switchblade. He followed me into a section of tenements that was so run down and filthy even the desperate inhabitants of this quarter refused to live there. The street was empty. Not a single light shone down from the broken windows. It was so still that I could hear my pursuer's nearly silent footfalls over a block behind me.

"There was a flurry of footsteps and a cold breath of air brushed my cheek. He had me in his clutches almost before I knew he was there. His grip was inescapable, even for me. Eyes dark as nothingness burned with unholy passion in a fierce, glowing face. Lips, black in the moonlight, parted tenderly to reveal sharp fangs. This was a blood vampire, and from my studies I knew I had but one chance. I had just fed, and I was at my peak strength, so it was almost possible. I whipped out my knife and sliced at his exposed neck. Even before the blood began to flow, I latched onto the wound with my mouth and sucked up a mouthful of the deadly, bitter blood. The vampire screamed, and battered at my head to dislodge me, but I clung fast. He snarled and bit into my neck. Aching white pain shot through my veins as he began to feed. I am not sure whether I fainted from pain or loss of blood.

"I woke up cramped and shivering behind a row of dustbins. But I was alive, or more accurately, I still existed. The vampire's blood had resurrected my body and was in the process of transforming it. Every nerve shrieked and my body convulsed and shook as it changed from dead human to dark angel. I staggered into a deserted apartment, pulled the door closed, and collapsed onto pile of rubbish. I writhed in rat droppings and filth, biting my tongue to keep from screaming. I knew that if anyone found me they would kill me, because I was a truly terrifying sight. My flesh bubbled and heaved on my bones as it transformed into healthy new tissue. My hands warped into claws and I could feel the fangs growing in my upper jaw. As my senses grew more acute, the pain that I had thought unbearable intensified until I fainted.

"When I awoke, the pain was gone and it was night once more. I stripped off my rags and was thrilled to see that I looked just like I had yesterday.

"Except I was even more powerful than before. I heard every whisper in the night and could smell the water in the horse trough two blocks away. I could move like the wind, and like the wind I sped out of my awful tomb and arrived at the trough just moments later. It felt wonderful to be rid of the worst of the filth."

Molly shifted in her chair. "So where did you go?"

"Home. When my mother found me in bed that morning, I told her that I had been sick and delirious for the past day, and had only been able to find my way home when the fever broke.

"Claiming fragile health, I opted to stay in Sevastopol and set up a clinic instead of subjecting myself to the rigors of the front. But the war came to me. The British and French blockaded the harbor and surrounded the city to the south and east. In early October our leaders sent everyone who wasn't in the military out of the city. I tried to leave with my family, but the Russian Army requested that I stay and work in the makeshift hospital they were setting up in the Assembly Hall. The first of the wounded arrived when the bombardment began in mid-October. There weren't nearly enough cots; most of the wounded lay on the floor. The once beautiful hall echoed night and day with their moans and sobs, and reeked of blood, excrement, decaying flesh, and the stinking yellow mud of the trenches. Even safe behind the hospital's thick walls, the staccato of musket fire, the constant boom of the cannons, and the shriek of incoming bombs grated on our nerves. I amputated hundreds of soldiers' arms and legs, ignoring their pitiful screams and inhaling the intoxicating aroma of their spurting arterial blood.

"But late one night Anna, my favorite Sister of Mercy, discovered me administering my own form of mercy to a dying soldier."

Molly gasped as she imagined the huge shadowy hall, lit only by a few flickering lamps and rippling with the moans and sighs of the sleeping wounded. The woman would have been exhausted and totally unprepared for the sight of the glowing white demon with dripping, red fangs and black eyes that flickered and burned with desire.

"What did you do?" she asked, hoping against hope that the nurse survived.

"What could I do? I was mad with lust. The pulse in her soft throat and the smell of her fear filled me with undeniable passion. I had caught her up and my fangs were deep in her throat before she was even able to scream. But her thoughts reached me even through the haze of my desire: "Please don't kill me. My children will die without me. I will keep your secret, I promise."

"Fortunately for her, I was already sated with the soldier's blood and was able to stop before I drained her. I left for Paris that very night."

"So how did you wind up here?" Molly asked, breathing a sigh of relief and hiding her contempt for the beast sitting across from her.

"When I arrived in Paris, I found that most of the vampires had moved to the southern United States to feed on the slaves. I followed them and lived like a king on one of the barrier islands off the coast of Georgia. I remember the still summer nights, raucous with frog song, and the moon shining through live oaks dripping with Spanish moss. I bought slaves and fed from them until they weakened and died, and then I bought more. The supply was endless. But then the Civil War began. It was as bad as Sevastopol, and like Sevastopol, the South was doomed; so I moved to New York City. It was a huge metropolis even then. And, for a vampire, there is safety in numbers." His eyes glittered like starlight on black ice as he watched the look of helpless horror that Molly had plastered on her face to cover her rage.

"I see that I have shocked you." His lips formed an unrepentant smile.

It was that smile that did it. The vampire's nasty smirk finally broke Molly's fragile hold on her temper, and she vaulted up out of her chair.

"You are so freakin' evil; you don't deserve to exist."

Fury overwhelmed her.

Her whole being centered on ridding the multiverse of the thing in front of her.

She reached for Flick.

But before she could move she felt the memory of Micah's hand on her wrist, pulling her back from her blade.

"Bad move, Miss Molly."

The words echoed in her brain, paralyzing her.

In a flash, the vampire's handsome face morphed into a nightmare.

She watched in horror as his eyes became bottomless, black pits of rage and his lips pulled back, revealing wicked fangs.

"How dare you judge me!"

The vampire's claws reached for her throat.

Oh shit oh shit oh shit. Now what am I gonna do? I may need to at least try and kill the evil bastard after all—just so he doesn't kill me.

But before the claws touched her a brilliant white light lashed out at the vampire's eyes. Screaming in rage and pain he clutched at his face and doubled over.

Vibrant heat radiated from Gram's talisman as it continued to fill the room with light.

JUMP!

The voice in her head was as clear and strong as if Asmodius were standing right beside her. It brought memories of all the life-saving jumps she'd made in Damia.

But this wasn't Damia.

Could she do it?

And where would she jump to? It had to be somewhere close. She definitely couldn't jump back to Tamerlane's.

JUMP! NOW! Asmodius's voice was furious with fear.

The vampire was recovering. In moments he would be on her.

Gathering up all her rage and terror, she flipped them into power and reached out until she could see the Web-lines. She chose one, and jumped...

And landed in an exhausted heap on cold concrete. Brick walls surrounded her on three sides. Concrete stairs with a fancy wrought iron railing led up to a sidewalk bustling with the feet and lower legs of pedestrians. She was back in the basement stairwell next to Iskander's brownstone. She needed to get up on that sidewalk full of people and into the coffee shop where she was supposed to meet Philadelphia.

It took nearly all her remaining strength.

24

A Bit Later

he Silver Spoon was as upscale as the rest of the neighborhood. Armani-clad customers sipped coffee, read newspapers, stared at laptop screens, and chatted at marble-topped tables. Molly hoped Philadelphia would get here soon. She didn't have any money, and the barista had looked a little too long at her non-designer blue jeans and Grant sweatshirt. But Molly was beyond caring what the barista thought. She curled up in an overstuffed leather chair and shook. And waited, for what seemed like forever. Just as the barista headed toward her, Philadelphia strode into the shop.

"Oh good, you're here in one piece, but you're pale as a vampire!"

Molly groaned and glared up at her.

"Something hot and sweet will put you right. What can I get you?"

"A tall mocha breve with sugar, please." Molly sighed in anticipation and forgave Philadelphia for the bad joke.

Her instructor sighed wistfully. "If I drank half and half in my coffee I'd be a blimp." As she headed to the counter to place their order she pointed to a small table in a corner and said, "Let's sit over there."

Molly chose the seat that put her back to the wall.

"So, how did it go?" Philadelphia asked as she handed Molly her latte and dropped gracefully into the opposite chair.

"Not so good."

"Bother. What happened?"

Molly clutched the hot mug with both her cold, shaking hands and took a sip. The frothy goodness rolled down her throat like a warm massage and made a comforting pool in her belly, which slowly unclenched. She took another sip, closed her eyes, and let the warmth, sugar, and caffeine radiate through her as she tried to decide what to tell this powerful stranger. Philadelphia was an adept, which made her a suspect; but she was a woman and she didn't teach at Grant, so she probably had never heard of Shandra until she was murdered. But she taught students from Grant at the Academy and might know about Shandra from them. And if she was an eternal, she could be a man who had taken a woman's body and so Flick might have been fooled into thinking the killer was a flesh and blood man. Her stomach clenched once more as she realized how impossible this monster would be to identify, let alone catch.

Best not to trust anyone.

She took a sip of her coffee and shuddered.

Philadelphia waited patiently while the barista's potion worked its magic.

"He turned into this horrible monster and tried to grab me." Molly finally said.

"Oh dear." Then Philadelphia's lips tightened and she leaned toward Molly.

"Vampires are quicker than thought. Why didn't he get you?"

"I jumped."

"Really!?" She sat back in amazement and then frowned. "No way!"

"Really. I did. I was so scared I just did it." Gram's talisman was tucked safely under her sweatshirt and she was definitely not going to tell this woman about it and about how it had helped her.

Philadelphia looked doubtful, but then shrugged. "That would explain why you're so exhausted. Jumping in this world is hard work." Then she touched Molly's shoulder. "I'm so glad you escaped. There's no telling what he might have done. Why did he attack you?"

Molly shifted uncomfortably in her chair.

Because she'd been stupid, stupid, stupid.

"Because I called him an evil monster that didn't deserve to exist."

Philadelphia's mouth dropped open and her eyes widened with shock, which quickly turned to anger. "Ye gods!" she said gripping the edge of the table with both hands, "Of course he attacked you. Iskander is a nasty piece of work with a vile temper to match. And yours is obviously not much better." She sat back, took a sip of coffee and regarded Molly speculatively. "A sword and a quick temper are a dangerous combination."

Molly's heart sank and fear slithered up her spine. She knew exactly what her instructor was thinking.

And what every other mage and adept in the Web was thinking. "I didn't kill Shandra."

"I hope not—for your sake."

Her latte had lost its taste, but it was still hot and sweet and she needed the warmth, caffeine, and sugar. She was nearly finished when Philadelphia asked, "Did you at least find out what you needed to know?"

"Yes."

—

Damia • Afternoon

"How was your class?" Tamerlane asked, looking up at her from his chair and setting aside an open tome that sparkled with magic.

Molly's caffeine and sugar jolt suddenly expired and her whole body ached with exhaustion.

"Fine. Philadelphia took me to see a vampire," she said, collapsing into the easy chair beside him. She was too drained and too embarrassed to give him the details of her disastrous visit. And besides, she had questions for her mentor, and she wanted to ask them while she had a chance. He'd started some new project, and once her weapons practice and classes were finished, he dove back into his studies, totally oblivious of everything.

"Ah, yes. She always does that one first," he said, reaching for his book.

"So," she said quickly, "suppose someone very dangerous and very evil was about to attack you. Would you kill him?"

Tamerlane's hand snapped back from the sparkling book and his stern, piercing eyes searched her face. A split second of fear surged through her, reminding Molly of how powerful he was.

"Don't tell me you killed the vampire!"

"No, I didn't."

He relaxed back in his chair and went into teaching mode.

"If you are under attack, usually the best thing to do is run."

"What?!" This was the last thing she expected to hear. "You would never run."

"Ah, but I would. And I have. Most fights aren't worth fighting. At the end of a sword fight, one of you will be either dead or badly wounded. If you don't fight, you both live, unharmed, to enjoy another day."

Molly flopped back in relief. It felt good to hear him say she'd done the right thing. But he hadn't answered the whole question.

"But suppose the person attacking me is evil. As a warrior mage, shouldn't I try to kill him?"

"And what is your definition of evil?"

"Someone who kills people."

"You kill people and will probably kill many more. Are you evil?"

The question smacked into Molly like a fist to her chest, making her gasp.

Was she evil?

With merciless accuracy, Tamerlane had asked the question behind her question, the one she'd been asking herself since she decided to become a warrior mage.

"I don't know. Am I?"

"Only you and the gods know the answer to that. But I can assure you that killing someone doesn't *always* make you evil."

She wasn't sure she agreed with that, but she really wanted to.

"Then what is evil?"

"It's indefinable and you don't stumble upon it very often, but it exists."

So they were back where they'd started.

"So let's say this person was evil..."

"If the person you're referring to is the vampire you met today, I doubt that he was evil. Vampires aren't, by definition, evil, although some may be."

"This one was! He was cruel and he enjoyed killing."

"Have you ever watched Asmodius play with his supper?"

Molly shuddered. Yes, she had. Way too many times.

"But is he truly evil?"

"No."

"However, it's hard to be objective when you are the supper, and I imagine you were the metaphorical equivalent of that vampire's supper."

He was right. The vampire was a predator, and he'd had been playing with her. She could see that now. Thank the gods, once again, that she hadn't tried to kill him. Either he would be dead, or, more likely, she would be dead.

Either outcome would have been bad.

Tamerlane reached for his book again. But then he paused, and picked up his pipe instead. "You seem to be struggling with ethics. We were going to get to this in your Magical Ethics, Etiquette, and Philosophy class, but I think you need to hear some of it now."

What Molly really wanted to do was sleep, but Tamerlane was correct. So she settled in for a lecture.

"As a warrior mage, your code of ethics is exactly the same as any other mage or adept," he said, packing tobacco into his pipe. "It requires that you harm no one."

First there had been "Run!" and now "Don't hurt anyone." These were the last things she expected to hear from Tamerlane.

"So why all the weapons practice?"

Tamerlane reached out to a bunch of wood slivers stuffed in small, cut-crystal vase and selected one. He scowled briefly at its tip, which promptly burst into flame. Holding the flame to his pipe, he lit the tobacco, puffing out gray clouds that reeked of cedar and citrus. Molly dragged herself out of her chair and opened the door. A chilly breeze swept in, but it was better than breathing smoke.

"A warrior mage has a more direct and physical approach to problem solving than other mages. As you may have noticed, this means that you frequently come into direct, physical contact with those who are causing the problem. You are no use to anyone if your adversary kills you, so you must be able to defend yourself. Thus all the weapons practice. However, with luck, you may be able to solve the problem without a fight, or leave before one starts, or disable your adversary and take him prisoner. If this is not possible and you must kill him to save your life or those you are defending, then you may do so. If it becomes obvious that by sacrificing your own life, you will save the lives of your loved ones or those you are defending, then the warrior's code requires your death."

He sat back and smoked and waited for the inevitable questions.

Molly only had one.

Sort of the same one she'd started with.

"But if the person I'm about to fight is not only the cause of the problem, but he's really dangerous, and killing him would not only solve the problem but make it so he couldn't harm anyone else, shouldn't I kill him?"

"Only if it's obvious that if you don't kill him, he would kill you and those you are defending that very day—not some hypothetical time in the future. A mage must be non-judgmental. Just because you decide someone is evil doesn't mean they are. No one, even an adept, is able to see far enough into another's soul to determine this. Your adversary may actually be following the path he was meant to follow in this life. Therefore, a warrior mage only kills to save his own life and those he is defending. He does *not* kill because he has decided someone needs killing."

25

Tesseract Academy • Midmorning

he next morning the Librarian transported Molly to her Anatomy and Physiology class, and she was, once again, suspended in black infinity. But this time she wasn't seeing stars, she was staring in dumbfounded awe at thousands of whirling galaxies.

She shuddered and opened the door into her class.

She found herself in the middle of Aunt Althea's garden in Northeast Portland. Purple-blue asters, lemon-yellow marigolds, deep orange calendulas, and a red rambling rose with just a few remaining blossoms glowed in the sunshine. Fat orange pumpkins lolled on spent vines, and blueberry bushes showed off their bright red fall foliage. The air was loaded with the smell of green herby things and a gazillion bacteria and fungi busily decomposing garden debris. Muscles Molly hadn't even realized were tight began to relax as she breathed in great breaths of the delicious air.

Far in the back of the garden she heard rustlings and hummings and headed toward them. The humming became a soothing, wordless song sung by a woman busily weeding out a row of spent bush beans. She was kneeling, so most of what Molly saw of her was her rear end clad in black leggings. As Molly approached, the woman turned to look up at her. Her face was smudged with dirt and her brown hair, streaked with gray, was piled up on her head and halfheartedly clipped in place. Her hazel eyes sparkled as she regarded the intruder.

"Hey, Aunt Althea. Tamerlane didn't tell me you'd be my anatomy and physiology instructor!"

"Tamerlane didn't know which of us would be teaching you. The Librarian keeps track of that sort of thing. Actually, I'm teaching you auric healing, Max will be teaching you anatomy today. I'm so glad you're taking these classes. Healing is a very important skill for you to have—not only for yourself, but for your companions. Warriors are dangerous people to be around."

An image of Shandra's body sprawled on the cold pavement like a bloody rag doll stabbed into her, and her fear for Adam and Diana sent shivers up her spine.

"Yeah, I know that," she said.

Her grandmother's closest friend stood and touched her on the shoulder. A jolt of warmth and well-being soothed the slight stiffness left over from this morning's weapons practice and boosted her sagging energy level back to normal.

Molly was so surprised that she forgot to ask who Max was.

"How did you do that?" She remembered how she felt when she had first arrived in Damia—frightened, exhausted, and in pain. Queen Flora's touch had had the same effect then as Althea's did now.

"It's the most basic, yet most difficult, healing principle of all. Most students are unable to understand it well enough to use it. I'm sure the Little People of Damia taught you that all things—even the ones we call 'inanimate'—are alive and have a spirit. This garden has a spirit, and every plant, animal, bug, bacterium, and rock within it has a spirit. I take care of them and I give them plenty of love and their spirits are strong. As I touched you, I sent my love out to the garden and asked it to please give you a healing. You felt the result. The multiverse and every soul within it is here to heal you. The trick is knowing how to ask and being willing to open up and receive what you are given."

"Madam Rue told me pretty much the same thing."

"Who's Madam Rue?"

"I don't really know. You'd have to meet her. She's this really strange woman I met in Damia."

Molly told her about the gypsy with her caravan full of shadows, shades, and memories and how she had shown Molly her own body of light and taught her to heal it.

Althea was fascinated. "That's exactly what I'll be teaching you, only in a bit more detail. And Max will be teaching you physical anatomy and physiology. Come into the house and I'll introduce you to him."

The walk back through the garden was an education in itself. As they passed a large evergreen shrub, Althea stopped and said, "Molly, this is Rosemary."

A mist formed above the plant. A pair of blue eyes appeared in its center and gazed at Molly intently. The mist coalesced into the shape of a tiny woman with wavy silver hair that sparkled like sunlight on water. She wore a gauzy gown that exactly matched her eyes. A feeling of safety and well-being radiated out from the plant, and Molly felt her mind sharpen and clarify.

A voice inside her head said, *Good morning, Molly. You need me, and I am here to help you.*

"Um, good morning. Are you a fairy?"

Silver laughter rippled through her brain, soothing it and quickening it at the same time. *No, silly, I'm a plant spirit. My name is Rosemary, and I give the gift of mental clarity and alertness. Take a sprig from the tip of one of my branches.*

Molly picked the tender green leaves and crushed them between her fingers. A burst of piney, sweet fragrance filled the air. It reached deep into her brain and tweaked it gently.

I will help you remember what Max has to teach you.

The spirit faded back into her plant with a shimmer of blue light.

"Thank you, Rosemary," Molly said, tucking the sharp scented sprig into her curls.

You are most welcome.

They arrived at the back of an old Craftsman home painted sage green with soft cream and deep plum trim. French doors opened out onto a flagstone patio where a young man was standing. He was tall, dark, and broodingly handsome. His black three-piece suit fit perfectly, and every hair on his head was in exactly the correct place. He stepped forward with a polite smile and extended a perfectly manicured hand to Molly.

"Molly, this is Max. Max, this is Molly Adair."

"A pleasure to meet you, Miss Adair. Please, come inside." And he stepped back and indicated the open French doors.

Althea waved goodbye and disappeared behind a giant artichoke plant.

Molly stepped into a sunny, yellow kitchen. Handouts, a pen for note-taking, and a glass of water sat in front of one of the chairs at the butcher-block kitchen table.

"I thought that since there are only two of us, the kitchen would be the most comfortable place for a class. Have a seat."

Comfortable wasn't exactly the way she would describe a one-on-one class with this handsome hunk. Romantic, maybe, or thrilling, but certainly not comfortable. Every girl in Tesseract Academy was probably drooling over him. She smoothed her hair, hoping it made it look better and not worse, and walked her best fashion model walk over to the chair. As she was sitting down she looked up at Max.

And gasped in fright.

Her well-trained muscles went on autopilot as she drew her sword, and dropped into fighting stance. In front of her, a human skeleton raised its arms and took a step backward. But its fixed grin never changed—how could it?

And then the jawbone began to move up and down and Max's voice said, "Oh, nicely done! This is the first time I've ever been threatened at sword point. I suppose it serves me right for start-ling a warrior mage. And, by the way, the bone that moves when I talk is called a 'mandible.'"

With growl of exasperation, Molly resheathed Flick, dropped heavily into her chair and glared at the grinning skeleton. "What'd you do that for? I might have killed you!"

"Ah, but you didn't. And it has provided an excellent oppor-tunity for instruction. A good scare causes your adrenal glands to release adrenaline, or epinephrine, as a pharmacist would call it. The adrenals sit atop your kidneys like so…" Two kidneys floated in the back of Max's abdominal cavity, and two small blobs appeared on top of them. "Adrenaline is a hormone that increases your heart rate and body strength, dilates your bronchioles, increases blood flow to your muscles and internal organs, and causes your body to consume more oxygen. It also cuts down blood flow to the skin, which helps control bleeding if you are injured. Notice your heavy breathing and increased heart rate, and you're obvi-ously irritable and a tad bit sweaty. Other effects are bladder and bowel contraction."

Fortunately for her dignity, Max had no way of knowing how close she had come to exhibiting those last two symptoms as well.

"Now, if you will look at your set of handouts on the table," the skeleton continued, "you will see that the top page folds out into a detailed picture of the human skeleton. As I demonstrate the shape and movement capability of each bone, label the corre-sponding bone in your handout. In two weeks you will be given a box of bones and I will expect you to be able to identify each one."

A bod like that, and all I get to see is its skeleton. Molly sighed, took the top page from the stack of handouts, and pinched her sprig of rosemary until she could smell its sharp, clean scent. She was gonna need all the help she could get for this class.

Tesseract Academy • Three-Month, Day 3

Molly stood suspended in black vastness sprinkled with uncountable sparkling stars. The door to her Who's Who class loomed in front of her. This was the only class this three-month that she would be taking with the other mages, and she was dreading it. By this time everyone at the Academy probably knew that her best friend had been murdered and that she was the main suspect. Her classmates would not only be strangers; they would be suspicious, hostile strangers.

She pushed open the door and walked into green twilight. Huge trees rose up around a smooth circle of leaf litter, their branches so high up that she could barely make out individual leaves and so thick that the clearing remained in deep shade. The excited chatter of a small group of mages cut through the cool silence. As Molly walked toward them they stopped in midsentence and stared at her. The look was quick and intense. Then they turned away, moved closer together, and resumed their conversations.

It had happened in an instant, and in that instant Molly realized that if Shandra's murderer wasn't found, she would never be truly accepted in the Web—even if she was never actually accused.

Pain and grief stabbed into her.

Philadelphia appeared in front of them dressed in brown, knee-high boots, green leggings, and a creamy, full-sleeved tunic cinched in with a wide brown leather belt with a silver buckle. Burgundy-colored lips compressed as she surveyed the scene.

"Good morning, mages. Molly Adair is new to Tesseract Academy. She comes from the USA West Coast region. Please make her welcome."

Molly was greeted with downcast eyes and a few half-hearted "Hi's."

Philadelphia glared at her class and continued. "Today we are going to meet a forest elf. They are wary, reclusive, and often dangerous individuals. And with good reason—for hundreds of years we have been destroying the forests they love and call home. Stay together and be silent. Speak only when spoken to."

She led them into the trees with Molly trailing behind.

◆

Damia • Early Morning

Three months after she had arrived, Molly and Tamerlane were sitting at the table finishing their breakfast. "So, I'm done with all my classes." Molly said, gathering up the plates. "When do I go back?"

"The Librarian will send you back after lunch, which, if you remember, was the time of day you arrived here. That way you will be in sync time-wise when you return. You've got the morning off. Rest, do something you enjoy. You look exhausted."

Tamerlane was right. She was totally exhausted. Her days had been filled with crazy-hard, mind-warping classes, hostile classmates, and grueling weapons practices. Her nights had been filled with terrifying dreams of hundreds of dead Shandras, having her brain wiped, and getting kicked out of the Web.

Much as she loved her mentor and cherished her time in Damia, she was so ready to go home and figure out who killed Shandra. It wouldn't bring her friend back, but it would, at least, bring a creature who had probably murdered thousands of innocents to justice.

And prove her innocence.

But how was she supposed to catch an eternal?

26

Wednesday, October 26 • Early Afternoon

After the cool silence of the Wildwood, the noise and confusion of Grant's halls blazed into her brain. Dozens of rapid-fire conversations pounded into her ears. Students rushing for classes in the packed halls nudged and jostled her. The girl ahead was wearing way too much Supermodel perfume, and the guy behind her needed deodorant.

And everyone seemed to be looking everywhere but at her.

Yup, Theo had been hard at work.

An itchy sensation crawled between her shoulder blades. Someone was coming up behind her, and they definitely weren't thinking of inviting her out for coffee. She spun around to confront Theo Peregrine in the act of reaching out to shove her.

Speak of the Devil.

"You are a murdering scumbag," he said, stopping short and pointing at her dramatically. With his tousled blond hair, designer jeans, and cool, white dress shirt, he looked like an avenging hero straight out of a teen romance.

Oncoming students skittered around the two angry students and kept going.

"As long as you walk these halls, none of us are safe." His eyes blazed with hate.

"I didn't do it!" she said, reeling with shock. Even Iskander hadn't managed to pack so much venom into his glare.

"Liar! They ought to kill you like a rabid dog, or at least wipe your mind and kick you out of the Web—

"But they won't have to, now will they?" His voice was low and his smile was pure poison. He turned and melted into the press of students hurrying to sixth-period classes.

Rigid with anger and puzzled over what Theo had meant, she stomped down the hall to Pre-Calc. She grinned as she spotted Adam and Diana standing outside their classroom door. She hadn't realized how much she'd missed them. Her anger drained away as quickly as it had arrived.

They looked grim. Their three-month must have been miserable. She'd only had one class at the Academy, but Adam and Diana had lived there, not only as social outcasts but also as friends of a suspected murderer. Their fellow mages probably hadn't been much kinder to them than they'd been to her. Diana looked exhausted, and she'd lost weight that she couldn't afford to lose. There were dark circles under Adam's eyes.

And then she thought of another reason why they looked so worn out.

"Oh, jeez, Diana, you had to spend your whole three-month turning into a werewolf," she whispered, and shivered as she looked into her friend's fierce blue eyes. "That must have been awful."

"The first day was," Diana replied, "Even Adam couldn't stand to be around me. He made me go see the school physician."

"She was just an animal," Adam said, looking tragic.

Diana grinned and smacked his shoulder.

"Ow."

"So anyway," Diana continued, "Dr. Lovelace gave me something that dulled the symptoms so I could at least function and wouldn't kill anyone."

"Lucky thing there was a fix," Molly said, squeezing her friend's hand. She had learned not to hug her during the change; it was too scary for both of them. "So, besides that, did you guys have a good three-month?"

"It was okay," Adam lied. "Where were you? You weren't in Dragon Lodge."

"She was at Tamerlane's," Diana said.

"How did you know?" Adam scowled at Diana. "And why didn't you tell me she was there?"

"Because I didn't know until just now. I smelled it on her." She grinned at Molly. "You positively reek of the Wildwood and that awful blend of tobacco he smokes."

"I can't smell a thing," Adam said, moving up close to Molly and sniffing dramatically.

"That is because you are not a werewolf."

"You're right," Molly said, pushing Adam gently away and staring at Diana in amazement. "I was at Tamerlane's doing catch-up classes."

Adam glared at her. "I am so jealous. It must have been amazing."

The bell rang.

"Let's meet on the bleachers after school," Adam said as he headed into class. "I've got to tell you all the stuff I found out during the three-month."

—

Tears streamed down Molly's cheeks as she stared at Shandra's empty seat. The computer lab was having its usual, calming effect, and every muscle in her body went limp as tension and grief poured out of her. She looked up into the serene gaze of Miss Matsuda. The tech nodded sympathetically and went back to her screens.

Molly brushed away her tears with the back of her hand and slumped in her chair. Images of her friend flickered through her brain. Shandra doing a silly victory dance after scoring a soccer goal. Shandra laughing as they walked home together and replayed their day. Shandra yelling at Zach Jefferson. Shandra nibbling on the top of her pen as she concentrated on a forensics lecture. It felt good to just relax and remember her. She hadn't been able to do this since Shandra had been killed.

So why was she doing it now, three months later, in the middle of a computer lab? And with Mr. Liu, one of her main suspects, sitting right behind her. He looked exhausted, like he'd been up all night, and he was staring at her. She could feel his gaze drilling into the back of her neck.

Molly straightened up and focused, or rather unfocused, on the room.

The shimmering, pulsing lines of power that connected everything to everything else came into view. The dim glow of the computer screens made the lab look like an aquarium full of light blue, sparkly Jell-O that someone kept tapping with a spoon. She sighed with pleasure as she watched the intricate patterns, bouncing and nudging and criss-crossing each other. But the lines surrounding Jamal Green, Grant's feisty Dragon mage quarterback, sparkled brightest of all. Molly watched in amazement as all that energy flowed through the Web lines and into Ms. Matsuda's aura.

The computer tech was a psychic vampire!

But was she an eternal?

And was she powerful enough to steal a magic sword from between the worlds?

Maintaining her unfocus, she studied Ms. Matsuda's light body. It was more complex than a normal one, and tiny flecks of magic sparkled inside it. Not nearly as many as in a mage's, but they were there.

Could she hide her magic from other mages?

But Flick had said the killer was a man.

Could the lovely Ms. Matsuda possibly be a Mr. Matsuda?

She was taller than average.

That'd be really hard on her admirers, Molly thought with a grim smile.

But the smile faded quickly as she realized she had yet another suspect.

As she was rushing out of the computer lab to find Diana and Adam and tell them her news, Micah Ortiz, bracketed by two of his thugs, blocked her way. Dark, brooding magic crackled and sparked around him, making Molly's skin tingle.

"Hey, Miss Molly," he said with teasing intensity. "Tell me if this is a coincidence or not. A friend of yours gets offed this morning and we suddenly have, by my count, three—yes, three—new janitors. And they all seem very interested in you. Especially the one across the hall pretending to dust the trophy case.

"No, don't look at him, you idiot.

"Now, what do you know about this murder, hmmm, Miss Molly?"

Mirror lenses reflected her startled face back into her startled face and held it fast as his index finger gently traced a burning line from the corner of her right eye down to the corner of her lips. Micah's finger stopped there, but the line took on a life of its own. It brushed softly over her throat, down to her belly, and exploded into her pelvis.

As her traitorous body tingled and quivered, Molly remembered that Micah knew she had a sword.

And he knew where she kept it.

She pushed past the menacing trio and out of the building.

27

Wednesday, October 26 • Late Afternoon

he sun warmed her face and made her squint as she headed out the door and toward the football practice field. The last red, gold, and brown leaves on the tall trees that lined NE Thirty-third Avenue glowed in the afternoon sun. Molly slowly relaxed until her heart had stopped flopping around her ribcage like a frightened canary and she was breathing normally.

Adam and Diana were waiting for her near the top of the bleachers. They moved apart and Molly sank down between them. Having two good friends was a comforting thing.

"We better keep this short or you'll be late for soccer practice," Diana said, glancing at her cell phone."

"I'm not going," Molly said. She really didn't want to deal with awkward sympathy or outright rejection from the girls who had known more about her and her friendship with Shandra than anyone else at Grant besides Adam and Diana. "Maybe I'll start again later, if the coach will let me.

"I've found two new suspects," she said, changing the subject.

"Who?" they asked in unison. They looked so much like two surprised owls that Molly almost grinned.

"The first one is Micah Ortiz." Molly slumped back against the seat behind her as she finally allowed herself to recognize the truth. She was in lust with the most dangerous guy at Grant. And he might be a murderer.

Stupid. Stupid.

Anger, betrayal, fear, and sadness fought for top place inside her.

"He is getting pretty pissed at you," Adam said. "You've been asking way too many questions and finding out way too much about what he's up to. I don't know how many times I've told you to back off. Micah plays for keeps."

"Yeah," Molly said. She shivered as she remembered the gang leader's words on her first day at Grant. *If you ever mess with me or any of my men again, I'll get you, Miss Molly. And you'll wish you were dead.*

"There's just one problem with Micah as a suspect," Adam said. "He doesn't know where the sword is and even if he did, he can't dimension travel and he can't time travel."

"He does know where Flick is. He and Zach Jefferson surprised me in the hall the first day of school and I reached for my sword." Molly cringed at Adam and Diana's shocked expressions.

"Micah followed my hand into the pocket with his hand and stopped me before I could grab hold of it. If he was paying attention, he might have been able to get to Flick again."

"He is a senior, but they haven't taken the Dimension and Time Travel class yet," Diana said.

"It's not unusual for especially talented students to figure it out before they take the class, and Micah is definitely talented," Adam said. "Just thinking about him jumping through time and dimensions gives me the willies."

"I can't believe the Librarian let him into the Academy. He's a gang leader, for gods' sakes," Diana said.

"You might as well ask why it let Theo in. He is bad to the bone too. Or even you. Werewolves aren't known for their moral, rational behavior," Molly said.

"Dragons are strange beasts," Adam said, gazing off into the distance. "They see farther than we do, and my mom thinks that over the centuries the Librarian and the Academy have sort of grown together into a single entity. Like you can't tell where the Librarian leaves off and the Academy begins, which makes it totally strange. And it's almost impossible to get your mind around a thing that's timeless and limitless. But the Librarian has been known to make mistakes, or at least what any sane person would call a mistake. Percy's dad told him that Jack the Ripper was an Academy graduate. He was never caught because the adepts got to him before the Bobbies did."

"Oh, wonderful," said Molly.

Diana growled.

The three mages watched in glum silence as the football team began doing jumping-jacks and yelling out the count. Diana said, "So who's your second suspect?"

"Ms. Matsuda."

"Are you crazy? She's not a mage and she's not a man," Adam said.

"Yeah, I know it sounds impossible, but once I tell you what I found out during my three-month you'll understand." And she told them about Madam Rue and her magic tea that sent her back into Shandra's body on the night she was murdered. And she told them about feeling the life being pulled out of her helpless friend and then watching the sword plunge into her heart. And she told them everything that Iskander had told her about psychic vampires and eternals.

Adam and Diana stared at her in speechless horror.

"And Ms. Matsuda's a psychic vampire," she said. "I watched her suck a bunch of energy off Jamal Green less than an hour ago."

They looked back at the field. The quarterback was easy to spot. He faced one of the five columns of the grid of players, rocking out and running in place between exercises and yelling mild obscenities as encouragement to his teammates.

"Doesn't seem to have slowed him down much," Diana said.

"Yeah, Jamal could be an ADHD poster boy. Matsuda was probably doing him a favor." Adam replied.

"She is tall, and if you look closely, you can see the magic in her aura," Diana said.

"Not that much though," said Molly. "Can an adept hide his magic from other mages?"

"I don't see why not; mages are just as susceptible to illusion as anyone else," Adam said.

"And remember, eternals can change bodies like we change clothes." Molly said. "Maybe Flick felt a male inside a female body."

"She's new this year and single," Adam said with a tragic sigh. "Yeah, I'd say she qualifies as a suspect." He was one of Ms. Matsuda's biggest fans.

The three young mages went silent and stared at each other in fear. They were trying to outwit and capture a creature who probably had centuries of magical experience and was even stronger and quicker than a vampire. Not only that, he could also jump time and dimensions and take on a new body, complete with new fingerprints and retinal patterns, whenever he wanted.

Yells and thudding sounds drew their attention back to the field. The team was busy smashing into one-, two-, and three-man sleds weighted with sandbags.

"Listen to what I found out about our other suspects," Adam said.

"Percy Pomeroy sneaked me into this cool place called the Records Room. It's full of all kinds of weird stuff and it's got files and files of information about everyone that's ever been in the Web. So I looked up Liu, Rathkin, and Thomas.

"Mr. Thomas probably didn't do it. He's been married for fifteen years, has three kids, and the most exciting thing he's ever done is climb Mt. St. Helens to take pictures right after it blew. But Rathkin and Liu are possibilities."

"They definitely are," said Molly. "Tamerlane had the Librarian remember where all the Grant adepts were at 2 a.m. this morning, and the only ones that weren't home asleep were Rathkin and Liu."

"But any of the other adepts could have jumped ahead from yesterday or something, killed Shandra, and be in bed on the night it actually happened," Diana said.

"Yeah, Tamerlane said the same thing, but I still think it's interesting that our two main suspects were out and about at the time of the murder."

"And wait till you hear what I found out about them," Adam said, pulling the conversation back on track. "Robin Liu's father was a gunman for the Suey Sing Tong, and Robin is an elder in that same tong. He teaches martial arts, and the Chinese community calls him Master Liu."

"What is a Suey? And what does it have to do with singing or tongs?" Diana asked.

"Back in the day, the tongs were the Chinese version of the Mafia," he said, eyes glittering with excitement. "Only meaner. There were lots of different ones in China, and most of them came to the U.S. with the immigrants. The Suey Sing is one of the Portland tongs."

"If they're that bad, why don't we hear anything about them?" Molly asked.

"Today the tong halls are sort of like community centers, but they control the International District. Who knows what they do undercover? A tong elder could easily be a master criminal...or a life-sucker."

"Is he single?" Diana asked.

"Yes, he lives alone in a tiny apartment in the International District. All the rest of his family are dead."

"That explains it. He smells like exotic incense and loneliness."

"How can someone smell lonely?" Molly asked.

"I don't know, he just does. What about Rathkin?"

"Rathkin is even scarier. He was a Green Beret in Vietnam in the late sixties, early seventies. He killed at least fifty men and was called up once on brutality charges that didn't stick. But get this: he's not a warrior mage. He got out of the military as soon as he could, went back to school for an education degree, and joined the Peace Corps. He requested remote, primitive areas and short assignments. There was a complaint from one place of undue use of force. He's never been married, and he's been Grant's principal for the last ten years."

"Rathkin was in the Vietnam War?" Molly was amazed. "He doesn't look a day over fifty!"

"Mages age well; but then, of course, so would an eternal," Adam said.

"He may not look old," Diana said, "but he smells old."

"You and your nose," Adam said.

"During the change, smells take on all kinds of emotions and textures. They tell me more than all my other senses put together. After this last full moon, when I came back to normal I felt half-blind and half-deaf. It was awful."

"So could you smell an eternal?" Molly asked.

"I doubt it, since I don't know what one smells like. I'm not good at smelling personalities either, just general feelings. Like Rathkin often smells angry."

"Of course he does," said Adam. "Old and angry, with a history of violence. I think that's a pretty good description of the sort of person we're looking for."

"Mr. Liu sounds good to me too," Molly said. "He's a warrior mage, isn't he?"

"Yes, one of the best, after Tamerlane, of course."

"That is hard to believe," Diana said. "He looks like he would blow away in a stiff breeze."

"I believe it," said Molly. "He moves like a fighter, wary and precise. He feels dangerous and exempt—like all the rules that apply to everyone else don't apply to him."

"All the adepts feel that way," Diana said.

"Yeah, but Liu really feels that way."

"Oh, I almost forgot." Adam said. "I checked Rathkin's and Liu's emails this afternoon and there was a very interesting message in Liu's mailbox."

"You read their emails?" Diana looked scandalized.

"Of course. I only had time to check their work mailboxes, and those mostly had stuff like questions from students and parents and meeting reminders, but there was an interesting message for Liu. It was from someone called Tiger Lily and said '8 p.m., Pioneer Square, tonight.'"

"I wonder who Tiger Lily is," Diana said.

Molly smiled. At last, something she could do.

"I think I'll take a trip down to Pioneer Square this evening and find out," she said.

"I'll come with you, because I think you will need my nose and ears. It will also be better than sitting around the house going insane."

"And I'm going to go see if Charlotte Matsuda is really Charles Matsuda. I've always wanted to do a stakeout like a real detective," Adam said.

"Okay. By tomorrow we'll have a few answers," Molly said, and started to get up.

"Um, wait a minute," Adam said, touching Molly's arm. He and Diana locked gazes. The air between them buzzed with intensity.

Finally Diana said, "Um, Molly, we've got some awful news."

"The adepts jumped ahead this morning," Adam continued. "They discovered that your corpse will be found in Wilshire Park early this Saturday morning. Apparently a suicide."

Molly closed her eyes and fought panic. She felt two pairs of hands reach out and support her. There was a low snarl. "You idiot," Diana said, "couldn't you have told her more gently?"

"Relax. She's tough. According to the stuff I read in the Records Room, she didn't tell us half of what she survived in Damia. Besides, there's no gentle way to tell someone they're going to be murdered."

He'd read her file! How could he? Anger surged through her, burning away her fear.

"See, look, her color's coming back already."

She opened her eyes, and glared at Adam. "I am so pissed at you. If you ever look at any of my personal info again I swear I'll break your laptop—maybe over your thick head."

"See, she's just fine."

But she wasn't.

Her fear returned with the chilling realization that she had been the intended victim all along. The monster planned to kill her and set it up to look like she'd been so sorry she'd killed her best friend that she'd committed suicide.

She was gonna die, and everyone would think she was a murderer. They would breathe a sigh of relief that the nastiness was all finished and wrapped up in a nice, neat package. Then they would go on with their lives and the beast, who had probably taken thousands of lives, would be free to take even more.

"But why?" She shivered and stared at her friends, who were still hanging on to her. "Why would he want to kill me?"

They had no answer.

Molly grabbed onto the one good thing she could find about the terrifying news.

"So that means I'm safe until Saturday morning," she said.

"Friday afternoon, actually. You'll disappear sometime after school," Adam said, giving her hand a squeeze.

"So we've got till then to catch the bastard," Molly said, squeezing him back.

A shout and a noise like stones falling on a Formica counter-top made them look up in time to see two lines of players collide. The team had started a scrimmage.

28

Wednesday, October 26 • Late Afternoon

arcus Aurelius Fox sat in his vehicle and glared at the house on Alameda Street. He reminded himself for at least the tenth time that he wasn't fourteen anymore. That he was, in fact, one of the most talented detectives on the Portland police force, and that he was here on police business. He climbed out of the black and white and stalked up the sidewalk to the front door.

An unanswered call on Shandra's cell phone had come in at 2:06 a.m., just minutes after Shandra had said she'd died. The techs had traced it to a cell phone belonging to one Molly Adair. Shandra's parents, who had been out of town at a convention at the time of their daughter's death, were able to confirm that she was—or had been—a friend of Shandra's.

Rathkin had also told him this.

And so, here he was, about to interview a young woman who was probably the granddaughter of his most detested teacher. He knocked on the door, which was immediately opened by a tiny woman dressed in a simple, full-length, silk dress. Wispy gray curls framed a deceptively sweet face. Estelle Adair hadn't aged a bit since she'd mercilessly drummed astrology and astronomy into his thick skull eleven years ago. But then, she was an adept, and they tended to age gracefully. Ice-blue eyes that almost exactly matched her dress peered up at him.

"Yes?" she seemed calm and only mildly curious, as if police vehicles pulled up in front of her house every day.

Marcus pulled out his ID and opened it with an expert flick of the wrist.

"Detective Fox, Portland Police. I have a few questions for Molly Adair."

"She's at soccer practice. I expect her home soon. Please come in and have a seat." She led him into a spacious living room and indicated a comfortable-looking armchair that reeked of magic. Marcus suspected that it probably wasn't too attached to remaining a chair and could very easily morph into something else, whether it had an occupant or not. He chose another, less edgy, seat.

Ms. Adair's shapely eyebrows arched up as she suppressed what might have been wicked grin. But she said innocently, in a voice any Victorian hostess would have been proud of, "I'll just go make us a pot of tea."

She disappeared through a door on the other side of the front entryway.

His stomach growled mutinously, hoping for something a bit more substantial than tea.

It hadn't been fed since breakfast.

A huge, black cat drifted into the living room. Glowing amber eyes locked onto Marcus's and sent a shiver of apprehension up his spine. It flowed up onto the chair that Marcus had avoided, hunkered down on the seat, tucked its paws under its chest, and continued to stare unnervingly at the hapless detective. Marcus ignored it and began a careful inspection of the living room.

Bookcases stuffed with novels, a few atlases, and coffee-table books flanked a formal fireplace. Nothing to make a visitor suspect that this was the home of an adept mage. A three-person couch upholstered in soft blue was a perfect complement to the peacock blues, rusty reds, and olive greens in the Morris carpet that covered the central part of the blond oak floor. Three huge multi-paned windows overlooked the front yard and a large rowan tree growing near the front door. Three rust-red armchairs and a few ottomans were grouped across from it. The chair that the cat occupied sat at a right angle to the couch and looked like it had been dropped haphazardly into the tableau.

He would be interviewing the girl here in the living room. And she would probably sit across from him on the couch. Not good. Her back would be to the window and her face would be in shadow.

He got up, inspected a few of the books in the bookcase, and then walked over to the couch and sat down.

There.

She'd need to sit in one of the three chairs facing the window.

Ms. Adair came in carrying a tray with a bone china teapot, two matching cups and saucers, two silver teaspoons, a milk pitcher, and a sugar bowl. Unfortunately there were no cookies or cucumber sandwiches. She deposited her burden on a small table and moved it to where she could reach it easily from the middle rust-colored chair. Seating herself gracefully, she picked up the teapot and began pouring. When she had finished, she looked up at Marcus and asked, "Milk? Sugar?"

What did she think she was playing at? This innocent-looking matron bore no resemblance to the holy terror that had remorselessly crammed his unwilling brain full of quincunxes, oppositions, apogees and perigees.

Or had she just mellowed with age?

Marcus didn't think so. She still had an edge—she'd just hidden it under layers of social convention, which demanded that she behave the way she was behaving and that he behave the way he was behaving. That, of course, was the whole point of social convention. It allowed people to get on with day-to-day business and work around messy emotions that would otherwise get in the way.

But a tea tray?

She knew exactly who he was and she was playing the situation for all it was worth.

The realization did nothing to soothe his hyped-up nerves.

He felt like a mouse trapped in a corner by a hungry cat.

Two cats, actually—the black beast in the chair was still glaring at him.

"Neither, thank you," he replied through clenched teeth and walked over to accept the dainty cup and saucer she offered him. Returning to the couch, he sat back and waited until she had taken a few sips from her own cup before he started on his.

To his intense relief, a small, athletic young woman chose that instant to come bounding in the front door, shattering the tension like a cue ball on an opening break shot.

"I'm home. We gotta talk..." she said in what parents euphemistically call an "outside voice."

"Oh..." she had spotted Marcus.

"Molly, this is Detective Fox from the Portland Police. He has a few questions for you."

For the merest split of a second, Marcus noted that the miniature Amazon went rigid with fright. The only change in her expression, however, was a slight widening of her steel gray eyes.

"Good afternoon, sir. Nice to meet you," she said, looking for a place to sit down.

The cat chose that instant to jump down from its chair and Molly immediately claimed it for herself.

Curse the animal.

Half her face was in shadow. A shame—it was such an open, expressive face. And was it his imagination, or did the chair's arms move just a bit closer together as if to embrace her when she absent-mindedly patted one of them? The cat jumped onto her lap and curled up, but not before it had looked her in the eye, exactly as if it were giving her a piece of vital information. And was that just the slightest nod that she gave it when it finished?

From what he had been able to observe in the way she carried herself and looked out of her eyes, this girl was not your average teenager. She was tough and intelligent, and her aura crackled with red magic. No kid gloves for this one.

"Miss Adair," he said, addressing Molly. "Last night Shandra Sheehan was stabbed to death just off Alberta Street."

Both women just sat there. Not a change in their expressions, not a movement of any sort. He might have just told them that the sky was blue. This wasn't news to either of them.

Time to go fishing.

"From the pathologist's description of the entry and exit wounds," he continued, "the murder weapon was a sword that closely resembled a Japanese katana. Do you own a sword matching this description, Miss Adair?"

"No! Er, yes, actually, I do." Had the blasted cat dug his claws into her leg when she'd started to deny owning a sword? She would have been foolish to lie to a detective about something like that. Principal Rathkin had already told him about it.

"Where is that sword now?"

She looked over at her grandmother who simply nodded. She stared at Marcus as if she were trying to decide whether or not he was capable of comprehending what she was about to do. Finally she stood up and said, "My grandmother made a space for it in a parallel universe, so it's with me constantly." Watching Marcus closely, she pulled a katana out of thin air. Marcus was reaching inside his jacket for his Glock, but the girl was faster. Before his hand had even touched the gun, she was holding the sword out to him with the point of the blade resting on her shirtsleeve and the hilt on her open hand.

Marcus was stunned. Not by the materialization, but by the sword and the unbelievably swift move that had produced it. He stood and moved closer. It was a work of art. She could have sold it for many thousands of dollars. The light danced in waves and flickered like flames over the exquisitely arced blade.

And it sang to him.

The song pulsed out and caught at his heart. The sword told Marcus that its name was Flick and that it had taken two lives so far in its short but illustrious life. Before the excited blade could go into any detail, Molly said, "Shush, Flick," and continued to watch Marcus.

Marcus stared in dumbfounded amazement at the treasure in his suspect's hand. "Where did you get that sword?" he finally managed to inquire.

"A goddess forged it for me."

That didn't surprise him at all.

"I'm honored to make your acquaintance, Flick," he called after the sword as Molly made it disappear and returned to her seat.

So this was the murder weapon, and surely he had the murderer as well. Judging from the way she moved and handled that sword, she was probably as good as any martial artist he'd ever fought.

Could she kill?

Definitely.

She had been trained to kill. In fact she had already killed twice, by her sword's own admission. Did she have the opportunity? Yes. The body was found less than half a mile from here. She was in excellent condition and could easily have run up to Alberta, stabbed her friend and been home again in under thirty minutes.

But what was her motive? None that he could see now. And it would have to have been a good one. Trained warriors who owned swords like the one he'd just seen didn't run around killing people for no reason. But the police force wasn't overly keen on motive. He had been taught to tie the suspect to the time and place of the murder and let the courts and lawyers sort it out. So, motive would be nice, but not necessary for an arrest.

But, according to Shandra, he *didn't* have the murder weapon. She had been adamant that the sword was not what had killed her. So even if she hadn't been stabbed, she would still be dead. So why had Molly stabbed her? There were pieces missing here.

"Did you kill Shandra Sheehan?"

"No," she replied. And her steely eyes never left his and her expression never changed. A tiny twinge of apprehension skittered through him and set his muscles on alert. This was one dangerous young lady.

"Miss Adair, where were you at two o'clock this morning?"

Molly sat down and gave her statement, which was short and sounded well rehearsed. She had been awakened in the night by Flick crying out to her. When she had pulled the sword into this dimension it was covered with blood. It had told her that it had just killed Shandra. She had called Shandra's cell phone and had gotten no answer. Yes, Flick was sure she had been alive when it stabbed her and that she had died immediately thereafter. No, it hadn't been able to tell her who had actually used it to run Shandra through. Yes, she remembered the time she had called—it was 2:06 a.m.

Her story could be true. It corroborated the coroner's evidence and the evidence on Shandra's cell phone. But he was sure that she hadn't told him everything. When she'd finished her statement, he'd seen her shift just a tad bit uneasily in the comfortable armchair. The cat had shifted as well, almost as if it was trying to mask her telltale movement.

Marcus continued to sit and look at her expectantly, as if waiting for her to tell him the rest of the story. His ploy didn't work. Molly sat as if carved from stone, and that soft silence found only in wealthy neighborhoods stretched out uncomfortably.

"I know you were in that alley with your friend," he said, breaking the silence with a snap.

"No!" For just a moment Marcus saw panic in those hard, gray eyes.

"Oh, yes. The techs found a hair stuck in the blood of her death wound. It is exactly your color and length. Is there anything else you'd like to tell me, Miss Adair?"

Marcus watched the girl's eyebrows draw towards each other. They only moved a fraction of a millimeter, but it was enough to bring out two vertical lines above the bridge of her nose. The fear that had been tap-dancing behind those expressionless eyes had darkened to anger.

A warrior with a temper.

Not good.

The anger faded as quickly as it had come and she relaxed, but only just the slightest bit. Most people wouldn't have caught it, but Marcus wasn't most people.

"I couldn't just sit there. I mean, maybe she was still alive and needed help or something. I went to her house, but the front door was standing open and no one was there. Shandra's dog showed up, and when I asked him where she was, he took me to her. It was awful..."

Either she was an excellent actress, which he doubted, or she was truly grief-stricken. There were no tears or sniffles, just bleak sadness tinged with horror.

"Molly, tell me exactly what you saw."

After a moment's hesitation, she did, and her description matched the crime scene exactly, which meant that the body hadn't been moved since around 2:30, and Molly Adair was definitely a suspect. It would have been nice if he really did have a blood-soaked hair to prove beyond a shadow of a doubt that she'd been there.

But there was still something she wasn't telling him. Marcus could feel it in his bones. Waiting her out wouldn't work—he'd tried that already—so he stood and handed Molly his card. "Thank you for your time. Please don't leave the city. If you happen to remember anything at all that might be useful, call me immediately."

Estelle Adair walked with him to the door and out onto the front steps. She reached out and touched his arm. The simple gesture froze him in place. "She didn't do it, you know," she said.

"That remains to be proven," he replied, staring out toward the street. "The only witness she can produce so far is a magic sword."

"But Flick will tell you it wasn't Molly who stabbed Shandra."

"Last I heard they don't let magic swords testify in the state of Oregon. And even if they did, why should I believe it?"

"Because it's an even worse liar than Molly. In fact, I don't think it's capable of lying."

"That may be so," he replied, finally turning toward her, "but your granddaughter is still a suspect, and she will continue to be a suspect until I find evidence that positively incriminates someone else. And she's not helping me do that because she's holding back information—and so are you. Any other detective would have already taken her into custody and confiscated Flick."

"I almost wish you would." Estelle sighed and changed the subject. "You've done well for yourself, Marcus," she said. "The Librarian was right again."

"What?" The dreaded Librarian had been his constant nemesis. It had known way too much about him and never hesitated to remind him of it.

"It kept telling us that you were highly intelligent, honest, and amazingly talented. All we could see was a sullen teenager that was failing his classes and spending way too much time with gang members. When you dropped out, the Librarian forbade us to wipe out your memories of magic and the Academy. The only thing it did was block your ability to jump."

Marcus looked up into the branches of the rowan tree. Its remaining leaves were gold, and a few red-orange berries still clung to their stems. They glowed magnificently in the last rays of the late October afternoon sun. The color reminded him of the seething rage that had been his constant companion during his time at Grant High School.

He had found the Librarian on his first day there, and the sea of magic that had always before lapped gently at the edges of his consciousness came crashing down around him with the first touch of its powerful mind. Frightened and disoriented, he'd managed to stagger over to a study carrel and bury his head in his arms. When the world finally stopped spinning, he was surprised that the library was still there. In fact it was even more there than it had been. Everything was clearer and more intense, like someone had just wiped a thick layer of dust off everything. Shimmering lines of power crisscrossed the room, connecting every object and person, each of which nestled in a cocoon of glowing color that hinted seductively about what lay within.

What had happened to him? The black thing on the shelf tried to work its scaly way back into his brain.

Stifling a scream, he had scooped up his stuff and headed out of the library, out of the school and into the bright September sunshine. Something had forced its way inside him, pushed buttons and changed settings, turning him into a monster who could read people's deepest secrets. The world around him was suddenly bright and dangerous, like someone had turned up the volume. Trees basked in the sun, their great spirits shimmering and singing. Passing strangers' emotions splatted onto his consciousness like rotten fruit.

He had hurried along the quiet neighborhood sidewalks, trying to leave the madness and the feeling of violation behind him, but he soon realized he might as well try to leave behind an arm or a leg.

It was part of him now.

And it fascinated him.

It was impossible to ignore, but he found that it was possible to control. Searching desperately inside, he learned how to shape and stack himself so that he floated on top of the roiling sea of sensation instead of getting swamped. The trees became just trees again, and strangers kept their secrets to themselves. But he could still peek under the surface and see all the stuff that wasn't quite so frightening anymore once he knew how to turn it off.

He was hooked.

Ignoring his fears and misgivings, he'd eventually gone back to the library.

He never fit in at Tesseract Academy. He barely managed to scrape through the first year. His second and third years went downhill from there. His peers had treated him like the village idiot and he hated them. They were stuck-up, privileged snobs, brought up to believe that the world was their plaything. Their parents were mages—powerful, intelligent beings who took them all over the world and taught them all kinds of amazing stuff. He was the only mage at Grant who had regular parents. His father was a plumber who worked hard all day, came home, watched TV, drank cheap beer, belched, and farted. His mother was a high school history teacher who spent most of her free time curled up with a book—preferably a murder mystery. Marcus could never figure out what they saw in each other. Neither one of them had much time for him.

By the end of his junior year he'd had enough. The Alberta gangs fascinated him. Their strict hierarchy would be easy to use to his advantage, and he was impressed by how loyal the members were to each other. He'd figured out how to jump and travel through time and dimensions and had made friends with a few gang members. It would only be a matter of time before he controlled his own gang and was rolling in money. Unfortunately, when he left the Academy and dropped out of Grant, he found that he was suddenly unable to jump, dimension travel, or do anything but the simplest magic. Without those skills, he realized the gangs would eat him alive. Actually, they probably would have anyway. Long story short, he'd earned his GED and studied criminal justice in college—it had seemed fitting.

Now, years later, the memories were still painful.

He dragged his attention away from the glowing berries and glared down at the woman beside him. He'd thought he was done with these arrogant bastards when he'd dropped out, and he wasn't looking forward to dealing with them now.

"If you know anything that might help with this investigation, now would be a good time to tell me, Ms. Adair."

Estelle Adair looked up into his eyes for a very long time. Marcus could almost follow her inner debate. When she finally spoke, he realized he'd been holding his breath.

"I have no information that will help you find Shandra's murderer," she said.

He breathed out a sigh.

⌒

As soon as her grandmother stepped out of the house with the detective, Molly slumped back in the Chair and breathed out a long, sibilant puff of air that lifted the hair that curled over her forehead.

"Do you think he believed me?"

Yes, but he and I both know there's something you're not telling us.

Molly closed her eyes and clamped her jaw shut. She'd decided on the way home that there was no way she was going to tell Gram and Asmodius that the killer was an eternal. They'd never let her out of the house, even if she wasn't due to disappear until Friday afternoon. And she couldn't tell them Adam and Diana were helping her because Gram would tell their parents and they'd be grounded too—and totally pissed at her.

Seconds ticked by on the old pendulum clock. With a growl of disgust, Asmodius leapt up onto Gram's chair and began lapping milk out of the pitcher on the tea tray.

"Gram says you're not supposed to do that," Molly said. "It's unsanitary and it makes you fart."

What Estelle doesn't know won't hurt her, Asmodius replied. He flowed back down to the floor just as the party under discussion walked back into the room.

Her grandmother sat down and looked searchingly into Molly's eyes. She hated it when Gram looked at her like that. It made her feel like a bug under a dissecting scope.

"What aren't you telling us?" she said.

There was one thing she could tell them that they might not know. Then maybe they would leave her alone.

"Tamerlane got the Librarian to check on where the Grant adepts were at the time Shandra was killed," she said. "Rathkin and Mr. Liu were both out."

Gram jumped up and started pacing and Asmodius stared at her from the floor. They still looked suspicious, but her grandmother's expression quickly turned to concern.

"I wish we could have kept the students from finding out about this, but the news was all over the Academy in no time. I imagine someone has already told you about your death."

Molly nodded.

"I'm so sorry. But remember, this is only one possible outcome." She sat on the couch next to the Chair, and took Molly's hand. A tightness in the pit of Molly's stomach let go. Taking a shaky breath, she squeezed her grandmother's hand.

"Unfortunately, most of the adepts are convinced that you are guilty, and are not willing to waste energy protecting you from yourself. But some of us believe you are innocent, and we will do everything we possibly can to keep you safe and find the real killer.

"Thaddeus wanted you to stay away from the school, but we reminded him that you are the only one in danger. Not one of the futures we checked indicates that anyone else will be harmed. He finally agreed. There are already several detectives patrolling the school and the teaching adepts will be on the lookout as well." She smiled sadly at Molly and patted her hand. "However, I think you are your own best protection. It will be difficult for even an adept to overpower you."

But the eternal will have no trouble at all, Molly thought, as she smiled back at Gram with what she hoped looked like confidence.

29

Wednesday, October 26 • Early Evening

arcus needed to walk. It helped him think. And Alameda Street was perfect for walking. The homes were beautiful, with mature trees and landscaping. They had been built back in the day when developers built houses one at a time, not by the subdivision, so they were all different styles and sizes, and reflected enough of their owners' individual quirks to be interesting. As he paced through the neighborhood, he let the soft October evening calm his whirling mind and focus it on making sense out of nonsense.

Magic and murder were potent partners. He had a victim who had been stabbed through the heart with a sword. However, the victim's spirit insisted that the sword wasn't the murder weapon. He had a sword that gleefully admitted to having done it. He had a suspect who owned the sword and actually admitted that it had killed her best friend, but denied having done it herself, even though she admitted to being at the scene of the crime. So if he believed everyone, he had neither the murderer nor the murder weapon.

He believed the victim, but did he believe the suspect?

Probably. If Molly was lying, she was certainly capable of telling a more believable and less incriminating lie than that.

If Molly hadn't killed her friend, then someone else had reached into that tiny pocket between the worlds, taken Flick, murdered Shandra, and returned it to its hiding place. That someone would have to have been an adept, or at least a very talented magic user, and that someone would have to have known both Molly and Shandra.

Rathkin had told Marcus that Molly had moved to Portland a few months ago. So it was fairly safe to assume that if someone knew both girls, he or she would know them from Grant. So the killer was a talented magic user who either worked at or attended Grant High School and probably Tesseract Academy as well.

Molly was no dummy; he was sure she had figured out this much of the puzzle. In fact, she probably had plenty of other information that would be useful to him. So why hadn't she told him any of it?

"Because," he muttered savagely, kicking at a drift of maple leaves on the sidewalk, "if she tells me too much, she's afraid she'll be in custody, pacing a prison cell, instead of catching her friend's killer." Two blood red leaves lofted into the air, fluttering in spirals on a breeze that was turning chill with the setting sun.

So why would the killer hide the real cause of death?

Probably because the real cause of death would tell investigators something about the killer that the killer didn't want known.

So why not just stab her and be done with it?

Because he gained something from killing her that way. He had stabbed Shandra to incriminate Molly and hide the true cause of death.

But what would the killer gain?

Maybe it was her life force he was after. Marcus knew all about psychic vampires, but was it possible for one to completely and immediately draw the life out of someone?

If the blood chemistry and toxicology came back normal, and he had a bad feeling that it would, it was possible that a dangerous predator was stalking the halls of Grant High School. How many other students would he kill to satisfy his hunger?

The cool breeze amped itself up into a chill wind, and Marcus's blood turned to ice water. A mage who fed off the lives of others would be impossible to catch. He could jump times and universes to kill and kill again, with no apparent motive, no true cause of death, and nothing to tie one murder to the next.

His first impulse was to call the principal and tell him his conclusions. He was a mage and would immediately understand the threat to his students.

But what if Thaddeus Rathkin was the killer?

Unlikely, but possible. All the mages at Grant were suspects.

Whether he was the killer or not, the principal would have no option—if a police detective even mentioned that he was trying to figure out which one of Grant's teachers was a serial killer that made Hannibal Lecter look like a Girl Scout, he'd need to close the school. And if Rathkin closed down the school, that would make finding the bastard very difficult. He might even panic and run. And Marcus knew that this killer would be very good at vanishing without a trace.

If the monster vanished, not only would he be free to continue taking lives, but Marcus would be left without anyone to arrest for the murder of Shandra Sheehan—except Molly Adair, the owner of the apparent murder weapon.

An image of the girl flashed into his mind. Her eyes looked steadily into his and her lips were set in a straight, grim line. Waves of magic swirled around her, and her small, muscular frame looked ready to pounce at the slightest notice. Here was an individual who might have a chance of catching a creature like this. In fact, he suspected that she and her sword were designed for just this sort of task. She was also perfectly placed to gather information and observe.

But what if Molly was the killer? Highly unlikely. Why would she use her own very talkative sword to finish off her victim? Why not just leave her mysteriously dead?

The most logical explanation was that the killer had used Molly's sword to incriminate Molly. And she would have been any normal detective's prime suspect. Unfortunately for the killer, he wasn't a normal detective.

Marcus continued to walk.

It was dark now. The wind's cold fingers stirred the fallen leaves, making them whisper and chatter along the sidewalk. It tousled tree branches, making fantastic shadows that groped and glided over the well-kept lawns.

Marcus shivered and headed back to his vehicle. The more he shifted and rearranged the pieces of this puzzle, and the more he listened to his instincts, the more certain he became that he was dealing with a serial killer straight from hell.

By the time he'd gotten into the black and white and locked the doors, he had made his decision. He would grab something to eat and go back to headquarters to catch up on his paperwork. But first he would sneak into Grant High School and have a chat with the Librarian. It would know whether or not the creature he was imagining truly existed.

30

Wednesday, October 26 • 7:30 PM

ark clouds swept across the face of a near-full moon as Adam strolled slowly toward Charlotte Matsuda's apartment building, trying to look like an innocent pedestrian. His sensitive stomach was doing flip-flops and his hands were cold and shaking. He jammed them in his pockets. This had seemed like such a cool thing to do when he'd been sitting safe and sound on the bleachers in broad daylight. But the reality was terrifying. What if Matsuda was the eternal and somehow sensed he was there. He shivered as the moon sailed out from behind the clouds and a gust of wind sent the shadows of bare tree branches scrabbling across his path.

Several windows in the building glowed with light. Was one of them hers? She was in Apartment 2, and the building was three floors and took up half the block, so it was probably on the ground floor. But where? He needed to sneak inside and check out the apartment numbers. He headed up the steps to the lobby door.

Locked.

Shit.

Heart pounding, he studied the mailboxes to the right of the door. Yes, she was in number 2, and there were two other Matsudas in number 4, Reiko and Seiji, probably her parents. As he was turning to leave he looked inside and noticed an elderly Asian woman hobbling across the lobby toward the door.

Now was his chance. As she pushed the door open, he smiled and held it for her.

"Thank you," she said, so intent on getting herself down the steps to the sidewalk that she barely glanced at him.

Adam slipped into the building. The faint scent of Asian spices and cabbage clung to the beige walls and carpet of the dimly lit lobby. He tiptoed to the right and then left down the hall to the first door. It was apartment 2.

Turning on his heel, he tiptoed back out the door and along the right side of the building. The window facing the street was small and dark and covered with a curtain. Slipping behind the rhododendrons that screened it, he was just tall enough to peek through a gap in the curtain and see part of a red comforter and a black pillow. This was the bedroom.

Quick footsteps tapped on the lobby tiles. He crouched low in the bushes and watched as the door opened and a young man headed down the steps. His height and shadowy profile matched Charlotte Matsuda's.

Yes! He couldn't believe his luck.

He needed to see where this guy was going. Pushing his way through the shrubbery he started to follow him.

His quarry stopped and looked over his shoulder.

Shit. Too loud.

Heart pounding, he ducked down behind the steps. An agonizing eternity passed until the footsteps continued toward the parking lot. Almost sobbing with relief he peeked over the steps. Dry leaves and dark shadows skittered in the moonlight, but the dude was nowhere in sight. Adam headed, quickly and silently, for the parking lot and dropped behind a hedge when he heard a car start. The engine revved.

And then idled.

And then idled some more.

How freakin' long did it take to put on a seat belt?

Finally he heard the engine reverse and then start forward. Peering through the hedge, he watched as Charlotte Matsuda's blue Camry glided by, driven by a man who looked a lot like Charlotte Matsuda. It turned right out of the parking lot, and turned right again.

"Gotcha!" Adam whispered. Matsuda was definitely a man and a psychic vampire, but was he an eternal? And had he murdered Shandra? As he sank back into the shadow of the hedge and waited until his pulse quit racing and his stomach quit churning, the thrill of victory evaporated.

He needed more information.

Unfortunately, this wasn't the sort of information he could coax out of the Internet from the safety of his room. It was the sort of information that needed to be gathered from direct observation of a possibly dangerous person. It required steady nerves, the ability to defend yourself, and a sincere love of adrenaline rushes.

He possessed none of these.

He was gonna be edgy for days after this, and he'd be awake and jittery all night. Why had he volunteered to go creeping around in the shrubbery spying on people?

Diana. Exotic, dangerous, beautiful Diana. Of course.

And he was afraid for Molly. She was caught up in a dangerous web of lies, and needed all the help she could get if she was going to live past Saturday.

And he missed Shandra. She'd left a large, dark hole in his world.

She shouldn't be dead.

He wanted her killer brought to justice. He was a firm believer in justice. If there was no justice, what was the point of anything?

All good reasons to go check out Matsuda's apartment and see if he could learn anything else.

Gathering up his shattered nerves, he slipped across the front of the building, past the small bedroom window and turned the corner. The first window on this side was much larger and the curtains were open—probably because it looked out on a bunch of trees instead of the street. The ground sloped down and Adam had to grab the window sill and pull himself up to see in. Clouds covered the moon, leaving the room murky in the feeble light of the street lamps. He could just make out an oriental looking queen-sized bed, nightstand, and dresser. A large picture of a samurai and a woman in a kimono hung above the bed.

The moon came out and a beam of light speared into the room illuminating a horrible white face that stared blankly at him from behind the dresser. Adam gasped and dropped to the ground. Shit oh shit oh shit. Scrambling to his feet, he began running.

And then stopped.

The dresser was against a wall. There was no way anyone could get behind it. And that horrible face had been horrible because it was totally featureless and had gleamed pure white in the moonlight. Logically, it couldn't be a person. And Adam was big on logic. But it took all his courage and then some to pull himself back up to the window and check for sure.

A mannikin head holding a wig stared from the top of the dresser. Of course Matsuda needed a wig. Limp with relief, he dropped back down.

And froze.

There was an unmistakable tingle between his shoulder blades.

Someone was behind him in the trees. And that someone blazed with magic.

Was it Matsuda?!

He might have seen Adam or sensed his presence, gone around the block, and come back for the kill.

If Matsuda was an eternal, Adam could never outrun him, but he was gonna give it a good try. He ran like a madman for the safety of the busy street.

The world warped into slow motion and everything went sharp and crystal clear. With each slow step Adam checked for that blaze of magic, sure that it would be gaining on him. But it remained hidden in the trees.

Almost there. Just a few steps more.

The moment Adam's foot touched the street sidewalk, the presence moved. Just as he was taking his next step, inhumanely strong hands grabbed him and tossed him into the street.

Right toward the path of an oncoming car.

And there was no way that car could stop before it smashed into him.

If he didn't jump, he was dead.

He'd never jumped before, but his father had explained the theory. It involved mentally grabbing onto a line of power and using its energy to pull you toward it. He searched frantically for a line that was strong enough, and found one in the park across the street. He reached for it, willing himself to be there with every molecule of his being...and became a dizzying swirl in a heartbeat of frigid blackness.

With his next heartbeat, he landed in a bush.

31

Wednesday, October 26 • Late Evening

olly pressed her forehead against the train window and gazed down into the dark waters of the Willamette River. She and Diana were on the Red Line train, gliding across the Steel Bridge. The light rail reminded her of the ultramodern trains she and her parents had ridden when they'd traveled through Germany last year. Tears stung her eyes and made the window ripple like the surface of the river. Would she ever be able to think about them without hurting?

She lived in a totally different world now and was a totally different person. It was like the first fifteen years of her life had been chopped off and thrown away like an amputated arm. But even though the memories were fading, that life wasn't all the way gone. It still surprised her every once in a while by shooting a jolt of pain into her heart.

Oh, stop it. Crying over her parents wouldn't bring them back. And it certainly wouldn't find Shandra's killer, which she definitely needed to do or she'd be dead in a few days. Wiping away tears with the back of her hand, she looked up at the sparkling city lights and began to wrap her mind around the idea of dying. It wasn't death that bothered her; she'd already died once and was actually sorry when she'd had to return. But she was beginning to enjoy her new life and didn't want it stolen from her. And she really didn't want to face Shandra and try to explain why she hadn't brought her killer to justice.

Diana fidgeted in the seat next to her, bringing Molly back to the present. Closed-in spaces were beginning to bother her friend, and the feeling would only get worse.

"How did you ever convince Estelle to let you go out tonight?"

"It was easy. She knows that I'll probably be safe until Friday afternoon, and I told her I really needed to study calculus with you and Adam, since I'd forgotten most of it during the three-month."

The MAX, or Metropolitan Area Express, glided and bumped through Old Town, past the upscale restaurants and businesses on SW First Avenue, and turned right onto SW Morrison Street. Molly liked downtown Portland. Compared to Boston, it felt small and homey. Lots of green, not so many skyscrapers and not so crowded. Even at night the city felt almost safe.

But not tonight.

As soon as she and Diana got off the MAX at Pioneer Place, Molly's skin started to crawl.

"Someone's watching us." Molly whispered.

"I feel it too," Diana said. "But I can't tell who it is."

There were still people out walking, enjoying the moonlit evening. Any one of them could be the watcher. It was so bright that it was easy to see faces, but they didn't see anyone they recognized.

"We've got to lose whoever it is before we get to Pioneer Square," Molly said. "Let's split up."

"No. I am here to protect you. We need to stay together."

"I'll be fine. Watch." Remembering her lessons from the Little People of Damia, she concentrated on becoming one with the sidewalk.

"Ah, excellent! You're almost invisible."

"Good. I can never be sure if it's working," Molly said, stepping closer to the train kiosk and blending into it. "It was so easy in Damia, but it takes all my concentration here."

"If they can't see you, you will be safe enough. You go that way and I'll go this way and we'll meet at the Mr. Portland statue." Diana darted across the street and blended into a group of people on the sidewalk. Even Molly's sharp eyes had trouble following her. She was sure they'd be able to lose whoever it was. But as Molly headed toward Pioneer Square, she felt the watcher's eyes boring into the spot between her shoulder blades like the red dot of a laser scope.

Molly sprinted around the corner, keeping to the black moon-shadows as much as possible. She zigzagged, twisting and backtracking. She knew she was virtually invisible because no one paid any attention to her as she flitted past.

But the watcher stayed with her. In fact, he was getting closer.

She turned a corner and backed into the nearest doorway, holding her breath so her frantic breathing wouldn't give her away and blending into the stonework behind her for all she was worth.

Silence.

Molly waited until her lungs were ready to burst, let the air out and breathed in silently. She counted to a hundred.

A few people passed by, but no one noticed her. Hopefully she'd lost him.

Molly sprinted for Pioneer Square.

Diana was already standing beside the black bronze businessman, and Molly ran up to her with a sigh of relief.

Diana jumped and growled in annoyance. "Don't sneak up on me like that. It's dangerous."

"Sorry. Whoever it was, he followed me instead of you, but I think I lost him. Have you seen Mr. Liu yet?"

"Not yet." They stood in the inky shadow of the statue and scanned the red-brick square. At least Diana did. Molly was really getting into being Mr. Portland. This was one happy statue. Everyone liked him and he knew it. He made her smile.

Diana hissed and looked back over Molly's shoulder. "I can't see him yet, but I can smell him." They watched and waited. Diana faded back behind Mr. Portland's coattails, and Molly concentrated on holding up his umbrella and gesturing to someone in the distance.

Robin Liu stepped out of a shadow. He moved on cat feet and his eyes were everywhere. Molly held her breath and became one with the bronze. She could feel Diana tense beside her. He slipped past them, down the steps and toward the fountain.

"I smell peppermint and leather. The Ortiz creature is somewhere behind Mr. Liu, but I can't see him and he doesn't seem to be coming any closer." Diana whispered. Molly tingled with fear. Or was it excitement? Had Micah been following her or had it been Mr. Liu? Or had it been someone else? The feeling of being watched was gone.

Mr. Liu was approaching a girl huddled in the nook beside the fountain.

"We've got to get closer so we can hear what they say," Molly said.

Diana began to stroll in the general direction of the fountain. Molly detached from Mr. Portland, blended into the brick, and followed her. The splashing water would make it hard to hear. Hopefully Diana's sharp ears would pick up something.

It looked like the adept was asking the frightened girl a bunch of rapid-fire questions and she was answering them in short, sullen sentences. She was much younger than Shandra and she had the piercings, tats, shabby clothes, and wary eyes of a street kid. Just as they were nearing the couple, Mr. Liu said something, jabbed the girl sharply on the shoulder and walked away.

Diana gasped and stopped in her tracks. Molly ran into her and backed off with a shudder.

"What did he say?"

"He said, 'Watch out, or you will be next.'"

32

Thursday, October 27 • Late Morning

Molly's morning classes dragged by at the speed of a crippled tortoise.

She'd overslept and barely made it into first-period English before the bell, so Adam hadn't been able to tell her how his stakeout of Matsuda's apartment had gone. But judging from the dark circles under his eyes and the way he jumped at every sudden noise, it hadn't gone well. "I'll tell you all about it at lunch," he'd said as he headed for his second-period class.

When third-period bell rang, Molly practically ran to the front steps. Diana was already there, pacing the sidewalk and Molly paced with her.

When Adam finally appeared, Diana grabbed one arm and Molly grabbed the other and they headed for the QFC to buy lunch.

"So what did you find?" Diana asked, giving him an urgent shake.

"Impatient, aren't we?" Adam's eyes glinted mischievously for just a moment and then faded back to tired and frightened. "You'll never guess what happened."

"If we will never guess, then just tell us," Diana said.

"Can't you just say 'What?' like a normal person?"

"I am not a normal person." Diana growled and shook him a bit harder.

"Okay, okay, here's what happened..."

Adam told them everything that that he'd seen, and about the inhumanely quick and strong person who'd tossed him into the path of an oncoming car, and about how he'd saved himself by jumping.

"It had to be the eternal because it was so strong and so fast," he said. "Matsuda is a man and a psychic vampire and the only person besides you guys that could have known I was there. I think Matsuda murdered Shandra."

"So why didn't he come after you?" Diana asked. "From what you say, he was so fast that he could have found you and finished you off before you left the park."

"Oh gods, I never thought of that." Adam looked at her with wide, haunted eyes. "Maybe he'll try again later."

Cold dread squeezed Molly's chest and turned her legs to concrete. The monster had attacked another of her friends. If Adam hadn't been so quick and skillful, he would be dead.

Like Shandra.

Her mentor's words echoed through her brain: If it becomes obvious that by sacrificing your own life, you will save the lives of your loved ones or those you are defending, then the warrior's code requires your death.

She was gonna have to be life-sucker bait. It was the only way protect her friends and to bring the monster out in the open. Maybe she could kill him before he killed her. But even if she didn't survive, her friends and family would be safe, because she was the one he was after.

"I was hoping you could eliminate Matsuda, not move him to the top of our list." Diana said. "Wait till you hear what we saw."

They arrived at the grocery store and went to the deli counter. At least Molly and Adam did, Diana headed for the back of the store. "I'll meet you at the checkout," she said.

By the time Molly and Adam had their lunches, Diana was waiting for them by the door. As they headed across NE Thirty-third Avenue to Grant Park, Adam said, "So who was Mr. Liu meeting?"

"We don't know who she was," Molly said.

"But we should start at the beginning," Diana said. "As soon as we got off the MAX, we knew someone was watching us."

As Molly and Diana told their story, the three mages located a secluded spot under a huge Doug fir and sat down to eat. In the middle of Molly's account of her mysterious follower, Adam glanced at Diana and gasped in horror. Molly stopped in mid-sentence and looked over just in time to see her friend pop a cube of bloody, raw meat in her mouth.

"Gods, Diana. Too gross! How can you stand to eat that?" Adam shuddered and pulled his pasta salad farther away from her.

"Yes, it is tough," Diana replied, wiping a dribble of blood off her chin. "Steak would be better, but it is too expensive."

Molly looked fondly at her friends. All her fears and worries melted away and she began to laugh. It started out as just a giggle, but as the absurdity of it all settled in, it got bigger and bigger until she was rolling on the ground and laughing so hard she could hardly breathe. It bubbled up out of her and she relaxed into the sheer fun of it. When she could finally catch her breath, she looked up to see Adam and Diana staring at her like they were trying to decide whether or not she needed to be committed.

"What? You guys are hilarious. I can't remember the last time I laughed that hard."

"You think it's funny that your friend is reduced to eating raw meat? Who knows how many kinds of nasty bacteria are crawling around on it? That stuff could kill her!"

"I don't think so." Diana replied and looked over at Molly with a grin that could only be described as wolfish. "I am glad we amuse you." She selected another cube from the large, bloody pile and continued eating.

Adam groaned and turned to Molly. "So, how could whoever it was follow you if you were invisible?"

"I haven't a clue. But they did. And it only gets weirder." Molly sat up and took another bite of her ham sandwich, which had suddenly become much tastier, and continued the story.

"Did you talk to the girl? What did she say?" Adam asked when she'd finished.

"We tried to, but as soon as she saw us walking toward her, she ran away."

"And nobody followed you after that?"

"Not as far as we could tell."

"We've got more questions now than we had to begin with." Adam said, pounding his fist on the ground. "Is Mr. Liu the eternal? Was the street kid Tiger Lily? Is he going to kill her next? Who was following you?"

"And we have no time to find the answers, and that girl is in danger." Diana said. "We must report all this to the police."

Police! She'd totally forgotten to tell them about the detective.

"Um, when I got home from school yesterday, the detective that's investigating Shandra's murder was there. He asked me a ton of questions." Molly told them about her interview with Detective Fox and what Gram and Asmodius had told her about him.

"I can't believe the adepts kicked the dude out of the Academy and didn't erase his memory," Adam said.

"According to Gram, they wanted to, but the Librarian wouldn't let them."

"Lucky for us," Diana said.

"I'll call the detective right after school and tell him what we found."

"Do you want me to walk home with you?" Diana asked.

"Asmodius is meeting me. I'll be fine."

"I just hope Fox doesn't say anything to Estelle and our parents. We'll be grounded forever," Adam said. "And whatever you do, don't tell him about the eternal or we'll definitely be grounded."

33

Tesseract Academy • Just Before Midnight

hen Molly opened the door into Greek Mythology, her eyes widened in surprise. A full moon sailed high in a velvet black sky. Only a few stars managed to outshine its brilliance. At her feet, the broken bones of a giant gleamed white. In fact, bones littered the entire hillside that sloped up in front of her.

Oh, get a grip. Those couldn't be bones.

Closer inspection revealed that huge leg-bone-shaped objects at her feet were fallen marble columns. She was surrounded by a jumble of marble building parts. Blocks that had once been walls, slabs that had once been floors, sections of columns, and pieces of decorative friezes, and heads and body parts of statues all glowed eerily in the moonlight.

In a way, they *were* bones—the bones of a huge temple complex.

She had no doubt that they had been temples.

The place pulsed with power.

Krios, Zeno, and Elspeth stood farther up the hill staring at the ruins. When she joined them, Krios touched her shoulder.

"My condolences, Molly. It is a hard thing to lose a friend to violent death." Molly's eyes burned with sudden tears, but her instructor's sympathy took some of the weight of grief from her chest.

The rest of the class materialized one at a time, and the group divided like it had been cut with a sword. Jenz, Zeno, and Alim looked at Molly suspiciously and kept their distance, but Ophelia and Elspeth stepped up close beside her and gave her fierce, supportive hugs that brought more tears to her eyes. Krios watched his students' reactions with interest and then gathered their attention.

"Welcome to Elefsina," he said, sweeping his arm in a broad arc to take in the area behind them and down the hill to their left. They followed his gesture, murmuring in amazement when they realized they were in the middle of a town. Behind them stretched a shadowy, deserted street lined with parked cars and Mediterranean-looking stucco shop fronts with second-storey apartments. Far down the hill, the harsh, bright lights of a modern industrial port reflected on black water. "It's about twenty kilometers west of Athens, Greece. Since we're studying the Eleusinian Mysteries, I thought you should see where they took place."

Krios led his class uphill through the scattered marble ruins that glowed white and cast ominous black shadows on the moonlit ground. There was no sound except for their footsteps scuffing on the dry, stony ground. They stopped in front of a gaping black hole in the cliff face behind the site.

A pickup truck could have driven through it.

"Since the Eleusinian Mysteries involved a trip to the Underworld, a Plutonion, which is a gate to the Underworld, had to have been present," Krios said, pointing into the black emptiness.

Not a pickup truck. A chariot pulled by four huge, black stallions with blazing red eyes?

"This one is still open."

Oh gods, was it ever. The whole class took a step back as an icy draft swirled out of the cave's mouth and ran cold, possessive fingers over their faces and through their hair. This was not a healthy place to be.

"Right now, the year is at the midpoint between the fall equinox and the winter solstice. Those of you in Europe and North America are about to celebrate the festival of Samhain, or All Hallow's Eve. At this time the veil between the worlds is thin, and the air is thick with spirits. A perfect time to visit Hades and Persephone, the King and Queen of the Underworld."

A chill shimmied up Molly's spine and goose bumps swarmed and prickled down her arms. She looked at her instructor in horror.

He had to be kidding.

Persephone, fine. But Hades?

Hades made Darth Vader look like Santa Claus. The ancient Greeks were so frightened of the grim lord that they never called him by name. Instead they referred to him as "He Who Receives Many," "The Unseen One," or "The Wealthy One." The few temples built for him were only opened once a year and then only briefly. With terror and averted eyes, the priests sacrificed black sheep to him, dripping the blood into deep pits, and quickly closing the temple doors once more.

Any sensible person would have turned and run, but the mages stood like statues, fear and curiosity fighting for first place inside them. Their eyes were round with terror, but their lips were set in a firm line. Of course they were all gonna go. They were mages. They understood that death was a part of life, and that they needed to understand all they could about it. A chance to meet the Lord of the Dead was irresistible.

Krios held out his hands and a bouquet of small branches covered with rounded green leaves and white berries appeared in them. "This is mistletoe," he said, handing them each a branch. "It's your ticket into and out of the Underworld, so keep hold of it, whatever happens. It will get you safely into the throne room of Hades and Persephone. When you're ready to leave, lay your branch on Persephone's lap and thank the Lord and Lady for their hospitality. They will send you back."

Molly's fingers began to tingle as soon as the mistletoe touched them, and the branch shimmered. What exactly had her instructor just given her? She wasn't about to wander around the Underworld hanging onto something she didn't understand. She studied the branch more carefully and found that three different light patterns had been inserted into its aura. They were things of beauty, woven from strands of light in every color of the rainbow. And they were filled with power. Whoever had done them was a freakin' good spell weaver. One was definitely a protection spell, and one felt like a key, the thing that would help the mistletoe get her into and out of the Underworld. But what about the other one? She tried to move the branch in her hand to ease the tingle. It was stuck fast.

Aha!

Molly glanced over at Ophelia and grinned. The tiny mage was trying to shake off her mistletoe, and Alim was trying to pull his off.

Krios wasn't taking any chances.

"Prepare to trance," he said, after everyone had accepted the fact that there was no way they could lose their herbal passport.

"Pluck a leaf and chew it slowly and thoroughly...

"Spin slowly in a counterclockwise direction...

"Still your mind and open yourself to the divine..."

—

She was walking through a field of ripening wheat. The sky was picture-book blue and a warm breeze caressed her cheeks. She continued until she came upon a broad expanse of lawn dotted with groups of trees. People of all ages and races were strolling over the grass or sitting in groups.

Was this the Underworld?

Impossible! It looked just like the surface.

Well, maybe not exactly like the surface.

There were no shadows.

And there were no shadows because there was no sun to cast shadows. The beautiful blue sky was empty.

No way to tell time.

Which meant, of course, that in the Underworld, one time was like any other time.

A few soccer-field lengths away, the façade of a palace loomed, carved into a black stone cliff. Its classic Greek triangular roof line topped a decorative frieze, which topped a row of huge columns. Broad, black stone stairs led up to the columns.

Molly shivered and headed toward it. When she reached the steps, she stopped and looked up...and up. It was massive, black, and forbidding. Even though the plaza at the top of the steps continued invitingly past the columns and straight into the palace, Molly really didn't want to go in there. Because once she was inside she would be under a mountain, walking through timeless darkness filled with countless souls. She could see them from where she stood. The darkness writhed with them. Occasionally one would move past the pillars, become more solid, stroll down the steps, and join the others on the lawn. A man and a woman, holding hands and laughing, skipped up the steps and into the palace. Their fragile forms fell apart, leaving only their souls to glide through its crowded silence.

Would that happen to her?

Clutching her mistletoe, she followed them up the steps and into the dark.

It was a strange, creepy sort of dark. She could see clearly, but there wasn't any light.

Empty space stretched out above and around her with the hint of a black stone wall far in the distance. She glanced over her shoulder and gasped in fear. The columns and the bright lawn were gone. She was surrounded by emptiness—an emptiness filled with unseen souls that swirled and whispered around her, caressing her face and slithering over her arms.

In a panic, Molly looked down at herself and sagged with relief. She could see her body and feel the fabric of her T-shirt and the pressure of her hands. Her feet still stood on the black rock floor. She still had her body. A soft glow appeared in the distance, and Molly pushed toward it through the soft press of the surrounding souls.

It wasn't a pleasant walk.

She kept her eyes on the light, ignoring the wispy presences that swirled around her, plucking at her clothes and gently tapping her, trying to get her attention. All of her instincts warned her that if she paid attention to even one of them, she would lose herself in their invisible whirlpool.

The glow slowly resolved into a man and a woman seated on ebony thrones. They were leaning toward each other, caught up in what looked to be a friendly conversation, but as Molly drew nearer, they turned their attention to her. Molly's skin prickled and twitched, and her heart thudded against her rib cage as raw, remorseless power surrounded her. She stopped and bowed her head. Not just out of respect. She needed a moment to get her fear under control.

Persephone was radiantly beautiful. Her gleaming red hair was caught up in a single braid, and tendrils of curls had worked their way free to frame her lovely face. The floral pattern of her simple, black damask gown was set off with thousands of tiny diamonds—Molly had no doubt that they were real diamonds—that flashed and sparkled with a life and light of their own, creating the glow that surrounded the couple.

Beside her, Hades was an ominous shadow. Everything about him was black except for his tanned, weathered skin, a stark contrast to his queen's creamy white complexion. He was a warrior. Molly could see that from his upright, watchful posture, and, of course, his black armor. But it was his eyes that took Molly's breath away. They were two deep, compelling pools of darkness that sucked the soul right out of you, explored all its nooks and crannies, and then, if you were lucky, returned it to you.

Molly was lucky.

"Welcome to the Underworld, Molly Adair," he said. Molly blinked in confusion. Yes, it really was Hades who had spoken, but his voice was soft and gentle. And, oddly enough, once you got used to those eyes, there was comfort in their unbending gaze.

"And we will soon be welcoming you back," Persephone said. Her voice was firm and precise.

A cold dread seeped into her as she understood the meaning of the goddess's words. The eternal was probably going to kill her tomorrow and she was looking at her fate.

And then she realized that she'd had it all wrong. Of the two gods, Persephone was the one to fear, not Hades. She wasn't cruel, but there was no mercy or gentleness to be found in that stern, beautiful face. Her quick, fiery spirit cut straight to the heart of any issue—no matter how painful it might be for the one with the issue.

A blast of power slammed into Molly from the right.

"Don't be countin' your chickens before they hatch, Your Majesty!"

Brigga was standing beside her, fists jammed into her hips, a blaze of brilliance in the gloomy Underworld. Molly's mortal dread melted away. She was so glad to see Brigga that she could have hugged her and wept tears of relief onto her scorched-leather smith's apron. But she never got the chance, because at the same moment, Hades leapt up and pointed his two-pronged staff at Brigga. Black-violet light lashed from its tips. "Begone, Brigga. This realm is forbidden to you." The dark cascade encircled first Brigga and then Molly. Every hair on Molly's body stood on end and the staff's power sang dirges in her ears, but it came no closer. The magic of the mistletoe held fast.

"Nae, it is *not* forbidden," the goddess replied, pointing to the luminous cord that joined her body to Molly's.

"Ah, I see." The ultraviolet halo around them disappeared. "But your mission is futile. Your agent is doomed. All the power in the multiverse won't save her. Give it up, Bright Lady." The Lord of the Underworld set aside his staff and lounged back on his throne. "However, rest assured, I'm not looking forward to welcoming her soul. It will be angry and cause all sorts of unpleasantness. I have my agents on the surface watching to see if they can help her, but their reports give me little hope."

"We'll see about that!" Brigga replied. "Allow the Fates to spin out the thread of her life, Hades. Atropos has not yet cut the thread that binds her to the surface."

"Of course I will wait. I have no choice," he said with a shrug. "And, Fates willing, it will be many more of her years before I receive her soul."

"We wish you the best of fortune. Farewell, Molly Adair," Persephone said.

"Give the queen her token," Brigga said. "It is time to leave."

Numb with awe, Molly crept forward and bowed. She held her precious talisman over Persephone's lap and released it.

"Thank you great Lord and Lady for your hospitality."

The mistletoe fell into the lovely queen's waiting hand and disappeared.

The diamonds on her gown flashed green.

—

"Take a moment to process your experience and open your eyes." Krios's voice wedged itself gently into her consciousness.

Process her experience? There wasn't enough time in the multiverse to process that experience. The dark, potent power of the King and Queen of the Underworld had been brutal. It had stripped her soul bare. But instead of leaving her devastated beyond repair, she felt calm and light—as if she'd just dropped a ton of psychic garbage. And how do you process the fact that you're doomed, and your best friend's murderer will go free to kill and kill and kill again? And she wasn't much closer to finding him than she had been the night of Shandra's death. But on the bright side, she knew that not only Brigga, but also Hades and Persephone, were pulling for her. That had to count for something.

There was a muffled sob from Elspeth, and Jenz groaned. The class—yes, all six of them had made it back—lay sprawled just outside the gaping mouth of the Plutonium. They slowly sat up and gazed around them like shipwrecked sailors washed up on a welcoming beach. Then they all crawled over to comfort Elspeth and each other. Elspeth was in grateful tears because Hades and Persephone had arranged a visit with her grandmother. The Underworld was a lovely, restful place, and her Grandmother was happy to be out of pain at last. And then everyone else told their stories. Molly left out quite a bit of hers, and she suspected others had as well. But everyone's experience in the Underworld had been unique, and they'd each come away with a totally different picture of it and of its king and queen.

That wasn't surprising.

It had been the same with every god and goddess they'd visited so far.

Molly stalked through the packed halls to Pre-Calc. Hades had to be mistaken. She couldn't die now. If she died she couldn't expose Shandra's killer. And she needed to. Not just to get justice for Shandra, and not just to keep him from killing again, but because every cell and molecule in her body burned with rage and the desire to kill the monster who had devoured so many innocent lives. It had been simmering inside her ever since she had found Shandra's ruined body, but her terrible grief had blinded her to everything except numbness and pain. Her trip to the Underworld and Brigga's powerful presence had somehow cleared her mind and fanned her anger and resolve. Her grief was still there, but it no longer weakened her. Instead it had become a crystalline force behind her rage.

From its pocket between the worlds, she could hear Flick humming silver songs of daring exploits.

An arm slipped through her right arm, pinning it. She breathed in the scent of leather and peppermint, stared up into Micah's aviator lenses, and growled. She tried to jerk her arm free, but he held it fast and smiled down at her. It was a thin-lipped, intense smile that set her heart racing.

He was so incredibly cool, and when she looked at their energy fields, they were intertwined; Micah's purple-black, flashing, and intensifying and her own clear red. The couple ahead of them was hanging all over each other and their blue and green auras were doing the same thing. This was what attraction looked like. And, of course, Micah could see and feel it too. So what was wrong? Why was he always threatening her, and watching her, and trying to control her? Why couldn't he have walked up beside her and smiled like he was glad to see her and said something like "How's it going?" And then they could have walked together and maybe he would take her arm. But he would hold it gently because he knew they both enjoyed the touch and she wouldn't pull away.

"I thought I'd walk you to Pre-Calc and we could talk," he said, slicing through her thoughts. She'd gotten part of her wish. Sort of. But Micah didn't make small talk, and he didn't seem to care how things were going for her.

"About what?"

"About why you and Diana were stalking Master Liu last night. Do you think he killed Shandra?"

No way was she going to discuss Shandra's murder with one of her main suspects. Molly tried to escape again, but Micah held her tight.

"Answer me!"

"I don't know. Maybe he did. And maybe you did! Why were you following us?"

Micah dropped her arm and disappeared into the crowded hallway.

Molly couldn't decide whether she was relieved or sad to see him go.

34

 omeone was shaking her and she wished they'd stop. She didn't want to wake up—ever.

SMACK!

The shaker had slapped her.

The bastard!

She lashed out with her fist and felt the satisfying pain of contact.

"Ow! Damn it!"

Strong hands caught her wrists and pinned them to the ground above her head.

Molly looked up into Micah Ortiz's angry face. The mirrored aviator glasses were gone, and she wished they weren't. His eyes were black, empty pits in the moonlight and they were pulling her in. She gasped, closed her eyes in panic, and tried to knee him in the groin. He defended himself by simply pushing her leg away with his and lying on top of her. His minty breath touched her cheek.

"What are you doing here?" She asked. Her eyes were still scrunched closed as she struggled to escape.

"I was going to ask you that same question," he replied. "Do you even know where *here* is, Miss Molly?"

She stopped struggling and looked around. Tall Doug firs framed a nearly full moon floating serenely at mid-heaven. She was lying on grass, and there was a cedar chip path several yards away.

She must have taken too long to reply, because Micah answered his own question. "You're in Wilshire Park. Do you know how you got here?"

She shook her head and continued to look intently at the trees, the grass, the moon, anywhere but into those bottomless eyes that threatened to steal her soul.

Sirens wailed dismally in the distance.

"I've called 911. That's probably them. If I let go of you, will you be nice?"

She nodded and carefully studied a tree branch behind Micah's left shoulder as he let go of her wrists and stood up and away from her in one quick movement.

Then he began pacing and wiping his bleeding nose with the back of his hand.

A police car came roaring up NE Thirty-third, turned right onto Skidmore, and came to a stop as close to Micah and Molly as it could get. Detective Fox jumped out.

"What happened?"

"I was out for a walk and found Molly lying unconscious and called 911."

"You just happened to be out for a walk at one o'clock in the morning? And just happened to see a body dressed in black lying well away from the street? Come on, Ortiz, what were you doing here?"

"You're the one they have investigating Shandra's murder, aren't you?"

"Answer my question."

"Why is Grant suddenly crawling with detectives, and why are they all interested in Molly?"

"Answer the question." Marcus's voice was very low and threatening.

"Okay, okay. Like I said, I wanted to find out what was going down so I've been keeping an eye on Molly, cuz she seems to be right in the middle of it. I put a psychic tracer on her."

So that's how Micah had been able to follow her downtown.

"Oh, don't look at me like that, Fox." Micah's words sliced through her thoughts. "You would've done it too, if you'd been able to. So anyway, about half an hour ago, I felt it disappear. Like zip, it was gone. I got on my bike and headed for her house to check it out. I'm about halfway there and all of a sudden, wham, it's back, only now it's north of her house. I followed the connection and it led me here. She was unconscious—I mean really out of it. Shaking didn't do a thing. I was afraid she'd keep slipping away, so I slapped her."

"And that's how you got that bloody nose." Marcus said turning toward Molly to hide his grin.

"Yeah."

"I'm outta here." Micah turned and walked toward a sleek black motorcycle parked a few yards from Marcus's car.

"Ortiz," Marcus said in a sharp, deadly voice.

Micah stopped in his tracks.

"Take off the tracer."

"It's done."

Molly's left cheek tingled.

"And don't leave town. You're a suspect in a murder investigation. I want you in my cubicle tomorrow to sign your statement."

"Yeah, yeah, I'll be there," he said as he started toward his bike once more.

"Fuckin' cops," he muttered, just loud enough for them to hear.

As Micah roared off, the medics arrived in a flurry of flashing lights and bustle, and Marcus knelt down beside Molly. "Are you hurt?"

She took a quick inventory and said, "I'm okay. There's something wrong, and I don't know what it is, but I don't think it's anything those guys can fix."

She submitted to their pokings and proddings but refused to go to the emergency room.

Detective Fox drove her home.

⌣

The detective watching the house stared in astonishment when Marcus arrived with his assignment in tow.

"Honest, Marcus, I never saw her leave. There's an eight-foot wall around the whole back yard. She would have had to come through the front yard to go anywhere and she never did."

Marcus jammed both hands in his pockets, fists clenched in frustration. The detectives working with him had no idea what they were up against. They were not only next to useless, but also totally vulnerable. There was no way they could protect themselves from a mage. He wished he didn't have to use them, but if he didn't follow procedure, questions would be asked. "I believe you, Neil. Just watch the place for suspicious activity. Come on Ms. Adair, let's get you inside."

The back door was unlocked.

"It's Detective Fox. I have your granddaughter," he called into the kitchen.

Before he'd finished his sentence, the cat streaked into the room followed by Estelle in a swirl of rippling blue silk.

"Molly! Are you hurt? Why did you leave the house?" Her grandmother enveloped Molly in a fierce embrace. "You don't feel right. What happened?" she asked, holding her granddaughter at arm's length.

"I don't know. I was home in bed and then Micah Ortiz started shaking me and slapping me and I was in the middle of Wilshire Park."

Estelle smoothed her granddaughter's wild hair as Marcus told her what had happened. Then she kissed her on the forehead and then began pacing. "A tracer. That's a complex working. Even some adepts can't put one of those together. Why would he take the trouble?"

"If his story is true," Marcus answered, "he did it because he wanted to know what was happening with the murder. Having police detectives in the school makes him nervous."

"Of course it does," she said. "That boy has more angles than a dodecahedron, and I'd be willing to bet that most of them aren't legal."

"However, he could be lying."

"That's also possible," Estelle stopped her pacing and turned toward Molly. "You look dead on your feet. Go and get some sleep."

Actually the girl looked past dead. She glided out of the kitchen like a living ghost, not even bothering to argue. The cat followed her. Estelle watched her leave with a worried frown and turned to Marcus.

"This never should have happened. Only a top-level adept could find his way through our house shields, and we would have definitely noticed if he had. And Molly promised us she wouldn't leave the house without telling us. He must have planted a suggestion, although I can't think how. This won't happen again. We'll put a binding spell on her to keep her inside."

She flitted over to the stove and turned on the kettle. "Let me make you some coffee, you look like you could use it." The water boiled seconds later. Another flurry of movement and a press pot with ground coffee appeared on the counter. The mage poured the hot water into the pot and said, "But why would the killer abduct Molly, only to return her Wilshire Park?"

The screaming started just as Marcus was taking his first sip of the fragrant, restorative ambrosia that Estelle Adair called coffee. He slammed his mug down onto the table slopping the hot aromatic brew over the cuff of a sports jacket that was already begging for a trip to the cleaners. Cursing vehemently under his breath, he followed the screams to an upstairs bedroom and threw open the door.

The sight that met his adrenaline-enhanced eyes was enough to turn his blood to ice. Two naked Molly Adairs wrestled with two vividly colored Asian dragons, their fangs and claws flickered sharp and cruel.

"Get it off! Get it off!" The two Mollies shrieked in perfect unison as Asmodius, puffed out to twice his already ample size, bared his fangs and hissed in rage.

Heart pounding, Marcus reached for his switchblade, stepped further into the dimly lit room, and immediately realized that the situation wasn't what he'd thought.

It was, if possible, even more sinister.

His fear turned to bright, blinding fury as he pocketed the blade and searched for something to cover the naked teen. There was only one Molly. It had seemed like two because she was writhing in fear and disgust in front of a full-length mirror. And there was no dragon, only a picture of one, drawn in cruel detail over most of the front of her body. As Molly moved, the vicious, clinging image moved with her. Its tail caressed her left knee and its body undulated up her thigh and across her belly. Its back claws dug into her hips, its front claws grasped her left breast, and its fanged mouth opened wide, ready to bite into the tender flesh.

Every scale and whisker glowed with meticulous perfection—a monsterpiece of horror and beauty.

Estelle was right behind him. She gasped in anguish and reached for Molly. Her hands looked claw-like in the dimness and her hair stood out from her head with a life of its own. The cat snarled a heart-stopping litany of feline curses and his eyes glowed wickedly. The picture they made—a wild old woman and her vicious, black familiar casting huge, menacing shadows and stalking a terrified young woman—sent a chill of apprehension up Marcus's spine. It took all the self-control he had to step back and see what they were going to do.

The adept wrapped her arms around her granddaughter and the cat reared up on its hind legs and placed a paw on Molly's hip, the center point of the beast. Marcus watched as the luminous lines of power that clustered thickly around Molly swirled into a glowing whirlpool, spiraled down through the adept, and disappeared into the floor. There was a quick twist and rearrangement in the remaining lines, and the dragon was suddenly just a well-executed image. Marcus had totally missed the presence of the ever-so-subtle spell woven through its every tooth and scale and claw.

Now that the two mages had calmed her hysteria and defused the spell, Marcus stepped forward with the robe he'd found draped over a chair. Estelle snatched it and wrapped it quickly around her granddaughter. As she hugged the sobbing mage close, the cat stepped in, sniffed at the dragon, and looked up at Estelle. She pointed down to the jumble of clothes that Molly had stripped off as the pain of the dragon spell lanced through her. A handful of colored pens spilled out of a pocket in Molly's jacket.

"It was probably done with those."

"Yes, but why?" Marcus asked, trying desperately to hide his horror and appear calm.

"And now you can cross her off your list of murder suspects," Estelle said.

But could he? Molly could have drawn the dragon on herself. He remembered that when he was at Grant, there had been a few girls who decorated themselves with amazing designs done in colored ink. And he was willing to bet his next cup of coffee that those pens had Molly's fingerprints all over them. But he doubted that Molly could have faked her fear. That had been pure, honest panic.

And then there was Micah Ortiz. He only had the gang leader's word that he was following a tracer signal that had disappeared. Micah could have drawn that dragon.

"If she's not the murderer," he said, continuing his train of thought to its ghastly conclusion, "she is more than likely scheduled to be the murderer's next victim, and this is an attempt to drain her energy so she'll be easier to kill. Do you understand, Molly?"

"Yes," Molly sobbed. "Gram, you're squeezing me so hard I can hardly breathe."

"Sorry," her grandmother said and relaxed a bit. But she didn't let her go. Marcus could see the rage spilling off the tiny adept.

It was time for him to leave, but there were a few things he needed to say.

"I've placed a few undercover agents at Grant to protect you. They're disguised as janitors."

"Yeah, I know."

Of course she knew. He kept forgetting he was dealing with mages. "They have no idea what they're up against and I can't tell them, so give them a break and keep them in sight at all times."

" 'Kay."

"The detectives say that you have been having some intense discussions with two other students. Keep them out of this, Molly."

When Molly had called yesterday and given him all that information about Robin Liu, Charlotte Matsuda, and the principal, he'd guessed that her friends had helped her. Even she couldn't have pulled all that information together in one day. He'd interviewed both Diana Andrusko and Adam Aubrey several hours ago and done his best to drag as much out of them as possible, but he was sure he hadn't gotten it all. Did the three of them know that Molly was probably being stalked by an eternal? A mage who could kill with a glance and move with a speed and strength that would leave even Superman dead in the dust?

How could he allow her to leave this securely shielded house tomorrow?

But she couldn't hide forever. Sooner or later she would have to come out, and then the monster would kill her—and anyone who got in the way.

"But they're my friends. They ask questions," she replied, interrupting his painful thoughts. "What are they supposed to do? Sit around and watch me get killed?"

"Hopefully you won't have to sit around and watch *them* get killed," he said, and stalked out of the room.

Tomorrow had already started, and he had a gut feeling that it was going to be a nightmare.

35

Friday, October 28 • Late Morning

olly pounded downstairs in a fury.

It had taken them forever and two bags of cotton balls and two bottles of rubbing alcohol to wipe away that awful beast. When she'd come out of the shower, Gram and Asmodius had grabbed her and done a psychic clearing and balancing. They must have sneaked in a sleep spell too.

Rotten, meddling mages!

It was way late and she had to get to school.

Scrambled eggs, sausage, toast, and orange juice were waiting for her. As she was demolishing her second helping of eggs, Gram said, "You're not going to school today, it's too dangerous and you need to stay home and recover." She looked exhausted. Binding spells must be hard to cast.

"I'm fine. Hiding at home behind the shields won't help catch this monster."

"Oh, and running around with 'target' written all over you will?"

"Yes."

"No, it won't. You don't stand a chance. That monster is clever and cruel. I can't let you walk out of this house to your death."

She was thankful that Gram didn't know how small her chances really were.

"So when *will* you let me walk out of this house? I can't stay here forever, and when I do go out he'll be waiting for me. I won't have any more chance then than I do now."

Molly put on a jacket and her backpack and headed for the door with Gram right behind her.

"I've gotta do this. Let me go," Molly said, turning to face her determined grandmother.

They glared at each other for what seemed like ages until, with a sigh of regret, her grandmother released the binding spell.

"Do you have your crystal? You left it behind last night."

Molly nodded and pulled down her T-shirt so Gram could see it.

Then she kissed the tiny adept, hugged her fiercely, and left the safety of the house.

Asmodius glided out from under the rowan tree and fell in step beside her.

Molly sat in the library fidgeting and jumping at every blip and shimmer in the magically charged atmosphere. When was the stupid bell going to ring? Weapons practice had been totally exhausting, but at least she'd felt safe and it gave her something to do. But something was wrong. Outwardly, everything seemed calm and safe. The Librarian snoozed on its shelf. Students either pored intently or dozed over open books and homework assignments. But every cough and every rustling turn of a page cut into the silence like a knife. Something dangerous lurked just at the outer limit of her senses.

She could feel it.

It made the back of her scalp and the skin between her shoulder blades tingle.

She whipped around and looked up at the mural of famous people. Their eyes were alive and every one of them was watching her.

But none of them moved.

They just watched.

Her heart pounded in her chest and the palms of her hands prickled with sweat. Sitting still was impossible—especially with her back to all those staring eyes. She got up and started prowling along the bookshelves, occasionally reading a title or scanning a table of contents. But no matter which way she turned or where she looked, the back of her scalp still tingled and the skin between her shoulder blades itched. She noticed that Ms. Neal was keeping a careful eye on her.

Was she the watcher?

"I'm just being paranoid," Molly muttered and continued prowling.

Finally the bell rang, shattering the silence and pulling everyone to their feet.

It was a relief to escape into the roaring press of students. There was safety in numbers.

Or was there?

The itchy tingling between her shoulder blades remained.

Someone was following her.

She glanced back, and a thrill of fear shot through her. Micah Ortiz was behind her. An insolent shadow of a smile tugged at the corners of his mouth.

He was getting closer.

She felt the heat of him on her arm and shoulder just before he grabbed her elbow, anchoring her in place. Panic washed through her as she breathed in his scent and stared up into his mirror lenses. Students bumped and jostled around them as Micah leaned in close.

"Can you feel it? Watch your ass, Miss Molly." And then he was gone.

With a shudder of relief—or was it disappointment?—she turned into her Pre-Calc class.

Adam and Diana were on her like ads on the Internet.

"Where have you been?"

"And why did you tell that detective about us?"

"He came to our houses and grilled us last night."

"We are so grounded."

"I had a rough night, too." Gods, she didn't even want to think about last night. "And I didn't tell him. He must have guessed after I dumped all that information on him."

"You look like you've seen a ghost," Diana said. "Are you alright?"

"Micah Ortiz followed me from the library to here." Molly slammed her pack onto her desk and threw herself into her chair.

"Ah," Diana said. "I'll walk you to forensics after this class. The Science Block is only a little bit out of my way."

"My forensics class is in the computer lab today."

"I'll walk with you then," Adam replied. "My history class is sort of in that direction. If we move fast, I can just make it."

"I can't believe that anything could happen between here and the computer lab, but thanks, that would be great."

"No problem."

Class was a misery. Molly hadn't done her homework and had no idea what Ms. Denzel was blathering on about. She sat back, trying to look attentive, as the stream of numbers and formulae washed over her, accompanied by the rhythmic click of chalk on the blackboard.

And then the breathing started.

It was faint at first, and she thought it was just the mouth-breather behind her. But it gradually grew louder.

It filled the whole room.

Her body seemed to contract with each deep, sibilant exhalation.

The walls started closing in and the smell of chalk dust was suffocating.

Adam and Diana just sat there looking bored and taking the occasional note.

Couldn't they hear it?

Terror clutched at her heart and stole her breath away.

Was she going crazy?

Of course you're not. Strengthen your shields, you idiot.

She tore her attention away from the breathing and focused on making her shields stronger and more resilient. She found another cord in her solar plexus. Damn, how could they have missed this one? She yanked it out viciously and repaired the damage.

The breathing stopped, the walls receded, and the smell of chalk dust faded into the background aromas of ripe gym bags, hormones, deodorant, and over-applied perfume. The lecture continued, and it still made no sense whatsoever.

But at least the breathing had stopped.

When the bell rang, she almost dragged Adam out of the room.

"Hang on, hang on," he said, stuffing his calc book into his pack and grabbing his jacket off the back of the chair. "What happened?" he asked as Molly pulled him out into the hallway. "You looked like hell."

"Oh, jeez, Adam, it was horrible. The room started breathing and crushing in on me. It was him, just watching me and sucking away my energy."

"Yeah, your shields were weak. I felt you strengthen them. Is it gone now?"

"Pretty much. I had to pull out a cord he'd stuck in me. But I can still feel him pushing against my shields. It's like he's telling me that all he has to do is push a little harder and he'll have me again."

"This is nuts." Adam draped a comforting arm casually over her shoulders and added his shielding to hers. It felt good, like a warm blanket tucked over her on a cold night. Molly relaxed into it and recharged herself. "Sooner or later that creep is gonna get you, and I don't even want to think about what'll happen then. You've gotta call your grandmother and have her take you home."

Jason Cleft from their Pre-Calc class came up behind them and gave Adam a playful shove. "Nice move, Aubrey."

"Beat it, Cleft."

Jason snickered and continued past them.

"Fine. So I go home and sit safe and sound. What then? Do I just sit there forever? How dumb would that be? Our only hope is to catch him when he grabs me. Just keep an eye on me and if I disappear, find a cop and make him call Detective Fox. They're never far away—look, there's one over there. Oh shit, there's Micah."

He was about ten feet behind them, but his presence was palpable. Students unconsciously moved out of the way as his dark, menacing aura slid over them. Molly suppressed a hysterical giggle as the theme from *Jaws* began playing in her head.

Adam just growled.

They reached the computer lab. Adam saw her safely inside and rushed off to his history class.

Her classmates' heads and torsos glowed in the light of their screens. Keyboards clicked all around her. Strangely enough, she felt safer here than she had anywhere else in the school.

Was it because all the computer electronics somehow blocked the attack?

Or was it because the killer was in the room with her and didn't want to call attention to himself?

Mr. Liu sat unobtrusively at a computer in the back of the room and Ms. (or Mr.?) Matsuda lurked in her web of computer screens at the front of the room. Whatever, it was a relief to be able to relax and turn her attention to her assignment and the Internet. She typed the first web page she wanted to visit into the search engine and hit Enter.

Up came a picture of Shandra's corpse sprawled and bloody on the pavement.

Paralyzed with horror, Molly stared helplessly at the gruesome image, as scenes from that awful night flashed mercilessly through her head.

Flick, dripping blood that gleamed black in the moonlight.

Shandra's warm, happy greeting on her cell phone, asking her to leave a message and she'd call her back.

Shandra's dog, Keiser, whining in front of that awful, black space, begging her not to go in.

Shandra's sad, bloody body suddenly illuminated by the flash of a streetlight.

Darkness.

Shandra's dead eyes staring at her.

Darkness.

The streetlight kept blinking, flashing the nightmare scene on and off, on and off.

With a sob, Molly clicked the back arrow.

Shandra's dead eyes still stared from the screen.

She tried closing the tab.

The eyes blinked.

Stifling a scream, she clicked the X repeatedly, desperately trying to leave the Internet.

There was a waft of jasmine and sandalwood and a gentle hand touched her shoulder. She looked up into the stern eyes of Ms. Matsuda and realized that behind that gentle, ultra-fem exterior lurked someone you really wouldn't want to cross.

"Where did you find this picture? It has nothing to do with your assignment. I suggest you move on to something more productive," she said softly.

"I can't," Molly sobbed. "As soon as I started working, the computer put this up and won't let me change it."

"Hmm. May I try?"

"Please," Molly replied, getting up.

Ms. Matsuda sat down at Molly's computer, confirmed that it was impossible to navigate away from the page, tapped in a few codes that Molly didn't understand, and said, "This is strange, almost as if someone has tampered with your computer. Let's see if turning it off and rebooting it will help."

They did, and it did. Why hadn't she thought of that?

As the tech made her way back to the front of the class her words finally sank in. Someone had tampered with her computer. No one else but her seemed to be having any problems. Ms. Matsuda or Mr. Liu could have done it easily. Did Micah have the computer savvy to do it? Rathkin? Maybe, maybe not.

And the killer had, yet again, cut into her soul, leaving it bleeding, weakened, and vulnerable.

Was the monster watching her right now and feeding off her fear? She checked her shields once more and made sure there were no cords. She spent the rest of the class doing every calming, strengthening exercise she could think of and trying to look busy. She wasn't fooling Ms. Matsuda. Those glittering dark eyes watched her constantly.

When the bell rang, she bolted for the door. She was supposed to wait for Adam and Diana outside the computer lab, but right now she really, really had to pee. The restroom was just down the hall. If she went in, maybe she would give the eternal a chance to nab her, and Adam and Diana would be nowhere near. They'd be safe.

The restroom smelled just like any other restroom at Grant. The odors of cheap perfumes and disinfectant clashed brutally, barely managing to hide the underlying whiff that reminded you that well-used toilets squatted behind those metal doors. But fear had fine-tuned her senses and a wave of nausea roiled through her empty stomach as she entered the toilet stall nearest the door.

A group of girls trooped in and headed for the mirror.

"I totally hate cutting up dead frogs."

"Yeah, they're all clammy and cold and they stink."

"And the formaldehyde is making my fingers all yucky," the third said.

The echoing, blow-by-blow account of the dissection was entertaining and she relaxed and closed her eyes. Molly's sympathies were definitely with the frogs.

"Did you ever find the gall bladder?"

"Yeah, it was that nasty little green thing next to the liver."

"I swear mine didn't have one. Maybe he got gall stones and had it taken out before he croaked." The girls snorted with laughter and went into the rest of the stalls, slamming the doors behind them.

Molly got up, snapped her jeans, turned to flush the toilet, and froze in terror.

A black figure, crackling with magic, crouched on the seat she'd just vacated. It had no eyes, no nose, no mouth, and no ears. Its face was a black, fleshy disc with slight bumps and indentations where all those features should have been. Before she could catch her breath and scream, one black-gloved hand ripped off her talisman and the other struck the side of her neck.

As she spiraled down into unconsciousness, she heard the toilet flush and the latch to her stall slide open. An inhumanly strong arm scooped her up.

36

dam was frantic. Molly was supposed to have met them outside the computer lab, but she was nowhere in sight.

"She went in that bathroom," Diana said with a sniff.

He'd forgotten Diana's spectacular sense of smell.

"Then go in and get her."

Diana followed her nose to the restroom and slipped inside.

There was a detective just down the hall who had given up all pretense of being a janitor. He'd whipped out his badge and was interviewing a bunch of girls. Their eyes were bright with excitement and they were all talking at once.

"Yeah, one of the stall doors was closed."

"Are you sure?"

"You were too busy with your makeup."

"Yeah, it was the first stall."

"No, the second one. I was in the first."

"No, you weren't, you were in the second one."

"She must have left while we were in the stalls."

"I heard a toilet flush."

"Yeah, so she must have left."

Diana pushed open the restroom door. Panic shimmered in her eyes.

Adam almost ran over to the detective. "Excuse me, sir."

"I'll be with you in a minute," the man said, and turned back to the girls.

"Please listen to me." Adam barely restrained himself from grabbing the man and shaking him. "I'm a friend of hers. She's being stalked by a murderer. I've been keeping an eye on her all afternoon, but I've had to be in classes so I couldn't watch her all the time. But I do know that she went in that restroom."

The man gave Adam an intense, measuring stare. Adam had never had a cop look at him that way before and it gave him the creeps. The guy's face was an unreadable mask, but his stare cut into him like a laser and left him sweating. He had the distinct feeling that the cop had discovered all his guilty secrets, and was gonna make him pay for each one. To his intense relief, the assessment only lasted a few seconds. Apparently the detective decided that he was at least worth trading information with and said, "I watched her go into that restroom. These girls went in just after her. They came out, but the subject never did."

Adam fought down the cold fear that was turning his stomach into lead.

"You have to believe me when I tell you that you haven't just lost her, the murderer has her. I don't know who he is, but he's been after her all afternoon. She's probably not anywhere near the school by now. Please, you've got to call Detective Fox and tell him what you told me."

The man looked unconvinced. The girls' eyes were round with excitement. This would be all over school tomorrow.

"Look, if I'm right, and I am, and you don't make that call, you'll have her death on your conscience for the rest of your life. All I'm asking you to do is call Detective Fox before you start searching—because you're not gonna find her."

The detective reached under his jacket.

Adam was so keyed up, that for one heart-stopping moment he was sure the guy was gonna pull out his gun and shoot him, but he pulled out a cell phone.

—⁓—

Marcus's day had been exhausting and filled with dead ends, but he was now sure he knew who Shandra's killer was; unfortunately, he would have trouble proving it. And to make matters worse, the eastbound Banfield Expressway was a parking lot. An accident pulled over on the right just before the NE Thirty-third Avenue exit had jammed up traffic all the way back to I-5. He couldn't get around it, even with the red flashers on. It was just past three, and he'd hoped to be at Grant by now to make sure Molly got home safely.

His phone rang.

It was Estelle and she was frantic.

Molly was missing.

"Yes ma'am. I'm on it." He thumbed off the phone, stifling the urge to scream in frustration and throw the phone against the windshield. Instead, he turned on the siren, and applied himself to pushing through the traffic and pissing off most of his fellow drivers.

The phone rang again.

As he listened to the worried detective recount the details of Molly's disappearance, his mood changed from foul to thunderous. He had made the unacceptable mistake of underestimating his adversary. The life-sucking son of a bitch was superhuman. The words insane, desperate, and death wish also came to mind.

And now he had another possible murder victim on his hands and an officer who would spend countless sleepless nights blaming himself if she died. And it wasn't the man's fault. How can you even begin to protect someone from a killer who is able to skip through time and space, disappear, and change shape, if you don't even know that these things are possible?

Carefully keeping the rage and frustration out of his voice, he said, "You did the right thing, Troy. The killer probably got her while she was in the restroom... No, I don't see how he could have either, but I'm betting he did. Tell Principal Rathkin that the high school is closed and off limits to everyone until further notice, then call for reinforcements, clear out the school, and finish your search. I want to be sure he doesn't have her hidden somewhere on the premises, and I don't want anyone else disappearing. Any questions?... Fine, I'll be there in a few minutes."

He broke the connection and began uttering a long, vicious string of invectives.

And then he made another call.

"Detective Finder," the phone said after one ring.

"Jamie, a student has just disappeared from Grant High School. I think it's connected to the Sheehan murder." There was a charged silence at the end of the line. This was what they'd all been dreading.

"Then you'll be needin' to get on it," Jamie said. "Who is it? If you have her pic and info, I'll do the APB."

"Her name is Molly Adair. All her stuff's on top of my desk. Thanks, Jamie, you're a saint."

"So you owe me. Go get 'em."

When he finally squeezed past the accident, he sped toward the exit.

Searing, white light exploded in his head and pain gripped the back of his neck. Blinded and in agony, he just barely managed to stop the car without driving off the ramp.

This couldn't be happening.

Molly was probably fighting for her life somewhere, and here he was having a stroke or an exploding tumor or something.

Shit. Shit. Shit.

A woman appeared. She was dressed in dove gray boots and leather leggings. A scorched brown leather apron fit snugly over a grubby white sleeveless tunic. Her feet were firmly planted about two feet above the pavement in front of his car, and her clenched fists rested on her slim hips. Her hair gleamed in a golden, swirling aureole around her angry face. Raw power surged out from her in waves, sending spasms of pain ricocheting through Marcus's head and raising the hairs on the back of his neck and arms.

Shit.

All these years and the gods had to choose now to start messing with him.

"Look, Lady, this really isn't a good time. Could you call back later?"

"NAE! I WILL SPEAK WITH YOU NOW!"

The words ripped through his already tortured brain, causing him to writhe in agony and grab his head. "Fine. Anything you say. Just lower your voice and cut the power or I'm gonna faint."

"Ah, my apologies."

The pain stopped immediately.

"Ye be more sensitive than most in this benighted world."

"Yeah, that's me, Mr. Sensitive," he said, massaging his temples.

There was a gentle tap on his window and he looked around into a face full of piercings and a pair of worried eyes. He rolled down the window.

"Hey, man, are you all right? Should I call 911 or something? You don't look so good."

Marcus sighed and glanced over at the impatient goddess hovering over the hood of his car.

"I'll be okay. It's just a headache that came on real sudden. Thanks for stopping."

The good Samaritan didn't look like he was buying it, but apparently decided that he'd done the best he could, and who was he to give advice to a cop? He shrugged and said, "Okay, man, take it easy," and walked back to his car.

Marcus glared at the goddess. "Now, who are you and what do you want?"

"My name is Brigga. I made Molly's sword. I want you to rescue Molly."

Marcus looked at the woman in front of him with a glimmer of hope and new respect. He noticed her broad shoulders, muscular arms, and intense fighter's stare, and decided that it wouldn't be a good idea to piss her off.

In fact, it would be a really bad idea.

"That's exactly what I was trying to do, ma'am, when you ran me off the road," he replied.

"Well, you were nae makin' a very good job of it. You don't even know where or when she is, now do you?"

"No, do you?" he asked.

"O' course I do, you simpleton, I am a goddess!" she said, puffing out her shapely chest, doubling in size, and somehow managing to look even more dangerous.

Marcus regarded her anxiously.

But then, just as quickly, she shrank back to human size and said sulkily, "But the gods have very little power in this world, and I need your help."

The tension drained out of him and he breathed a sigh of relief. With the goddess's help, there was a good chance that Molly wouldn't wind up glaring at him above an autopsy table and that that he might actually be able to kill the eternal.

"Where is she?"

"She will be at Grant High School at midnight."

Marcus groaned and rested his forehead on the steering wheel as he imagined his colleagues faithfully searching the city for a murderer and his victim that wouldn't be there till midnight, and when they arrived, they'd be where everyone had already looked.

"Where in the school?" he asked as Brigga appeared in the passenger's seat. The phrase "God is my co-pilot" popped into his head. He was so giddy with relief that he only just managed to keep from bursting into hysterical laughter as he accelerated up the exit ramp.

"In the outbuilding next to the theater, in the room named S-4," she replied.

The science block. He knew right where that was.

And now for the million-dollar question. He thought he knew the answer, but he wanted to be sure.

"Who's the killer?" he asked as he drove up the exit ramp and onto NE Thirty-third.

"That I dinna know. Even in this world, the killer has managed to put up a shield strong enou' to block me out. The only reason I even noticed that she'd gone missing was because Flick started screamin' like a banshee when it lost touch with her."

"So Molly is safe until midnight?"

"Aye."

"Should I wait 'til then and go in and get him?"

"You could do that. But there's a tiny wee chance that things might shift in the multiverse between then and now and they will nae be there. It would be best if you went now."

"I'd love to go now, but I can't move through dimensions."

"Aye, and I cannot transport you either, but you used to know, didn't you?"

"Yeah, and I was good at it."

"I imagine you were," the goddess said, grinning wickedly. "That may be why the mages blocked you. But I believe the time has come to give you back that talent."

"You can do that?" he asked.

She looked at him impatiently.

"Of course you can, you're a goddess," he said quickly.

"All you need do when the time comes is start to reach for the time and place as best you can, and I will guide you through the blocks."

Marcus turned into Grant's parking lot.

The officers were well into the process of clearing the school. Streams of bewildered faculty, staff, and students poured out the doors and into the late afternoon sunshine.

He pulled into a parking space and stared ahead, collecting his thoughts. Students were heading away from the school through Grant Park, chattering excitedly and kicking at fallen leaves. The evergreen trees in the park loomed like dour old maids over the dainty deciduous trees dressed in the last tatters of their dazzling fall finery. The grass was brilliant green in the red-gold light and the air smelled of spices and smoke. He never ceased to marvel at the way life went placidly on and how the world continued to be breathtakingly beautiful—even when horrible things were happening. It was both unsettling and reassuring.

A pickup truck pulled in two spaces down from him. Three officers emerged, lowered the tailgate, and let two Alsatians and a basset hound out of their carriers. The dogs, bright eyed and bushy tailed, leaped down onto the pavement and pranced over to their partners. At least the Alsatians did. The basset hound needed a little help getting off the tailgate.

The K-9 team had arrived.

Troy English, the detective who had called him about Molly's disappearance, was hurrying toward the team, and Marcus managed to intercept him well before he got there.

"Have you found anything?" he asked.

Officer English glowered back at the school and said, "Nothing, nada, zip. Just her backpack in the bathroom stall. It's like she disappeared into thin air."

Which she did, Marcus thought, but I can't tell you that.

"The dogs were a great idea," Marcus replied. "And you have her backpack for scent. If she's anywhere in that school, they'll find her. But if you come up with nothing, lock up and have your men start checking hospital emergency rooms and patrolling Alberta Street. I have a few leads to follow up. I'll get back with you later."

"I'll get them started," he said heading towards the K-9 team.

"Thanks, Troy," Marcus called over his shoulder as he strode back to his car.

"No problem."

Leaning against the door on the driver's side, he called Jamie Finder again.

"Hey, Jamie. How's it going?"

"I've issued an AMBER alert. All units have been notified, and I've sent out her picture and notified security at the airport, train station, and bus station to be on the lookout for her."

"Thanks, Jamie. If English's crew doesn't turn up anything at Grant, they'll start checking hospital emergency rooms and patrolling the surrounding neighborhoods. I have a few leads to follow up, and I'll be pretty much unreachable for the next nine hours or so. If anything comes down while I'm gone, cover for me, okay?"

"I hate it when you pull stuff like this. What am I supposed to tell them, that you're taking a really long potty break?"

"You'll think of something."

"Why the hell can't you at least stay in contact like you're supposed to?"

"Because I can't—look, I'm going, even if you don't help me out."

There was an exasperated sigh at the other end of the line, and he knew that Jamie was remembering all the other impossible cases Marcus had solved with almost no evidence and no leads.

"Okay, I'll do it."

Marcus sagged with relief. "Thanks, Jamie."

But the line was dead.

Footsteps came running up behind him and he turned to see Molly's two friends skid to a halt. Their faces were white and filled with fear.

"We know who the killer is," Adam said.

37

Friday, October 28 • Early Evening

iana growled, grabbed the dashboard, and silently cursed her mother. It was almost moon-rise. The woman would be late to her own funeral, which, if she didn't hurry, would be happening soon. To be fair, it wasn't *all* her mother's fault.

When the adepts had discovered that Molly's corpse would be found in Wilshire Park on Saturday morning, a few of them had decided to keep watch at the park through Friday night starting right after school and try to prevent the tragedy. Mother had had to take the first shift because no one else could make it and the adept covering the next shift had been late. It was after five o'clock by the time she had been able to drive Diana out to Forest Park and her appointment with the full moon.

Most of the adepts believed that Molly had killed her best friend and had adopted a wait-and-see attitude. "That's what happens when you give a sword to a teen with a temper," Rathkin had said. "If she kills herself, it's not the Web's problem."

Unbelievable! How could he be so cruel?

And hardly anyone had believed her when she'd told them who had *really* killed Shandra and nabbed Molly. But she was sure she was right. Her nose didn't lie. And that detective had believed her. It was almost like he'd already known. But where was he now? No one seemed to know.

Rush-hour traffic was awful, but they were finally speeding through Forest Park.

"Mother, there's not much more time. Let me out!" At least that's what she tried to say. What actually came out was an angry growl. But the woman beside her seemed to understand and answered calmly.

"We're almost there. Very soon, my love." They were speaking Ukrainian, or at least her mother was. English had become impossible for Diana.

Demeter's tears! Doesn't she understand that I'm losing control? Diana could feel the moon like a cold fire on the horizon, and it was driving the beast into a frenzy. They were cutting this way too close!

Her muscles twitched like they were wired directly to Lady Moon and She was pumping silver jolts of power into them. The beast was sure the car was shrinking and was seriously considering jumping out the window. And oh, dear Goddess, she could almost hear the blood pulsing in the big artery that quivered on the side of Mother's neck, and she longed to sink her fangs into the tender flesh and taste its metallic sweetness. She was insane with hunger. Her mind twisted in shame and confusion as the scents that used to signal love and comfort now urged her to rend and kill.

Diana slammed against the console as her mother swerved onto a back road.

Her head felt like it was splitting apart and every joint in her body was on fire. She howled in panic as she watched her fingernails turn into claws that scrabbled on the dashboard.

The car stopped. She beat furiously at the door handle with useless paws and then lunged for the window, which was way too small.

"Diana, go out my door!" Her mother was standing outside the car.

Snarling with rage she struggled over the console, and leaped out. She was free and her body surged with power. The luscious smell of prey made the saliva flow under her lolling tongue.

It was just standing there.

It would be hers in a heartbeat.

She leaped at the pale, soft throat.

An invisible hand came out of nowhere and swatted her to the ground.

"Diana, get control of yourself. You are a mage!"

The beast groveled and whined because that's what any sensible wolf would do in the presence of an angry alpha female. Diana groveled and whined because she'd almost torn out her mother's throat.

"Hush! And listen to me." Her mother held up a backpack. "You will need this at moon-set. I have put a change of clothes and a jacket in here. The ones you have on will be ripped to shreds. There's a package of Wet Wipes in the side pocket. Use them." She stashed the pack behind a tree. "Stay deep in the woods. I will see you in the morning. Good hunting, my daughter."

A fresh breeze smelling of Douglas firs, dead leaves, and rich earth blew away the stink of the car. It was underlain with layer upon layer of smells that gave her a more detailed picture of the forest than if she'd been looking at it in broad daylight. And, yes, there it was. The scent of a young buck. Diana snarled with savage joy and loped silently downhill through the forest and toward the rising full moon.

The night and that buck belonged to her.

38

Saturday, October 29 • Just After Midnight

olly stared in horror at the blank, black mask of the eternal. He was sitting crosslegged on the floor in front of her, pulsing with remorseless, insatiable hunger. The same hunger she'd felt last night as she'd stared up into that featureless parody of a human face. The memory of those terrible hours poured into her brain with searing cruelty, leaving her breathless, weak, and terrified. He had stripped her naked and tied her face up on a cold, metal table. He'd started at her right knee with the black marker and slowly moved up her inner thigh. Pain, like the pain of a hundred wasp stings, followed the line up to her crotch and on up to her right hip. Bearing it in silence was impossible. She screamed and screamed, begging him to stop and knowing he wouldn't, because she could feel him savoring her agony

and slowly sucking out her life. The searing pain continued over to her left hip, circled her belly and ended just short of her right nipple and then moved back down toward her knee, completing the outline of a vicious dragon. His breath came in short gasps and he moaned in ecstasy as he began to meticulously draw in each scale, talon, and fang and color them in with burning reds, blues, greens, and yellows.

Mercifully, she had fainted.

Molly snarled in rage and fear at the memory, and struggled to stand.

A wide cloth wrapped snugly around her legs and waist trapped her in a cross-legged position and a binding spell held her completely immobile.

"Now, now. Be still or I shall have to gag you. There is no one near to hear your cries, but it is always best to be cautious. I've also taken the liberty of moving us a bit ahead in time to avoid the search parties. It's midnight, the witching hour." The eternal's voice was a soft, deadly whisper.

A brilliant moon lit up the night and filled the room with a silvery glow. There was enough light to make out colorless shapes and a bit of detail. But the featureless face that floated in front of her glowed with its own light, like another, darker moon. Molly surveyed her surroundings—anything to avoid looking into those smooth, empty, ravenous sockets.

She was in the forensics lab in the science block at Grant. If she walked out the door, she would be in a courtyard. If she turned left and started walking, she would cross the baseball diamond and the football field and finally reach NE Thirty-third. But she wouldn't be doing that anytime soon. The door was closed, and no doubt locked, and the only things she could move were her eyes.

A human skeleton grinned at her mockingly from its stand in the corner, and a knife lay on the floor directly in front of her. Its blade was not quite a foot long and it was shaped like Flick's. She had no doubt that it was razor sharp. A white cloth was wrapped around its top six inches.

"I think a forensics classroom is the perfect place for a murder, don't you? Unfortunately, no one will know what happened here. They will find your disemboweled body in Wilshire Park and it will appear that you killed yourself. See, I've even written your suicide note for you."

He held a piece of paper out to her, and Molly's unwilling hands reached out and took hold of it. The handwriting was a perfect imitation of her own. She was not surprised to read that she was consumed by guilt and that she hadn't meant to stab her best friend in a fit of temper. Her only honorable option was to take her own life. And since she was a warrior, she would commit *seppuku*, like a samurai.

His black-gloved hand plucked the note out of her unresisting fingers and pocketed it.

Grief and hopelessness turned her heart to lead. She would die knowing that almost everyone would believe that she had committed the horrible crime of killing a friend in uncontrolled rage and then taken the coward's way out and killed herself. *Seppuku* and the samurai code of honor meant nothing in this time and place. And worst of all, Shandra's death would go unavenged while her own death-agony would feed this monster and free him to kill again and again and again.

She couldn't let this happen.

"And so it ends," her captor said, interrupting her thoughts. "You have been a worthy opponent. Your life force is potent and sweet and has fed me well. I intend to take my time and savor every last bit of it."

Molly felt her hands reaching for the knife. She resisted the motion with all her warrior's will, but her hands didn't even slow down. The left one grabbed the handle of the knife and turned it so it pointed toward her lower belly and the right one, protected by the white cloth, curled around the blade itself.

Nooooo! Quick. Think of something to keep him talking!

"At least tell me who you are," she said as her hands moved the knife, point first, toward her belly."

"I will tell you what I can. You are a dying a warrior's death and so deserve to hear my story."

The knife stopped and Molly almost sobbed in relief.

"My name is Akimoto Takatomo and I was born over three centuries ago in Japan. I was an Elder or *Roju* for the shogun Takugawa Tsunayoshi. But first and foremost, I was and am a sorcerer. Because of my position, I had access to the Emperor's library in Kyoto, a treasure trove of arcane knowledge. One day, as I was exploring one of the oldest sections, I found an ancient parchment amongst the paper scrolls and folding books on one of the top shelves."

This was sounding familiar.

"The text described how a sufficiently skilled sorcerer could draw the life force completely out of another human being and use it for himself. It promised that anyone who mastered this technique and managed to devour ten strong lives in rapid succession would possess not only superhuman powers, but also eternal life."

Gods! How many more of those awful scrolls were out there?

"I was a brilliant scholar and my research had already been of great service to the empire. With the gifts this technique promised, I would have the time and energy to make even more phenomenal discoveries. There would be no limit to what I could do."

"Once a month I disguised myself as a common laborer and walked the slums of Kyoto looking for beggars and prostitutes. I became amazingly strong and I could move like lightning. I also relieved Kyoto of some of its worst vermin."

Molly looked at the monster before her in horror. As far as she was concerned, he had ceased being human with the first innocent life he'd consumed.

Keep him talking. The longer he talks, the better.

"So how did you manage to kill ten men all at once and not get caught?"

The life-sucker stretched luxuriously, "Have you ever heard the story of the Forty-Seven *Ronin*?"

"No."

"A pity. It is Japan's most iconic story."

At this point Molly could have cared less about a bunch of whatever they were, but she did care about staying alive. "Tell it to me, please."

"We have some time, so I shall.

"It all began in the early spring of 1701 in Edo, the shogun's capital city. Today it is called Tokyo. Naganori Asano-Takumi-nokami, a young feudal lord, committed *seppuku* because he had committed the unthinkable crime of drawing his sword within the confines of Edo Castle and wounding a high-ranking official, Yoshinaka Kira-Kozukenosuke. Forty-seven of Asano's three hundred twenty-one now masterless samurai, or *ronin*, vowed to avenge him and restore his honor by killing Kira.

"One snowy winter night they assembled in Edo and attacked Kira's mansion. They found Kira huddled in an outhouse and gave him the honorable option of committing *seppuku*. Kira, of course, was a coward and refused. So they decapitated him like a common criminal and put his head before Asano's grave, thus declaring their master's honor redeemed."

"So what does all this have to do with you?" Molly asked.

"Patience, patience," he said, shifting to a more comfortable position. Molly watched him with envy. The immobile cross-legged position was killing her back and her armpits dripped with sweat that ran in annoying trickles down her sides.

"The shogun admired the courage and loyalty of the forty-seven *ronin*. Instead of executing them, he gave them the option of an honorable death by *seppuku*. I burned incense at my altars and poured libations in my gardens, called in several favors and made sure that I was one of the four lords who would attend their deaths.

"The surge of power from their departing life force was brutally powerful. It slammed into me, frying every nerve ending and energy connection in my body and reworking them into perfection. I was completely reborn, essentially immortal. I still need to indulge in the occasional human life, and every hundred years or so I need a new body—a minor inconvenience."

Minor inconvenience? The creature lounging across from her might walk like a human and talk like a human, but he was a beast, a predator with no more feeling and connection to humanity than a cat has for a mouse.

"You are quiet," he said. "I take it you have no more questions."

Molly felt a sharp pain and realized that her hands had begun to push the point of the knife into the lower left quadrant of her belly.

"Oh, but I do!" Keep him talking. Keep him talking.

And to her intense relief, her hands stopped.

"What have I ever done to you?" Blood began to trickle down and soak the waistband of her jeans. "Why are you trying to kill me?"

"Oh, I think I'm doing better than just trying. But I will answer your question before I continue," he said, sighing with pleasure at the surge of life energy from the fresh wound. "We are killers, you and I. Right now you are young and inexperienced, and I am much stronger than you. But I travel the universes frequently, and in nearly every future I have visited you discover me and eventually kill me. Simple prudence demands that I kill you now and save myself from death in the future."

"So why not just kill me?"

"That, of course was my first impulse. But one doesn't survive for over three centuries by acting on impulse. Unfortunately, you are a mage and have very powerful allies. If you were killed, they would hunt the multiverse remorselessly for your killer and might actually succeed in discovering me. And so I decided on suicide. The police will tell them that the evidence is solid and they will believe them, grieve your death, and move on with their lives."

Relief flooded through Molly like warm sunshine.

The monster didn't know everything.

He didn't know that the detective in charge of Shandra's case was an ex-mage who understood about magic and dimension travel and knew that Molly was scheduled to be his next victim. Detective Fox might choose to allow the police to believe that her death was a suicide, but he and Gram, Tamerlane, Asmodius, Diana, and Adam would, indeed, "hunt the multiverse remorselessly" for her killer. Molly didn't give a flying fart what the rest of the adepts in the Web thought, but her friends would find him.

And he would never kill again.

"Your friend's death provided me with the extra power I needed to set up your suicide—this has been quite a bit of effort, you know." His blank eyes gazed at her reproachfully. "And killing you slowly is a much more efficient way to take in every last bit of your life force. I don't indulge myself in this way very often. It will be a most pleasant experience. If you relax and give yourself up to the pain, you may find a certain pleasure in it yourself."

Molly gazed in horror at the thing lounging before her and realized that she was in the presence of an evil so deep that it had no idea that it was evil.

"Do I know you?"

"Oh yes. I have disguised my face and voice because I can't have you telling tales in the other worlds. There are powerful beings there that would be very interested in your story and they could make things quite difficult for me.

"But enough questions."

His voice was thick with desire.

"It is time for you to die.

"Do it well."

39

Saturday, October 29 • After Midnight

fter the first few nudges from Brigga, the process of jumping had clicked back into Marcus's brain like it had never left. There was the reach into the shifting currents of space-time, and the "Got it!" feeling in the pit of his stomach when he latched onto the right time and place. Then the familiar lifting sensation, the cold blackness, the tilt and spiral, and he was standing in the courtyard between the auditorium and the science block. Moonlight twisted the familiar scene into an abstract of bone-white concrete and black shadows. A brisk wind sent dry leaves scrabbling like desperate fingers on a closed coffin lid. He jumped when Brigga appeared next to him.

"You owe me now, mortal."

And he had to agree. Being able to jump through time and space again was like suddenly regaining a missing right hand.

"But you need to practice time placement. You set yourself down a few minutes late. Quickly now, let me guide your hand to Flick. He cries out for the eternal's blood."

He reached out his hand and Brigga enfolded it with her energy. There was a pull and a feeling like water running over his arm, and then his hand closed around Flick's lacquered scabbard. He had the sword.

MOLLY'S IN DANGER!!!! TAKE ME TO HER NOW NOW NOW!!!!

"Be still, my bonnie blade, you will taste blood soon!"

And to Marcus: "Hold it by its scabbard in your left hand, hilt forward. Yes, like that. When you enter the room, make sure Flick is ahead of you. Now go!"

Marcus needed no other encouragement. He sprinted to the door like a silent shadow and gently turned the knob.

Locked.

Of course.

40

Saturday, October 29 • 12:30 AM

The exquisitely sharp blade slipped easily into her belly.

Molly shuddered as she felt the tug on her solar plexus increase to a strong, greedy pull as the life-sucker threw back his head and gorged on her life. His body arched in ecstasy, his breath came quick and short, and his lust filled the room like a living thing.

Seconds later, the pain blossomed, shot through with black fear. It swept across her belly and flowed in a jagged current out her arms and legs. It was a blood-red curtain of agony closing out the rest of the world.

Soon there would be nothing left except herself and her pain.

The door to the classroom slammed open.

"Freeze!"

MOLLY! I'M HERE. USE ME.

Fox stepped into the room, gun in one hand and Flick extended toward her with the other. He looked rumpled and mean as a scorpion, but to Molly's desperate eyes, the detective was a thing of beauty.

A heartbeat of horrible stillness hung like an exclamation point, and then everything began happening in excruciatingly slow motion, giving each horrid scene time to embed itself in her memory.

Molly pulled up her last bit of strength and threw it into a mental scream: *FLICK! KILL!*

The eternal turned.

The gun popped and the bullet slammed into his forehead.

The eternal blasted the detective with a sizzling burst of power that smashed him back against the doorjamb and left him lying on the floor in a senseless heap.

Flick zinged out of its scabbard and thudded into the eternal's side, impaling his evil heart. The binding spell released, and if it hadn't been for the support of the cloth wrapped around her waist and upper legs, Molly would have toppled over. Her hands dropped to her sides sending the knife clattering to the floor, opening the wound. Blood gushed onto her lap, drawing out her life force as cruelly and surely as the eternal.

But she was free and the eternal was dead.

I need to fix myself, she thought, and blacked out.

So peaceful, and the pain was gone. She was drifting in soft darkness.

"Molly! Attend to me," a voice said. "You are dying. Find your-self. You know how to do this."

Ah, yes, of course, that's what she was going to do. And yes, she could do it. Madam Rue and Aunt Althea had made sure that she could.

She reached out and found herself. But she wasn't the bril-liantly shining being that she remembered. The fountains of light were mere trickles and the rest of her power centers were closing down like wilting flowers. Brigga stood next to her, feet firmly planted in the black void, hands on her hips. She watched Molly expectantly.

"Lady, please help me," Molly said, and held out her hands toward her goddess, who smiled and took her in her arms. Pure bliss filled her and she expanded until she felt like she was touch-ing every part of the multiverse, and that all the possibilities con-tained in it were hers. Reaching into her light bodies she knitted up the gaping holes. Then she recharged her power centers, bal-ancing and adjusting as she went.

"Time for you to return. There be more to do," Brigga said, releasing her and giving her a gentle shove back into her body.

Molly opened her eyes and groaned in disappointment. Her guts throbbed with pain. She felt like a herd of elephants had just stomped over her and she was so tired. She wished she could have stayed wrapped in Brigga's arms.

Moonlight still chopped the classroom into black and white stripes and patches. Detective Fox was still lying crumpled on the floor, and the life-sucker was...

"Nooooo!"

Oh gods, please, not Tamerlane!"

Her mentor lay on the floor in front of her. His craggy, aesthetic face was serenely composed. He might have been sleeping, except for the fact that Flick was buried to its hilt in his side and there was a bullet hole in his forehead.

Molly howled in agony.

The kind, patient teacher that she'd loved dearly had never really existed.

She'd spent the last three months with a monster who was planning to kill her.

Her whole body shook with wracking, bitter sobs.

"You bastard!" she howled and began pummeling his chest with clenched fists.

Molly, don't! He's not...

Iron-strong hands grabbed her wrists.

...dead.

Tamerlane's eyes snapped open.

Eyes that blazed with hunger and hate.

His lips drew back in a parody of a smile as her life force began to gush out of her and into him like water from a garden hose. She was too weak to pull away.

"Defend yourself, lass!" Brigga said as Molly spiraled into oblivion once more.

"I don't want to. I'm so tired and I hurt." She was floating in comforting blackness.

"Aye, fine. Give up then. The monster will have won and you'll have some explaining to do to Shandra!"

Shit!

With a sob, she reached out to Brigga, who scooped her up in a fierce embrace. Brilliant light sang through her once more, filling voids and knitting up her tattered heart. Keeping its hold on the goddess, her spirit slipped back into her body. Wracking pain gripped her as she stared into Tamerlane's fierce eyes. They were shining with victory and lust.

"Ah, so sweet." He arched up and shuddered. His body convulsed, working Flick out of his side. It fell on the floor with the clang of well-tempered, but useless steel.

"So much glorious power. Where is it coming from? You should be dead by now."

Nausea dragged at her belly as he pulled more and more light out her solar plexus and gazed into her eyes with a hunger so obscenely great that Molly decided that all the power in the multiverse would never satisfy it. She searched those eyes for traces of the Tamerlane she knew, but there were none. Despair and disgust twisted her heart as her mentor, whom she had loved like a grandfather, moaned with pleasure and sucked away her life. And when he'd had his fill, he was going to kill her and toss her away like a piece of trash. Her eyes burned and hot tears slid down her cheeks.

"Hang on, Lass. You're not beat yet!"

Molly sensed a slight movement just out of her field of vision and her eyes flicked toward it. The detective was inching along the floor toward his gun. Hope flooded through her like water down a parched throat.

The life-sucker—she couldn't think of him as Tamerlane—hadn't noticed her glance. He was too busy with his personal orgy.

Fox was nearly there. Just a few more inches.

But her captor had been paying attention after all. He turned and raised his arm to fling another bolt of energy at her would-be savior. But he stopped, with one hand upraised and the other gripping Molly's arm. His eyes went wide with amazement.

The shadow of a nightmare slid into the classroom, followed by the nightmare itself. A gigantic wolf stood in the doorway. But it wasn't just a wolf. It was some darkly demented artist's macabre vision of a wolf on way too many steroids. It placed one paw between Fox's shoulder blades, smashing him back down to the floor and stared avidly at Molly. It drew back its mouth, pulling its muzzle into a frightening mass of ridges and baring wicked, cruel fangs. Its deep snarl reverberated in Molly's chest and echoed ominously through the room. Sapphire eyes that glittered with crazed intelligence pinned Molly to the linoleum like a bug on a collector's corkboard. White magic flashed and sparkled in its aura.

"Diana!" Molly stared at her friend in awe.

Tamerlane lashed out at the creature with a bright bolt of power, causing Molly to nearly faint again, because he'd pulled all that energy out of her. The effect on the werewolf was far from devastating; in fact, it was like pouring gas on an already blazing fire. The lightning sizzled through the magical creature's aura, turning it into a storm of light. The beast lunged at them, and with a howl of unholy joy seized Tamerlane by the throat. A quick jerk and a sickening snap cut short his awful screams. Diana opened her jaws and growled. The limp, gory body flopped back to the floor. Tamerlane's head lay at an impossible angle and his eyes stared vacantly out the classroom window. A thin line of blood oozed out of the corner of his mouth.

Then Diana turned those baleful blue eyes on Molly, and they gleamed with a fierce, loving intelligence. She gently touched Molly's hand with a huge paw bristling with needle-sharp claws, trotted past the dumbstruck detective, and out into the night.

Molly sagged in relief against the cloth binding and gazed numbly after her. It felt wonderful to just relax.

Molly, he's still not dead!

Of course. How could she have been so stupid?

She grabbed Flick and glanced over at the dazed detective.

"Do it. Quickly," he said. "I'm so sorry."

She forced herself to look down. Tamerlane's throat was a mangled, bloody mess, but the bleeding had already stopped and his eyes glittered up at her with rage. She gasped in horror as his neck snapped back into place. With a cry of panic, she yanked her mentor's head up by his hair and sliced through his neck.

Blood gushed out in two ghastly fountains, spray-painting the moonlit walls and disappearing into the black shadows. She held up the head, her fingers tangled in the white, silky hair. With a stab of grief, Molly realized that she'd never touched it before. Tamerlane had never allowed her close enough for that to happen. Tears stung her eyes and white-hot pain seared through her belly as fresh blood gushed from her wound.

The hair disintegrated in her hand as the eternal turned to dust.

"Molly, listen to me!" It was Fox's voice. She was spiraling down into safe, soft blackness. She didn't want to listen. She didn't want to think. She just wanted to....

"Take heed, Lass, This be important!"

Why couldn't they just leave her alone?

"What?"

Was that her voice? It sounded like it was a hundred miles away.

"When they ask you what happened, tell them the truth, but not the whole truth. Tell them you don't know who was trying to kill you or why. And don't tell them you killed him. Just say I shot him, which I did, remember?" Fox's voice was a thin thread of sound.

"Yes."

"And for gods' sake, don't tell them about the werewolf!"

" 'Kay."

Welcome blackness washed over her.

⁓

Will Molly be okay?

Marcus jumped and looked down at the shimmering blade that lay beside Molly's open hand. After the tiny warrior had fainted, he had checked out for a moment, staring at the pile of dust that had once been the most powerful mage in the Web, watching in mesmerized fascination as the wind through the open door began to scatter it around the classroom.

"Aye, my brightness, give her time and she will be right as rain."

The detective stood and winced as pain stabbed through his back and chest—that werewolf had been heavy.

That's good, because I have lots and lots of amazing stories to tell her. Tamerlane lived a long, long time and killed lots and lots of people!

Marcus grinned; Flick was the proverbial bloodthirsty blade. But it wasn't really the blood it thirsted for, it was the stories.

"And you can tell her every last one of them when she gets better, but right now I have to put you back where I found you."

Rats.

He wiped away Tamerlane's dust and slid the indignant blade back in its scabbard. Brigga guided his hand to its pocket between the worlds. Twice was enough. He knew Flick's address now.

"Come sit beside her and hold her. Molly's tether to this world is loose and she needs a human touch."

"She needs an ambulance," Marcus said, and called 911.

"911. What's the address of your emergency?"

"Grant High School, room S-4."

"What is the nature of your emergency?"

"This is Detective Marcus Fox. I have a young woman with an abdominal stab wound."

"Stay on the line; I'll be right back, okay?"

He could hear the click of a keyboard and knew she was beginning the process of summoning medics and police officers to the site, like so many genies out of a bottle.

A glint of gold caught his eye. He bent closer to see what it was and swore silently. The wind had blown the dust from the mage's gold signet ring. The griffin on its ruby cabochon glared up at him in the moonlight. The ring and his boot knife, the only other piece of metal he'd worn, had not disintegrated with him. The ring pulsed with magic. Marcus shuddered to think of the number of forensic tests it would foul up. The techs didn't need to find this. He hated to mess with a crime scene, but hell, he'd already hidden the murder weapon. Why stop now?

"Are there any other victims?" The dispatcher was back and the questions began. As Marcus patiently answered them, he pulled a pen out of his pocket, stuck it through the ring and headed out the door with it. The courtyard was mostly concrete, but there were a few beds planted with small trees and bushes.

"Do you know if there is someone we can call about her injury?" the dispatcher asked.

"She lives with her grandmother, Estelle Adair." he said and began digging into the nearest bed with tip of the pen. When the hole was deep enough, he pushed the ring in with his improvised tool and covered it up. He would show Estelle where it was later today and let her deal with it.

When the dispatcher had all the information he could give her, he hit End and called Jamie.

A sleepy voice mumbled, "Detective Finder."

"Hey, it's Marcus."

"Christ, Fox, it's one in the morning. Where the fuck are you and what've you been doing?"

"I'm at Grant. I've found her and she's been stabbed. The medics are on their way. Can you call off the APB and AMBER alert while I deal with them?"

Marcus heard a sigh of relief.

"Excellent! How did you find her?"

"You wouldn't believe me if I told you."

"Well, you'd better think of something fast, twinkle toes, because you're gonna have to tell Inspector Sharp a story that he *can* believe. I'll get the APB."

"Thanks, Jamie."

But the line was dead.

Switching on the classroom light for the medics, he noticed Molly's ashen face and quickly wrapped her in his rumpled tweed sport coat. She should be on her back with her feet elevated, but he was afraid to move her. Instead, he heeded the words of the goddess, sat down beside the wounded warrior, and held her gently against his chest.

41

Monday, October 31 • Late Afternoon

olly slumped on the couch in the family room and watched the rain spatter against the windows and run down the glass in rippling sheets, nearly hiding the West Hills. The dreary weather totally suited her mood. The Chair was sitting beside the couch, exuding comfort and support from every thread in its upholstery. Asmodius lay curled at her side, his rumbling purrs and warmth were calming and soothed her aching wound, but they weren't enough. Tamerlane's betrayal had loosed the dark monster of doubt inside her. If you couldn't trust someone who was that close to you, who could you trust?

No one, obviously.

But how could you live with your heart closed to everyone around you? How could you live without love? It was impossible.

"How could he have fooled everyone for all those years? I mean, you're adepts. Aren't you supposed to be able to see into a person's head?"

The purrs grumbled to a halt as the big cat sat up and regarded her with sad, amber eyes.

None of us are infallible, Molly. Adepts are like anybody else; we only see what we want to see. Tamerlane was a spectacularly powerful mage and a real asset to the Web. His knowledge and insight helped us through more tight places than I can count. But mostly he fooled us because he honestly believed he was a good man and that what he was doing was right. I knew him for years and he never gave me cause to doubt that. Conviction is very convincing. He was a loyal friend to both Estelle and me, and we grieve with you, my dear.

"But the Librarian..."

Who knows what that inscrutable lizard was thinking?! Asmodius plopped grumpily down on the couch and curled up. There were no more pleasant purrs.

The doorbell rang and Molly heard Gram's quick footsteps head toward the front of the house.

"Good afternoon, Estelle. I've brought Molly's backpack. We're done with it. In fact, we've closed the case. Are you sure she's ready for visitors?"

"Thank you for coming, and yes, she is more than ready to have someone besides Asmodius and me to talk to. She's moping herself into a bad place."

Oh, come on, she was not...Well, maybe she was. And she did need to talk to Fox. She had a ton of questions for him.

"Let me take your coats. You're soaked."

Oh jeez, who else had she invited? Molly struggled up into a sitting position, winced at the pain in her belly, and ran her fingers through her hair, which probably made it look even worse, but at least it wasn't all smashed down on one side. Asmodius rumbled in annoyance and crawled up on her lap.

Fox, Adam, and Diana trooped into the room. The two guys just stood there grinning like idiots, but Diana knelt down beside the couch and gave her a gentle hug.

"I am so glad to see you! The last time we met was awful. That place smelled like death and evil hunger and made my fur stand on end. Your soul must be shattered."

"Aunt Althea is helping me. She says I'll mend." Tears welled up and Molly hugged her friend closer. She had worried that being with Diana and Fox would be uncomfortable because it would remind her of all the pain—not just the pain of a knife biting into her guts, but the pain of being hunted down and tortured by someone you loved, someone that you thought had loved you. And it did, of course it did, but it was a good thing. Diana knew firsthand what she had endured and was horrified, and that horror somehow validated her own. She wasn't this crazy girl in a cell all alone with her nightmares anymore. There were people here that could share them with her and make them both more real and less frightening all at the same time.

"Thanks for coming." She held Diana at arm's length and looked into those beautiful sapphire eyes. They sparkled with tears and joy, and that haunted look was gone.

"And thank you for saving our lives. Fox and I would be dead right now if you hadn't appeared."

"I guess werewolves are good for something!"

"Oh yeah! But how did you find me?"

"Werewolves smell magic," she said. The wrinkles on her nose when she grinned looked just like the wrinkles on her muzzle when she'd snarled and bared her fangs. If it hadn't been for her laughing eyes, the effect would have been quite disturbing. "I went to Wilshire Park to see if the mages had found you yet, and I smelled Tamerlane's magic. The air was thick with it even up there. It was an easy matter to follow it to its source."

"None of the mages saw you," Gram said from the kitchen. She was pouring coffee, and its marvelous aroma wafted into the family room. "You were sneaky, but not quite sneaky enough. The news was full of wolf sightings Saturday, and animal control officers are still working overtime trying to find you. They're beginning to think it was a Halloween prank."

"Tipsy-toeing through a city the size of Portland without being noticed is not easy for a werewolf," Diana said grumpily. "And I would much rather have stayed in the park; it smells nicer. But I had a friend to look after." Diana kissed Molly's forehead and sat cross-legged on the floor beside her.

Gram bustled in with a tray loaded with mugs of coffee, a bowl of raw sugar crystals, a pitcher of half and half, and a plate of Althea's chocolate chip cookies.

"Help yourselves and have a seat," she said plunking the tray down on the coffee table. She ladled sugar into one of the mugs, added a generous slug of half and half, gave it a stir and handed it over to Molly. Diana grabbed a cookie, and Adam settled into the chair across from her warming his hands on his mug and gazing out the windows. Fox scooped up a mug and a cookie and lowered himself cautiously into the Chair. He only jumped a little when it shuffled forward so Molly could see him.

"You look amazingly well," he said, studying Molly. "I'm surprised we're not having this chat in a hospital room."

"You must have taken the easy Unicorn classes," Molly said.

"Yeah, plant devas and magic mushrooms were a kick," he said, grinning crookedly.

"She healed almost too quickly," Gram said. "By the time we got to the emergency room the wound had already started to close up. It was all Althea could do to convince the doctors not to cut it open again, put in drainage tubes, and pump her full of antibiotics. They had to be content with IVs to replace fluids and electrolytes."

"Brigga helped too. I would have given up a couple times if she hadn't talked me out of it, and she's the one who provided all the healing energy. The bastard couldn't believe his luck—totally blissed him out. But he was even hungrier for my life. If Detective Fox had come just a few seconds later, my whole stomach would have been ripped open. Of course, if you'd come just a minute or two earlier, I wouldn't have had this," she said, touching her wound.

"I did the best I could." Molly saw real pain in his eyes and regretted her words.

"And you were freakin' fabulous!" she said, reaching over and patting his knee. "But did you really expect to stop an eternal with a gun?"

"No, I expected you to whack the scumbag's head off," he said, looking all smug and self-righteous.

"Sorry, my bad. But I did eventually get it right."

"Yes, fortunately for both of us, you did," he replied, gently squeezing her hand.

"Molly, did Tamerlane ever say why he wanted to kill you?" Adam had questions and he wanted them answered.

"Yeah, he did," Molly replied, smoothing Asmodius's silky fur. "He time-traveled a lot, and in every future he visited, he said that I had killed him. So he decided to kill me before I killed him." Tears stung her eyes. "He probably didn't even think twice about killing me. For the whole three months I lived with him, he was feeding off me and figuring out how he was gonna do it. And he made me suffer so he'd be able to pull even more energy out of me. How could he do that?" Tears were streaming down her face and the room went still. Diana was weeping right along with her, Adam was studying his hands, and Fox looked bleakly out the windows. It was Gram who finally answered her.

"I do believe that Tamerlane was quite fond of you, but you must remember, an eternal is a self-centered predator and humanity is his prey. And as far as he was concerned, it was either him or you. He was killing to defend himself. Every time he looked at Flick, he must have seen his death."

"Yeah, I s'pose." Molly sniffed and wiped impatiently at her tears. Of course it made sense, but it still hurt and it would keep hurting for a long time.

"We all did our parts, but the real hero is Molly," Fox said, interrupting her glum thoughts. "If it weren't for her, that monster would still be alive and free to kill again and again, and he would still be lurking in the Web. The adepts should be very grateful."

"Yes, she was amazing," said Diana. "She not only deserves their gratitude, but also a formal apology."

"That may take a while," Gram said. "Believe it or not, some of the adepts are upset that Molly killed Tamerlane! But they'll come around eventually."

Molly didn't give a rip what the Web thought. What really mattered was that they'd beaten the bastard and she'd played her part well. It made her glow with happiness to know that her friends and family loved her and were proud of her. She was also glad that she'd rid the multiverse of a life-sucking nightmare.

"How did you figure out that the killer was Tamerlane? Did Brigga tell you?" Molly asked, looking over at Fox.

"While he was in our world, Tamerlane stayed heavily shielded. Brigga didn't know who had grabbed you, but she was able to tell me where and when he'd taken you. And she helped me jump after you. But that's not all the help I had." He shifted in the Chair, sighed, and continued. "I see dead people, and lots of other things most mages can't see. Shandra and I attended her autopsy together."

Everyone except Asmodius and the Chair gasped. Asmodius blinked.

"How was she?" Molly asked.

"She was royally pissed, but in control of her situation. Very few of the newly dead can communicate as clearly as she did. She must have been an amazing person."

"So go on," Adam said before Molly could tear up again.

He told them about the autopsy and how he'd figured out that the killer was an eternal.

"But you knew who the eternal was before you went after Molly," said Diana.

Fox nodded.

"How did you know?" she asked.

"Among the three of you, you had almost all the information you needed. You should have been able to guess. Your list of suspects was a great help to me. It saved me valuable time. But I was able to eliminate every one of them."

"No way!" said Adam.

Fox grinned.

"It was easy to eliminate Robin Liu and Principal Rathkin. Molly told me that Liu looked really tired in Forensics lab the day of the murder, and when I interviewed Rathkin Wednesday morning, he was exhausted and looked like he'd slept in his clothes." He regarded them expectantly.

"Of course," Adam said, smacking his forehead. "If either of them had been an eternal that had just killed, he would be fresh as a dew-fed fairy and raring to go! And since he didn't think any of us would figure out that an eternal was involved, he would have no reason to fake tiredness and every reason not to. What about Ms. Matsuda? Is she a guy or not?"

"Wait," Molly said, "Did you ever find out what Mr. Liu was doing in Pioneer Square Wednesday night?"

"And who is Tiger Lily?" asked Diana.

"One question at a time, please." Fox settled back in the Chair and took a sip of coffee. Molly decided that he was enjoying this way too much. "Master Liu is closely involved with the International District community, and he keeps track of the street kids. When he started noticing some of them disappearing, he began investigating and found that the white slave trade is alive and well in Portland. Operators snatch kids off the street, chain them in vans and drive them down the coast to serve as prostitutes."

The room exploded.

"That so totally sucks!"

"How could anyone do that?"

"It's just evil!"

"Tiger Lily is one of the cooks at the Sisters of the Road Café, a restaurant that serves the homeless community," Fox said, dragging the conversation back on track. "She is much more approachable than Master Liu."

"Just about anybody would be," said Molly.

"The girls talk to her," continued Fox. "When one has information for him she sets up a meeting. The evidence the two of them have provided to the vice squad has already led to the arrest and conviction of one operative."

"No wonder he looks so tired all the time," Molly said. "Maybe we can help."

"I don't think so, they're doing just fine on their own," Fox said. "But he has offered to help you with your martial arts training."

"When's he gonna find time?"

"He'll figure it out. He wouldn't have offered otherwise. If I were you, I'd take him up on it. He's no Tamerlane, but he's a close second."

Molly tried to wrap her mind around the idea of having her dreaded forensics teacher as a weapons instructor. The best she could do was mutter, "At least he's more my size."

"So what about Ms. Matsuda?" said Adam.

"Charlotte Matsuda is definitely female," Fox replied, grinning at Adam. The person you saw was her younger brother, who does look amazingly like her. And they share her car. If you'd checked the mailboxes, you would have seen that he and his wife live on the second floor."

"I did, but I thought they were her parents," Adam replied, slumping back in his chair.

"When you are collecting facts, never assume anything. She may not be a man, but she is a psychic vampire—you were right about that. However, she uses her ability carefully. Her hobby is doing Japanese tea ceremonies, and because she can absorb stress and tension and create tranquility, she is quite successful at it. You saw her traditional wig on her dresser; I'm surprised you didn't notice it wasn't her regular hair-style."

"It was dark," Adam said, sinking even lower in his chair.

"Just like a man," Diana said. "But I'm glad we don't have to sit in computer lab and pretend that he is a she!"

"It would have been really hard to keep from snickering every time one of her admirers threw himself at her feet," Molly said, and she actually giggled, which hurt her belly.

"So who pushed Adam into the street? Tamerlane?" Diana asked.

"Probably. He must have been listening to your conversation about Ms. Matsuda and decided to confuse things a bit," Fox said.

"So how did you know it was not the Ortiz creature?" Diana asked the question that Molly had been dying to ask, but somehow couldn't.

"Micah Ortiz has been raising hell in this neighborhood for years, and I've watched him grow from a cocky little kid to a powerful gang leader. I know him well enough to know that he has his own twisted code of ethics. He's perfectly capable of killing—in fact he's a favorite suspect in several unsolved gang murders—but I doubt that he would kill either an innocent student or a fellow Web member. And as far as I know he isn't able to dimension travel, and believe me, I'm watching closely and dreading the day he learns. Also, if he were the killer, he wouldn't have called 911 when he found her in Wilshire Park."

Molly relaxed back onto her pillows and carefully stowed this information beside everything else that she'd been able to find out about Micah. Each piece was a treasure, a way of getting closer to him. But how close did she want to get?

"And what about Rathkin? Where was he at two o'clock Wednesday morning?" Diana asked.

"You were so sure he was the killer," said Adam with a grin.

"He was out looking for Shandra." Fox replied.

"How did he know?" Diana asked.

"Philadelphia had a vision. She saw a young African American woman lying on concrete in a pool of blood. She'd been stabbed through the heart. A woman's voice said, 'Her killer is in the Web. Call Thaddeus.' And so she did. Her description of the woman didn't match any of the Web mages, but it did remind Thaddeus of Shandra Sheehan, Molly's best friend. Unfortunately, Philadelphia's warning came too late to help Shandra. Rathkin lives in Northwest Portland, and by the time he got to Shandra's house it was deserted, and he began a methodical search for Shandra. It took him a while since he didn't have Shandra's dog to guide him. And then he remembered that when he'd arrived at Shandra's house, he'd noticed a young woman jogging with a dog a few blocks away. She was about Molly's height and build."

"Oh, jeez, no wonder he thought I'd done it, and when the mages jumped ahead and found my suicide, that was all the proof he needed."

"But, since his story corroborated your story, it actually helped prove your innocence."

"Okay, so you figured out who it wasn't, how did you figure out who it was?" Adam was sitting on the edge of his seat, eyes flashing with curiosity.

Everyone turned to the detective, who sat back and smiled at them over steepled fingers, basking in the attention like the contented Fox that he was.

"Once I knew who it wasn't, it was a simple matter to figure out who it was. Who else could it be? Tamerlane was the obvious suspect—if you had the advantage of looking at him from an unbiased point of view. He was close to Molly—contrary to popular belief, strangers and distant acquaintances are poor murder suspects—and I have no doubt that you had told him about Shandra," he said, looking over at Molly.

She nodded. Her heart sank as she realized that she had unwittingly betrayed her friend.

"He also had plenty of opportunity and the skill and power to pull off the killings. So I had another chat with the Librarian. We went over the histories of all the other Grant adepts, just in case, and there was nothing to suggest that any of them was an eternal. All their families have been in the Web for centuries, they're all married with kids, and none of them have had any personality changes or mysterious absences. Then I asked about Tamerlane. It turns out that he walked into a library years ago and headed straight for the Librarian. Your gatekeeper tells me that it saw a brilliant, idealistic young man who already had quite a bit of magical knowledge. Perfect mage material. He was admitted on the spot. Tamerlane was that rare combination of competitive athlete and avid scholar, so he joined the Ouroboros Lodge and trained as a warrior mage. I believe he was a year ahead of you, Estelle."

"Yes, he was." Her eyes were filled with sadness and memories.

"He had no family, and he never married or formed any close attachments. After serving the Web with distinction for several years, he asked to live in Damia where he could more easily pursue his studies and train the occasional student. This was the profile I'd been looking for, and I was sure I had the killer."

If the detective had been expecting applause, he didn't get any. The room was silent with thought. Asmodius and Estelle looked devastated, but Adam and Diana were frowning.

"When the Librarian looked at me that first time it felt like it was burrowing into my soul. I cannot believe it didn't see Tamerlane for what he was," Diana said.

"How do we know it didn't?" replied Gram, and her eyes were hard as diamonds.

"What about the dust? How did you explain that?" Molly asked, filling the uncomfortable silence that followed her Grandmother's remark.

"I didn't," Fox replied. "I told them that the perp moved toward me after I told him to freeze and I shot him and he turned to dust. The techs found the bullet and lots of DNA fragments in the dust, so they had to believe me. They're not happy about it though, and we're all hoping the press doesn't find out that the only thing left of the killer's body is a pile of dust.

"What I want to know, young man, is where was the adept who was supposed to be guarding my granddaughter?"

Molly was very glad she wasn't Detective Fox right then. The man actually blanched. She'd always thought that blanch was a stupid word, but she couldn't think of a better one to describe that quick, terrified paleness. He definitely blanched.

"I asked Master Liu if he would guard her," he said, a bit too quickly. "After the students had left the lab, Ms. Matsuda found him slumped over his desk at the back of the computer lab with nasty bruises over both carotid arteries. Tamerlane must have gotten to him just before he went after Molly. It would only have taken an instant." The detective studied his hands like he was trying to read his fortune. Anything to avoid Gram's basilisk stare. Molly almost felt sorry for him.

"I see," Gram said. "I shall have to thank Robin for his effort. He's recovered and back to normal, I hope?"

"He's fine, but strikes to the carotids have been known to kill. He was lucky," the detective said, raising his eyes to meet hers. But something caught his attention and he glanced to his left.

He smiled, and Molly was sure his eyes misted with tears.

She followed his gaze and cried out with joy.

Shandra Sheehan stood framed in the doorway between the hall and the family room, looking absolutely fabulous in a tiny black dress dotted with neon pink skulls. Black fish-net tights and knee-high black leather boots with stiletto heels completed the outfit. Her brown eyes sparkled and her gold nose-ring gleamed. When she had everyone's attention, she gave them two thumbs up and disappeared.

⁓

After her friends left, Molly laid back and drifted into a deep sleep. Their visit had boosted her spirits, but it had left her exhausted. Soft footsteps pulled her from a delicious dream that involved two naked bodies, gentle, caressing hands, and the faint scent of leather and peppermint. She woke to find Gram standing beside her, looking worried.

"What?" she asked, impatient to return to her dream.

"Micah Ortiz was just here."

Molly was suddenly wide awake.

"He's...dangerous."

"I know."

"Of course you do," her grandmother said with an exasperated sigh.

"He said he can't believe you're still alive, and—I'm quoting him here—to get your 'butt out of bed and back to school'. He asked me to give you that." She pointed toward the coffee table and left the room.

It was a perfect red rose in a cut crystal bud vase.

Molly's whole body tingled as she took the flower in her hands. Its sweet fragrance engulfed her long before she buried her nose in its softness.

But this rose had thorns.

And each velvet petal was edged in black.

Acknowledgements

Ulysses S. Grant High School is, indeed, a Portland public school. I am grateful to all the teachers and students who kindly answered my questions about what had changed at Grant since our sons went there almost two decades ago. However, as far as I know, it is not a Mage Web magnet school; and all the teachers and students in my story are pure fiction.

Many thanks to:
You, for reading my books.
Jessica Page Morrell, my editor. Your meticulous suggestions and criticisms helped me to craft a much better book.
Dick and Karen Seymour, my first readers.
Your input and support are invaluable.
Michael S. Howard, PhD, for your editing and your invaluable alchemical advice and suggestions.
Damon at the Multnomah County Medical Examiner's office, for describing its offices and autopsy room layout and giving me the quote:
"If you're in Montana and you see hoof prints,
you don't look for zebras."
Gary D. Telgenhoff, DO, Las Vegas, Nevada forensic pathologist and "CSI" consultant, for patiently answering my questions about autopsies and writing Dr. Thanophoros's description of the entry and exit wounds.
If there are mistakes in the autopsy account, they are mine.
Todd H. LaVielle, my talented and patient website manager, for giving your mother so much of your precious time.
Ture Ekroos, for your beautiful cover art.
Becky Mellinger and **Johanna Norton**, for proofreading.
Adam P. Forrest, for designing the book.
Alexandra LaVielle, for posing and making faces for my cover illustrator.

And last, but certainly not least, I give thanks to my dear family—my husband, two sons, and two daughters-in-law—for your patience and love. And for believing in me.

About the Author

C. LaVielle began her grown-up life as a biologist because she is fascinated by people, plants, and animals and what makes them tick.

She became a wife, a mother, and a healer specializing in tarot divination and energy work.

She traveled to many marvelous, mythical places—from pyramids to temples to standing stones to cathedrals.

And became, at last, a writer.

She has discovered that magic is real. And it makes fantastic fiction.